WHEN TROUBLE SLEEPS

WHEN TROUBLE SLEEPS

Leye Adenle

Abuja – London

Leye Adenle is the author of the award-winning *Easy Motion Tourist*, and a contributor to *Lagos Noir* (Akashic Books, 2018) and *Sunshine Noir* (White Sun Books, 2016). His short story '*The Assassin*' was shortlisted for the CWA Short Story Dagger 2017. Leye is from a family of writers, the most famous of whom was his grandfather, Oba Adeleye Adenle I, a former king of Oshogbo in South West Nigeria. Leye lives in London. He has appeared on BBC Radio 4's 'Open Book' and is a regular panelist at literary and crime festivals.

First published in 2018 by Cassava Republic Press
Abuja – London
First released in the USA in 2019 by Cassava Republic Press
www.cassavarepublic.biz

ISBN (NIG) 978-978-55979-1-2
ISBN (UK) 978-1-911115-63-2
eISBN 978-1-911115-64-9

A CIP catalogue record for this book is available from the Nigerian National Library and the British Library.

Designed and typeset by AI's Fingers
Cover & art direction by Michael Salu
Printed and bound in Great Britain by Clays Ltd, Elcograf S.p.A.
Distributed in Nigeria by Yellow Danfo
Distributed in the UK by Central Books Ltd.
Distributed in the US by Consortium Book Sales & Distribution
Distributed in South Africa by Pan Macmillan

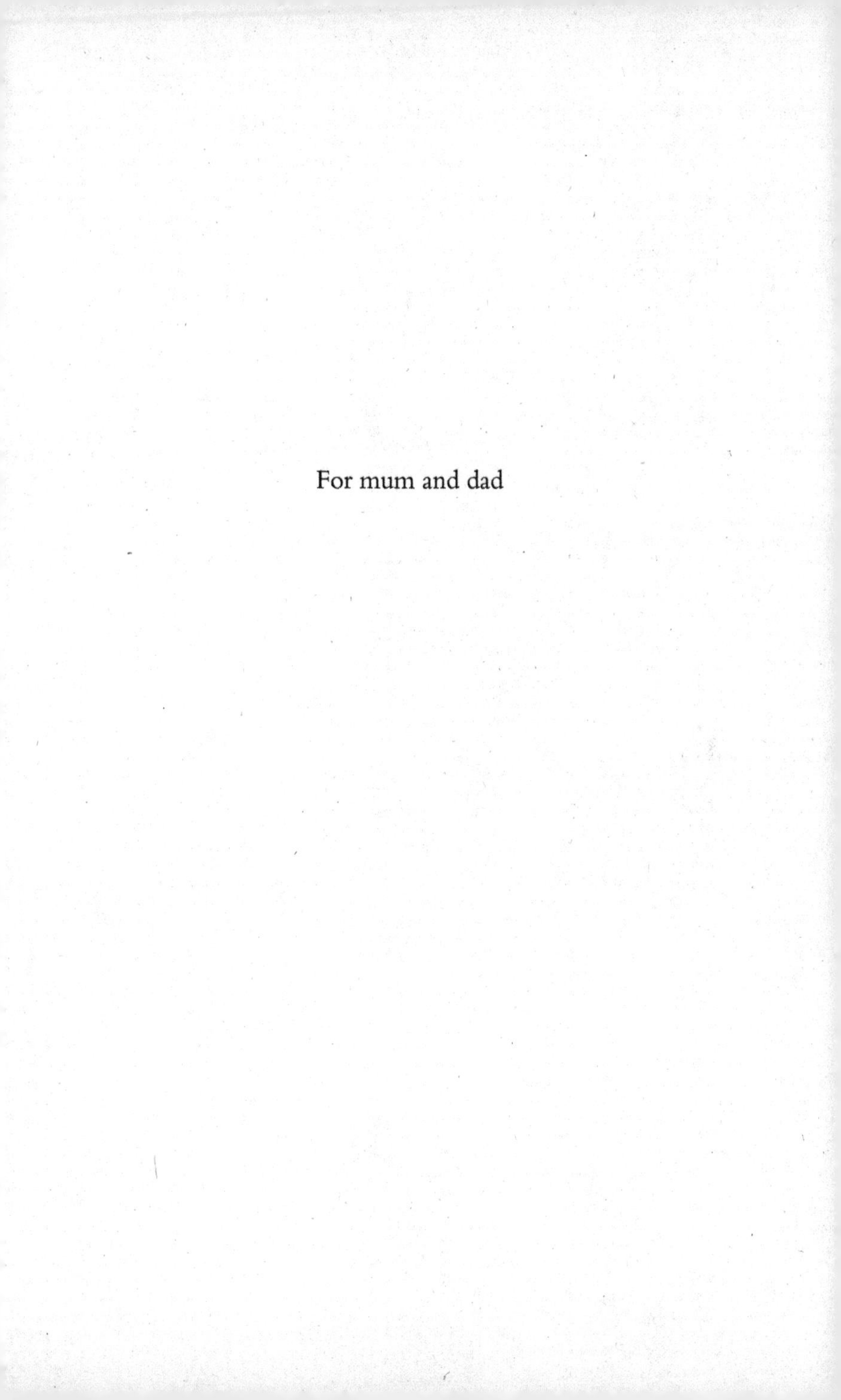

For mum and dad

Prologue

'Have you ever been on a private jet?'

Chief Adio Douglas stretched his hand over Titi's shoulder in the back of the Mercedes S-Class. Titi shook her head. 'You will experience it today,' he said.

Titi curled her feet up underneath her, careful not to scratch the black leather with the heels of her Manolo Blahnik sandals, and she folded her body into his arms. She looked up at his face. 'Is that the surprise?'

'No. I've got an even bigger surprise for you.'

'Where are we going? Should I have brought my passport?'

'We're going to Abuja. To the Villa.'

Titi unfurled herself. 'To Aso Rock?'

'Yes. I am meeting with Mr. President himself.'

'Wow. I will meet the president?'

Douglas laughed. 'No, my dear, I will meet the president. You will wait for me in the presidential suite of Transcorp Hilton.'

'Is that the surprise?'

'No, baby.' He pulled her back onto his chest and stroked her arm. 'It's a big surprise.'

Police officers at the gate stood aside and saluted as the limousine drove past them onto the Execujet secluded ramp close to the private wing of Murtala Muhammed International Airport.

Agents of the Department of State Services, who had been riding ahead in a Ford Explorer SUV, jogged alongside the Mercedes holding their Israeli TAR-21 assault rifles in both hands, buttstock to the shoulder and muzzle tilted to the ground. The limousine stopped close to the upturned wing tip of an Embraer Phenom 300. An agent scanned the shimmering the tarmac littered with private jets before opening the chief's door.

Douglas's white agbada billowed in the kerosene-laden wind as he pulled it over his head. Titi, in her black tunic dress, walked around the armoured car to join him. The boot of the Mercedes opened and DSS agents fetched Douglas's briefcase and Titi's weekend bag.

Just behind the cockpit, the aircraft's door began to open downward. Through her sunglasses, Titi watched as the door stopped its descent a few inches from the ground. She looked at Douglas.

'Can I take a picture?'

He smiled. 'Sure. So long as I'm not in it.'

She turned her back to the aircraft, held her phone high in front of her and pouted. On the screen she saw the pilot climbing down the steps.

'Didn't you say your ex-boyfriend is a pilot?' Douglas said.

Titi's hand dropped to her side as she turned to look back at the pilot.

The young man was standing by the steps with his hands held behind his back, his eyes hidden behind his Aviators and his head slightly tipped upwards. He stood still like a soldier.

Douglas placed his hand on Titi's back. 'Let's go,' he said. Her body resisted his push. 'Is anything the matter?' he asked.

Titi turned away from the pilot and looked up at Douglas.

'Is anything wrong?' he asked again.

She slowly shook her head.

'OK then, let's go. I don't want to keep the president waiting.'

Douglas and Titi waited for a DSS agent who had carried their luggage onto the plane to descend the steps, then with his hand on her back, he ushered her in front. The pilot remained still.

'Wait,' Douglas said.

Titi stopped, her hand on the cold handrail.

'Titi, meet our pilot for today: Captain Olusegun Majekodunmi. Did I get that right?'

The pilot nodded.

'Olusegun, meet my girlfriend, Titi.'

Titi did not look at the pilot. The pilot nodded but did not look at Titi.

They sat in the middle of the narrow cabin in beige leather seats facing each other. Neither spoke during the jet's take-off and short climb. Titi kept her sunglasses on, staring through the window.

'Are you OK?' Douglas asked when the jet had levelled out.

'Did you know?' Titi said. A tear appeared below her sunglasses before dropping onto her hand.

He unclasped his seatbelt and leaned forward.

'You knew,' she said, removing her sunglasses and placing them on her lap. The lenses were wet.

'In a couple of months, I will be the Governor of Lagos State. You will come and live with me in the State House.'

'You are married.' More tears ran down her face.

'Yes. And so what?'

'He is my fiancé.'

'And who am I to you? A sugar daddy?'

'You are married, Chief. You are married.'

'You lied to me, Titi. You lied to me. But I forgive you.'

Titi buried her face in her palms.

Douglas held her hand, but she slid out of his grip.

'Why?' she said, looking up at him, mascara leaking into the powder beneath her eyes.

'I will be governor; he is just a pilot. A glorified driver. I want you to choose now. Do you want to come with me, or do you want to remain where you are?'

She shook her head and turned to the window, closing her eyes to the brilliant sunshine; searching for the window blind.

He stood, leaned over her and reached for the blind. Looking out of the window his face creased. 'That's strange,' he said.

She looked out of the window to see what he'd seen, then she looked back at him.

At that moment, the engines roared, her sunglasses floated off her lap, and she lifted in her seat, her body held down only by the seatbelt around her waist.

Douglas, who had been on his feet, lost his balance, cracked his head against the sidewall and fell to the ground.

Titi became dizzy. Magazines, cups, and a silver tray darted about the cabin as the jet flew nose down and she began to black out.

1

'He found me.'

'Who found you?'

'Malik.'

'What do you mean he found you? Amaka, what's going on?'

'The bastard called me and threatened me. Did you tell him I was looking for him?'

Someone ran past Amaka's window, placed his hand on the bonnet to stop himself from falling, then dashed between the cars ahead. Something looked odd about his sweaty, shaven head: a huge lump on the crown.

'Gabriel, I've got to go. I'll be at yours soon.'

Amaka put the phone down, leaned to the side and placed her face against the window to try to see the man that had run past her car, but he was gone. Then, another man ran by her window. She turned around. A lot of people were running towards her car from behind. They were holding sticks and planks, and at least one wielded a machete. She turned to look ahead, holding the steering wheel and leaning forward for a better view. A shirtless torso slammed onto the window on the passenger side, jolting her. The man pushed himself off the car, leaving an imprint of his chest in sweat. He banged on the roof and continued running up the road with the rest, waving a plank above his head. One young man held a tyre over his head; worn smooth with its wire threading exposed. Another held up a five-litre jerrycan of a liquid he was trying not to spill.

More men ran up the road, sliding off car bonnets and using their fists to threaten drivers who protested. Amaka looked back and saw even more squeezing past cars and jumping over bonnets. She called Police Inspector Ibrahim.

'Hello, Amaka, I'm on my way,' Ibrahim said.

'To where?'

'To the crash.'

'What crash?'

'The plane crash. Near your house.'

'A plane crashed near my house?'

'Yes. A small plane. Didn't you hear the explosion? I heard it from the station.'

'No. I'm not at home.'

'Where are you?'

'Oshodi.'

'What are you doing there? You should be in bed, Amaka.'

'I'm fine. Listen, there is something happening here.'

'Amaka, do you understand what I just said? A plane crashed into a building very close to your house.'

'I heard you, but they are chasing someone and I think they will kill him.'

'Who is chasing someone?'

'A mob. They are going to lynch him. You have to get here fast.'

Amaka opened the door and stood on the ledge to see what was happening ahead. The men were gathered to the side of the road. They had caught him.

'Where exactly are you?' Ibrahim said.

'Oshodi market. They are attacking him right now. Come, now!'

'Amaka, stay in your car. Whatever you do, don't get involved. Do not leave your car. Amaka… Amaka?'

'Yes?'

'Do you understand? Do not get involved.'

'How soon can you get here?'

'I can't come. I told you, I'm on my way to the crash site. Whatever you do, don't get out of your car. Do you understand?'

'Sure, sure.'

She hung up and stepped onto the road. The man was now on the floor and the mob was attacking him with improvised weapons as a crowd of onlookers cheered, some holding up camera phones. Amaka closed the door behind her and flicked on her camera phone as she started walking towards the mob.

2

Alfred Rewane Road was blocked. People on the bridge at the Falomo roundabout had exited their cars and lined up along the kerb, some of them pointing out the smoke rising behind the mansions of Oyinkan Abayomi Drive, others recording with their phones. A lot of them had their hands on their heads; some stood open-mouthed, others talked on their phones, spreading news of the plane crash.

Inspector Ibrahim told Sergeant Bakare to kill the siren. It was making it hard for Ibrahim to think. The signal from central control in Panti ordered every available officer to be mobilised. Every available officer. That meant traffic wardens, desk officers, even detectives on active cases. A plane crash in a residential area was enough of a disaster, but this was not some regular neighbourhood; this was Ikoyi, old Ikoyi, where the old money lived.

The smoke looked as if it was being pumped out by a factory, then all of a sudden, a flash and the smoke turned orange. A split second later the sound of the explosion reached the bridge. A woman shouted to Jesus to save the poor souls but there was no saving anybody down there. The irony, Ibrahim thought. He knew these people – the same people who would make a call and divert state resources to guard their homes; people who could get a senior officer relocated to a post in Boko Haram territory for not understanding that the job of the police was to protect the rich. Too often he had been 'requested to provide officers' whose job would be to escort teenage brats to parties with even more brats – police officers who could be doing police work but instead carried shopping baskets behind bleached-skinned mistresses. He knew them like only a high-ranking police officer could. Rich criminals, that's all they were. They represented the cases quashed, the investigations called off, the murders, the extortions, the thefts. These people didn't need protecting; ordinary Nigerians needed to be protected from them.

Ibrahim climbed out of the front door of the police van. His officers got out of the back and joined onlookers on the side of the bridge. Next to them, a young boy in dirty jean shorts and a brown singlet was the only person with his back to the unfolding scene. A worn travel bag was wide open between his feet. In it, in protective plastic sheets, the self-help books he had been selling in traffic before the crash. He was telling a group of worried-looking motorists and their passengers what he had witnessed. With his hand he demonstrated the moment of impact.

'It was facing down like this. It come down, wheeeeeeee, then it explode, bulah!'

More people crowded round the boy and he repeated what he had said, his recollection of the moment of impact becoming more detailed and the explosion more impressive. As he spoke, everybody on the bridge turned and looked up. A grey helicopter flew low and fast over them and crossed the lagoon in seconds. It went over the crash site before circling back, tilting sideways, then it hovered loudly, spreading the smoke beneath it.

'Navy,' Ibrahim muttered to himself. Early reports placed the crash at Magbon Close; another report had it at Ilabere Avenue – both close to each other, both home to billionaires living in modern multimillion-dollar mansions on plots that once housed colonial administrators. Most of the properties had stayed in the same families for generations; the dynasties of Lagos. The very type of Nigerians who flew in private jets. How ironic. He turned to the officer beside him – a slim and lanky, dark-skinned man with tribal marks fanning out from the tips of his lips.

'Hot-Temper, take Moses and Salem and go to Oshodi market. Where is your phone?'

Hot-Temper was dressed in the military-style combat uniform of the special anti-robbery squad, Fire-for-Fire. He brought out his mobile phone, an old grey Nokia with a monochrome screen, the characters worn off the rubber keypad.

'Save this number. It's Amaka. She said they are about to lynch somebody there.'

'For Oshodi market? Wetin she dey do there?'

'Who knows? You are not going to get there in this traffic. Take okada.'

Hot-Temper saluted his boss and turned around to scan the traffic. A line of motorcycle taxis was parked between stationary cars, their owners close by watching the helicopter hover over the crash site.

'Be quick,' Ibrahim said as Hot-Temper walked towards an okada. The three officers were commandeering motorcycles from young owners who did not have driving licences and who knew better than to protest too much with police officers. 'And follow her wherever she's going.'

Hot-Temper waited for a boy to pull his okada motorcycle out backwards from between parked cars and turn it round in the cramped space on the bridge. Hot-Temper swung his AK-47 over his back and mounted the vehicle. The boy held on to one handle and Hot-Temper raised his hand as if he was about to slap the boy.

'Come to Bar Beach Station tomorrow morning to collect

your okada,' Ibrahim shouted to the boy. 'Hot-Temper, call me when you see her, OK?'

Hot-Temper kicked the machine to life and revved.

The helicopter flew back the way it had come. Everyone on the bridge ducked as it passed overhead, then arched their necks to follow it as it disappeared.

'We are walking,' Ibrahim said to the two remaining officers. He tapped on the bonnet of the van. Sergeant Bakare began to open his door to get out but Ibrahim gestured for him to remain. 'Meet us there,' he said, and started down the bridge with his officers.

3

Somebody emptied a jerrycan of petrol onto the man, now immobile and bloody on the road. Another struck a match.

Black smoke rose with a swoosh and an orange flame licked his body, trapped in a burning tyre that had been forced down to his waist, encircling his arms. He leapt from the ground as the fire spread. The crowd backed away from his burning mass, kicking him and breaking planks of wood on his back. He fell to the ground, then he stopped moving and the fire engulfed him till all that was left was a smouldering black figure supine on the asphalt road.

Amaka held her phone in front of her pushed through the men surrounding their kill. The fumes from the burning tyre stung her eyes, the smell of cooking flesh turned her stomach, but she continued forward. The murderers and onlookers, feeling her shoulders push them out of the way, tarried to budge, but the sight of her, her clean smart clothes, her neat hair, her pretty, solemn face, her indifference to them, threw them and they retreated, giving her passage, because she did not belong among them. She confused them, perplexed them, mesmerised them, and rendered their murderous energy ineffective.

The killers formed a circle around their victim. Amaka, with her back to them and facing the dead man, recorded their faces across the rising smoke, pretending to be recording their victim, and like this she worked the circle, her back to the people, her face to the bonfire, her phone capturing the culprits' images.

A woman was fighting to get through the crowd, screaming, crying, clawing, snatching and grabbing at bodies in her way, dodging an elbow here, absorbing a repellent jab there. She looked like she was in her twenties. She was slender and tall, her dark-chocolate skin smooth and shiny, her hair short and tangled and browning at the twisted tips. She was in a white flannel skirt with a large rose embroidered on the front, a white sleeveless tube top, a pair of red pumps, with a red scarf around her neck and red coral earrings.

She broke through and ran towards the body that was too late to save. Amaka watched her through the screen of her phone. Men grabbed the woman to stop her from reaching the fire, but another group tried to snatch her from the ones trying to save her and appeared to be dragging her towards it.

A lanky man held a tyre over the girl's head, attempting to get it round her body but other hands worked to stop him.

Amaka tucked her phone into her skirt, ran past the fire, feeling its heat on the side of her face, and grabbed the belt of the man attempting to put a tyre around the woman. She yanked him until he fell backwards. He dropped the tyre and it rolled towards the smouldering body.

Another man was holding up a metal pipe, trying to get a good aim at the girl's head. Amaka grabbed his hand and he swung round, his fist bunched, but Amaka thrust her knee into his groin before he could deliver the blow. As the man collapsed onto the floor, Amaka and the young woman locked eyes. The woman was being dragged away into the crowd and she stretched out her hands to Amaka, her eyes wide and unblinking, mouth open. Her fingers stretched outwards as if they could somehow bridge the distance between her and Amaka; as if touching Amaka was all that was needed; as if

Amaka was the one who could save her and even her dead friend. Amaka stretched her hands towards the girl as splinters of wood flew past her face and tiny sparks danced before her eyes, obscuring her vision. Her knees gave way and she blacked out.

4

A man with sunken cheeks, his faded brown Ankara outfit loose around his gaunt frame, looked around the crowd before stooping to the ground and picking up the phone he had seen fall from the woman trying to fight the men.

As he stood, he looked around before putting his hand into his pocket. The phone vibrated. It startled him, but nobody noticed. They were too busy filming the thief they had caught. He looked down at the screen of the ringing phone. 'Guy Collins.' He looked at the woman the area boys had knocked out. He looked back at the phone. He frowned at the sky; at God who had seen him stealing the poor woman's property, and he answered the call.

'Amaka, where are you?' the caller shouted into his ear. He cupped his hand over his other ear so he could hear the man over the noise. 'Amaka? Amaka?' She was Igbo. He was Igbo. He bit his lips. He cursed. 'Hello?' he said. 'Who are you?' He turned his back to the action and began to edge his way out of the crowd.

'Who is this?' the man on the phone shouted. He sounded like a real oyinbo, not just someone with an oyinbo name.

'Where is Amaka?'

'Are you her friend?'

'Yes. Where is she?'

'You better come here now, now. They are going to kill her.'

'What?'

'She is on the road here. They are beating her. They are going to kill her.'

'What are you saying? Who's beating her? Why are they beating her?'

'The area boys. They have already killed one thief. They are descending on her now.'

'What? Who are you? Where is she?'

'She is at Oshodi market.'

'Market? Who are you? Can you help her?'

'Me? What can I do? You better come now-now, before they put tyre on her neck and pour her petrol.'

'Please help her.'

He ended the call and switched off the phone. It was too late for anyone to help the woman, but God saw that he had done all that he could.

A skinny young man stood with his back to Amaka's car and looked around. He opened the door and ducked inside. He snatched the handbag from the passenger seat and tucked it under his shirt. At first he walked quickly through the crowd, then he jogged along the road and finally he turned unto a narrow, overgrown passage between the walls of adjacent buildings. He sidestepped mounds of excrement and swatted at flies. He checked behind him before taking out the handbag. There was a notebook laptop inside. It felt light. He tucked it under his armpit and searched for its power adapter.

He pulled out a passport and flicked through its pages before sliding it into his back pocket. He found a mobile phone and its charger, a cardholder, and a wad of pound notes. He stuffed everything into his pockets. He threw out a compact mirror, a lip balm, a nail file, and a bunch of keys, unzipped a side pocket and felt inside. He grabbed the contents. In his palm there was a black SD memory card among four mobile phone SIM cards. He picked up the memory card and inspected it, then looked up as two men walked past the entrance to the passageway. He dropped the memory card and the SIM cards back in to the bag and tossed it away. As he walked away, the bag sank into the vegetation until only its thin black strap was visible, curled over the stem of a plant like a snake hiding in the foliage.

5

Chief Olabisi Ojo groaned and turned over in his bed. He was naked. He put his hand to his forehead and groaned again. The throbbing radiated across his eyes to the back of his head. Lying on his fat belly, eyes closed, he stretched out his hand and swept it over the sheets. He opened his eyes. The lights hurt. He turned his head and looked on the other side of the bed, rolled himself onto his side, paused to let the throbbing subside, then heaved himself up and sat on the edge. The headache intensified.

He looked round the room of the presidential suite at Eko Hotel. His vision was blurred. He tried to focus on the armchair on which his friend, retired Navy Commodore Shehu Yaya had sat, next to a stool cramped with glasses, a dirty ashtray, empty bottles of Star and Guinness, and one empty bottle of Remy Martin - the bottle the girl had brought. Where was she? He tried to remember her name. It hurt to think. Iyabo?

Pain tore through his right eye. Removing his hand from his face, he tried again to focus. He stood and walked out of the bedroom into the living area of the presidential suite. 'Iyabo!' he called out.

He wrapped his fingers round his gold watch before checking the time. 7am. He walked to the dining area. 'Iyabo!' He looked around. Her clothes were not in the room. He couldn't see a bag. He wrapped his fingers round his watch a second time.

In the bedroom he found his clothes on the ground beside Shehu's chair. He picked them up and patted the pockets of his trousers; from one, he retrieved a bound, inch-thick wad of one thousand naira notes. He held the money between his index finger and thumb as if he could tell if any were missing. He returned the money and from the other pocket he removed his wallet, spread it apart, and stared at its contents: hundred-dollar notes. Without removing the money, he counted two hundred and fifty notes. Next, he thumbed through each of his credit cards. Confused, he dropped the clothes on the chair. She hadn't stolen from him. She wasn't a thief. But she had left without telling him she was going. Or did she? When did she leave? Did they have sex during the night? He reached under his belly and held his limp penis. He couldn't remember.

He checked the time again, began walking back to the bed, and stopped. His eyes flitted from one bedside stool to the other, then to the floor. He returned to his clothes, picked them up, and patted them down once more. He felt his money and his wallet but nothing in his other pockets. He went to the telephone by the bed, dialled and held the receiver by his side to listen for his phone to ring somewhere in the suite. His eyes fell upon the stool by the chair. He replaced the handset.

Standing over the stool, he looked at the ashtray in the midst of empty bottles and used glasses. Pieces of a SIM card lay atop the ash and butts in it. He bent down for a closer look and saw his phone on the rug near the foot of the stool, its battery and the back cover next to it. As he went down on one knee to pick them up he noticed that the SIM card had been taken out of the mobile.

'Iyabo!' he shouted in the direction of the open door. His head hurt as he bent to pull on his Y-fronts and trousers. It didn't make sense. Did she remove the SIM card and break it? Why? Was she angry with him? Perhaps because he fell asleep? At the club she had made it clear that she wanted to fuck him –

and not for money. In fact, she warned him that the deal would be off if he as much as tried to give her any money. She was not a prostitute. Did he get too drunk and try to pay her after sex? Did they have sex? He just couldn't remember anything. He replaced the battery and back cover and slid the phone into his pocket. Why had she broken the SIM card? So he wouldn't have her number?

He went to the window and drew back the thick curtain. It was dark outside. Panicked, he looked at his watch again; it wasn't seven in the morning. He had slept till seven in the evening.

He tried to gather his thoughts. He'd arrived at the hotel around one. Or maybe two. Shehu joined him not long after. Iyabo arrived about 4am. He had met her at Soul Lounge. She did not look like a prostitute; she said she wasn't one. She spoke with an accent, like someone who studied abroad. She wore a skirt suit; she said she'd come from work, that she was a lawyer.

The last thing he remembered was seeing Shehu off – that was a few minutes after Iyabo arrived – but he strained to remember what happened next.

Pain seared through the crown of his head as he stood up. He groaned, held his head in his palms and sat back down in the armchair. It creaked under his weight. His eyes darted around as he tried to think, then they shot back to the ashtray. With his index finger he searched amongst the stubs and the broken pieces of his SIM card. He turned the ashtray over onto the table. Nothing. He flicked the ash off his fingers and rushed to fetch his phone from his pocket. As he slid off the back cover and removed the battery, it was as he feared: the memory card was missing. An alarm went off in his head. He looked around, pushing his hands down behind the corners of the cushions. On his knees he searched on the floor and under the chair. He pushed himself up onto one knee and shouted, 'Fuck!'

6

Horns were going off everywhere on Bourdillon Road, cars lined bumper-to-bumper remained static. Exhaust fumes hung heavy in the air. Okada drivers straddling their motorcycles used their feet to move their machines between cars, their handlebars scratching paintwork in the process. A mass of people walked down the road and the traffic police watched from the enclosure of the roundabout under the flyover.

Inspector Ibrahim and the two officers with him joined the throng of people heading towards the crash site. All around them, men with scratchy voices spoke the bastardised form of Yoruba popular amongst Lagos touts. Men shouting and waving fists bumped their shoulders into the police officers as they passed them.

A man pushed past Ibrahim and, after four steps, scratched the road with his machete. Ibrahim placed his hand on the arm of the officer to his right who had begun to raise his AK-47. In front of them, the man was now circling the machete over his head. Ibrahim looked behind. In the midst of the approaching crowd, there was a group of men holding up leafy branches and machetes. A shot went off while Ibrahim was still watching. He jolted. The crowd continued past him and the other officers, unperturbed. Ibrahim had seen where the shot came from. The barrel of the black pump-action shotgun was still pointing upwards.

'What is going on?' Ibrahim asked. Among the men walking towards them, one was loading cartridges into a shotgun. The man looked up at the officers and continued loading his weapon. As he passed between them, his shoulder pushed Ibrahim, who had to be stopped from falling by the officer to his side. Again, Ibrahim restrained his colleagues.

Another shot went off, this time closer. 'Jesus,' Ibrahim said. The sound of a helicopter made him look up. This time it was a green one. The army. Just as it circled back on itself and hovered, another one flew over the crowd, made a large arch, then hovered opposite the first.

The crowd were marching past Oyinkan Abayomi Drive. They looked like they didn't know the geography of Ikoyi. The officers went down the drive. It was much less crowded. Two lines of immobile cars, many of them with their drivers still at the wheels, stretched back to where the lagoon began. The trees on the lagoon side partially obscured street lamps that had just come on. A third helicopter flew in.

'What is going on?' Ibrahim asked again.

They continued past Mekunwen Road, choosing their route by the position of the helicopters above. At Macpherson, a white Toyota LiteAce bus was parked lengthwise, blocking the road. In front of it, men in civilian clothes, brandishing AK-47s, stood guard. Opposite, civilians and police officers stood with their backs to the lagoon and watched the noisy aircraft.

'Sergeant,' Ibrahim called, and beckoned to police officers amidst the onlookers. They were not from Bar Beach police station. They were probably posted to stand guard outside homes in the neighbourhood, Ibrahim figured.

There were four officers in all, one woman and three men, who all saluted and stood in front of Ibrahim.

'What is going on here?' Ibrahim said. He read the name badge of the plump female officer he had directed the question to. Fatokun.

'An aeroplane crashed, sir.'

'I know that. But who are those men there and why are you standing with the civilians?'

'They are not allowing people to pass, sir.'

'Which agency are they with?'

'Agency, sir?'

'Are they DSS?'

'No, sir. They are party loyalists.'

Ibrahim shook his head. It was a euphemism for thugs. He looked at the armed men by the bus. The men stared back. It was illegal for civilians to own assault weapons, but here he was, a police inspector, unable to do anything but watch and pretend not to see. The traffic jam had made it impossible for appropriate security agencies to get to the scene. Other police commands would have received the same signal he received, and in time they would arrive along with FAAN officials; meanwhile he appeared to be the first respondent. With two of his own officers, another five conscripted officers, and only two rifles and his service pistol between them, diplomacy was the only option.

'Do you know which party?'

'Sir, you haven't heard?'

'Heard what?'

'The plane landed on Chief Adio Douglas's house.'

'Crashed into,' Ibrahim corrected.

He knew Chief Douglas. Everybody in Lagos knew Chief Douglas. He sat on numerous boards and he was chairman of Douglas Insurance – 'the insurers to Lagos state' as Ibrahim once read in a newspaper. His house was on Magbon Close and he was going to be the next Governor of Lagos State. His opponent, a doctor who returned from practising in America, whose name Ibrahim couldn't even remember, lacked the money, the popularity, and the political clout to run against the ruling party. Chief Douglas on the other hand was a former central bank director and a former finance minister.

'Was he in the house?' Ibrahim asked. At least the plane had crashed into just one household, Ibrahim thought, then it occurred to him that Douglas was just one life; there were other lives that could have been lost: his family, his servants, his gatemen, not to talk of the passengers and crew on the plane. As a gubernatorial candidate he would have been travelling with his security detail. Officers who bade their family goodbye in the morning, not knowing they would never see each other again.

'He was in the plane.'

'He was in the plane that crashed into his own house?'

'Yes, sir. They are saying the other party bombed the plane.'

Ibrahim remembered the men brandishing machetes and firing shots. They were the party loyalists, and the men armed with AK-47s, not letting people through, were waiting for them. Reinforcements. Lagos was about to explode.

7

Chief Ojo stepped out of the presidential suite, closed the door behind him and removed the 'Do not disturb' sign from the handle. He stared at the glossy door hanger – he didn't remember placing it there. Downstairs in the lobby, waiting for the woman at the desk to get off the phone, he continued trying to put together the disjointed pieces of the night before, all of it muddled in the haze of his fantastic headache. Iyabo had been on the bed when Shehu left. He couldn't remember if he followed his friend to the door, out into the corridor, or to the lift.

'Good evening, sir. How may I help you?' the woman said, jarring Ojo out of his thoughts.

Ojo placed his key card on the counter. The suite had been paid for. Originally booked for a visiting diplomat, the man had been unable to use it and Ojo had asked if he could have it. All Ojo had to do was pay for the drinks he and Shehu ordered through room service.

The girl typed on her keyboard, all the while maintaining her smile. A printer began to spool out a sheet of paper onto a table behind her. She fetched the invoice and placed it in front of Ojo.

'What the hell?' he shouted, reading the total on the bill.

'What is the matter, sir?'

'What is this?' He waved the bill in front of her face.

'It is your bill, sir,' she said, uncertainty in her voice as she inspected it.

'For a few drinks? How much is Star and Guinness?'

'It is including the charge for the room, sir.' Her voice became quieter as she spoke, as if retreating.

'The room has been paid for by the liaison office. Check your records.'

'But sir, checkout time is twelve, sir.'

'Yes. I did not check out before twelve, so that makes two nights. Paid for.'

'Sir, you checked in the day before.'

'Yes. Late last night.' He slammed the invoice on her desk.

The girl leaned in closer to inspect the figures. She struck some keys on her computer and took her time to read what was displayed on the screen, comparing it with the sheet of paper.

'No, sir. I mean ....'

Ojo snatched the invoice from her and glared at it.

A short man in a black suit, white shirt and a kente tie appeared beside Ojo.

'Good evening, sir,' he said. 'My name is Magnanimous. I am the concierge. What seems to be the problem?'

Ojo looked at his watch. At the date display.

'Are you OK, sir?' Magnanimous said.

'I have been here for two days?' Ojo said.

'Yes, sir,' Magnanimous said.

'Two days.'

'Yes.'

'I have been in the suite for close to forty-eight hours?'

'That is correct. What is the problem?'

'I thought...'

'What, sir?'

'Nothing. Nothing. Do you accept dollars?'

Ojo paid his bill and hurried out to the car park. As he approached his maroon Mercedes, he strained to see if his driver was inside. He would have been waiting for two whole days.

The driver, a short, thin man in his fifties, ran up to Ojo.

'Oga,' he said.

'Where were you?' Ojo asked.

'I was talking to some people there,' the man said, pointing. 'We are discussing the plane that crash.'

'Plane crash? What plane crash?'

'Oga, you never hear? One plane like that crash into Chief Adio Douglas house today-o,' the man said. 'Less than two hours now. They say he was inside it. They say it is opposition.'

'Douglas? He was in the house?'

'He was in the plane.'

'OK. Wait. You are confusing me. Douglas was in the plane that crashed? What does his house have to do with it?'

'The plane crash into his house.'

Silence.

'Oga, that is how it happen. He is inside the plane and the plane crash into his house.'

'Who was flying it?'

'Oga, how will I know?'

Ojo was silent as he dwelt on the unbelievable information. He grabbed his phone before remembering that the SIM card was broken. The girl. Iyabo. Fuck. What did she do to him? Why?

'Anyway,' Ojo said to the driver. 'Where did you sleep?'

'Me? Inside the car.'

'When you didn't see me, why didn't you come and look for me?'

'Oga, me I do not know your room, now.'

'And you couldn't call me?'

'No credit on my phone.'

'So, if something had happened to me, you would just stay out here forever?'

'Me I know that you are OK, sir.'

'You knew I was OK? How?'

'Madam phone me.'

'Madam? Matilda called?'

'Yes.'

'When?'

'Yesterday like that kind 5 o'clock.'

'AM or PM?'

'Early morning. She say that I shoul' call her when we leave the hotel.'

'How did she know we were at the hotel?'

'Maybe you tell her, sir.'

'You are mad. Did you tell her?'

'No o.'

'So how did she know?'

'I don't know o.'

'She didn't ask you?'

'No. She said that when we leave, I shoul' call her.'

'What exactly did she say? And what did you say?'

'Oga, I have told you. She said, 'Abiodun, when you are leaving the hotel, call me and give the phone to your oga.''

'And what did you say?'

'I told her I don't have credit.'

8

Three black Toyota SUVs with blacked-out windows turned off Coker Road, tyres screeching, onto Ilaka Street in Mushin, close to Ikeja. The cars stopped in front of a single-storey house with a white fence topped with glistening barbed wire and plastered with two different posters showing the face of the same clean-shaven, gap-toothed, smiling man with a raised fist. On one of the posters he was in a white agbada and an abeti aja cap, in the other he wore a grey suit and nothing to hide his bald head. Above both portraits were the words 'Dr. Adeniyi Hope Babalola', and below them, 'Hope for Lagos', followed by details of his party. Two police officers standing in front of the black gates swung their rifles forward and held them ready as they watched the cars.

The first SUV was still moving when a tall albino man with translucent, short hair jumped out of the back and onto the road. He was dressed in a grey safari suit and brown leather shoes. On his left wrist, a gold Rolex Daytona; in his right hand, a two-way radio. It was dark, but he wore sunshades. He marched round the front of the car. The police officers opened the gates and he entered, ignoring the three Alsatian dogs that ran forward growling and barking.

He tried the handle on the front door, then he banged his fist on the bulletproof panel. Moments later it opened.

'Where is he?' he asked.

The shirtless young man in the doorway stepped aside.

The gubernatorial candidate was standing in the middle of the staircase in a purple jalabiya, his hand on the banister, body turned sideways with his legs on separate steps as if ready to retreat. 'Yellowman, what are you doing here?' Babalola said. He sounded as scared as he looked.

'We have to leave now,' Yellowman said.

The shirtless man looked at Babalola.

'Where are we going?' Babalola asked.

'To Prince.'

'OK. Let me change.'

'There is no time. We have to leave now.'

9

'We are coming from the hospital,' Chief Ojo said from the back of the Mercedes as Abiodun drove towards his house in Chevron Estate.

He had to have a good explanation for his more-than-one-day absence, but without his phone with which to co-opt an accomplice for an alibi, and without knowledge of how his wife knew he'd been at the hotel, he had been unable to come up with a lie that sounded half-convincing, even to him. He was in some sort of robbery; they took his phone – it would be easier to explain a stolen phone than a broken SIM card. He remembered the missing memory card and his heart skipped a beat.

He fetched his phone and put it in the seat pocket in front of him. He ended up in the hospital, but without any money to pay the bill... He fetched his wallet and the money he had on him and tucked them in the seat pocket… they wouldn't let him leave the hospital because he didn't have any money and... No. Matilda knew he was at the hotel.

He was attacked. Armed robbers. It was a sophisticated robbery. He was just leaving from a meeting with an important diplomat when they accosted him on the corridor. At the hotel. Men – they had to be men. They were dressed smartly in business suits. They pointed a gun at him and took him into a room – they had a key card and they took his phone and money and tied him up. No. They sprayed something in his face that rendered him unconscious. At least *that* bit was true – he had been unconscious.

He looked up. His eyelids retracted as the realisation hit him. That was it. That was what *really* happened. He was drugged by the girl.

Matilda was seeing off a neighbour when Ojo's car pulled into his compound. Ojo greeted the woman from two houses away and had almost made it to the door when Matilda said, 'Come here.'

With Abiodun, the driver, standing there, and the neighbour not quite four metres away on the other side of the gate, Matilda held her phone to Ojo's face and said, 'Look at yourself.'

Ojo felt sick in his stomach. On his wife's phone was a photograph of a man asleep. It looked like him. It was him. He had never seen himself asleep before. A naked girl was on top of him. From the angle of the picture and the position of her hand, she, the naked girl, had taken the picture. Her face was out of shot, but her bare breasts were pressed against his chest. He went to take the phone from his wife, to get a better look, but Matilda held it away.

'Don't even think about it,' she said and she slipped the phone through the neck of her blouse into her bra. 'I don't want to hear anything. You have disgraced yourself for the last time. My father wants to see you right away.'

'Matilda…'

She put up her hand to shut him up. She brushed past him and went into the house, leaving him standing with Abiodun.

'Madam has vexed o,' the driver said.

Ojo slapped him just as Matilda slammed the front door shut.

'Take me to Baba's house,' Ojo said and he climbed into the back seat of the Mercedes.

How did she get the picture? Did she also have the memory card? Had she seen what was on it? That would be very bad. Very, very bad. Maybe it was a setup – by the girl, Iyabo. He groaned. What had Matilda told Otunba Oluawo, the Lion of Yoruba land? She was his only daughter. Otunba, a senator in the second republic and a recurring decimal in all administrations since then, both military and civilian, was a man to fear. Even at eighty he was still handpicking senators and ministers and firing governors at will. He was not called the godfather of godfathers for nothing. A young politician once made the mistake of referring to the ageing politician as a relic of colonial times. The gentleman was a senator then. Otunba called to ask who his godfather was. The senator told a reporter about the private phone call and boasted of how he had replied that he had no godfathers. He went on the record, in print, to denounce the 'manipulative, selfish Nigerian concept of godfatherism that allows ageing gangsters, for want of a better description, to place unconstitutional quid-pro-quo burdens on people they manoeuvre into office.' He declared that he was not going to be one of those young men who fall prey to 'the greed of such unscrupulous dinosaurs whose interference in the political system has held Nigeria back.'

Two days later the Economic and Financial Crimes Commission – EFCC – invited the man for a meeting, detained him for four days, and when his lawyer took to the papers to lament the unconstitutional treatment of his client, the EFCC filed corruption charges just as the man's party disowned him and the president stopped taking his calls.

Now, Otunba had asked to see Ojo on the same day his daughter showed Ojo a picture of himself in bed with a girl. She had reported him to daddy.

Even though Ojo was Otunba's only son-in-law, Ojo was not part of the inner circle. He was a husband, not a son. This was what Matilda's eldest brother told him when he mentioned his ambition to run for the House of Representatives and asked how best to seek the old man's help. And so it had always been; Ojo was married to the only daughter of one of the most powerful politicians in the country, if not *the* most powerful, but the matrimony did not translate to direct manna; he still had to work for his money. He used his father-in-law's name to gain access to certain corridors of power where the doorkeepers were important enough to influence the awarding or quick processing of government contracts. All that, it now seemed, was about to come to an end. And God knows what the brothers would also do after the father had had his piece of flesh. And what if they got to see what was on the memory card? He felt sick again.

10

In a room in a white mansion on Banana Island, in pitch darkness and near total silence, a man shouted, 'Nobody move!'

A dog barked outside in the distance. Inside in the room, somebody coughed, cleared their throat, and coughed again. A phone began to buzz and then stopped. Outside, a generator roared before a metallic lid closed with a clank, reducing the noise to little more than a murmur. Seconds later the lights in the room came on and the air conditioner hummed back to life and its vents resumed their slow oscillations.

'You can continue now,' Prince Ambrose Adepoju said.

It was a large parlour with eight two-seater sofas arranged in a square. Men in native outfits were seated and other men in casual clothes stood behind the sofas. In the middle, on the Persian rug, two men in white kaftans sat in front of three large Ghana-must-go bags so full with bundles of naira notes they could not be zipped shut. Another man knelt by the money while a fourth, similarly dressed, sat with his legs to one side of an open briefcase that had neat stacks of hundred-dollar bills in it. By his side he had a stack of more dollars and he picked out another bundle from the briefcase, held it in his left hand, licked the thumb of his right, and with his fingers, began counting the money. He went through the wad in less than twenty seconds, placed it on the stash by his leg, and went for another bundle.

Ambrose was sat leaning forward on a sofa directly in front

of the man by the briefcase, keeping his eyes on the counting through thick-rimmed glasses with lenses that made his eyeballs look twice their size. He was in his sixties. He had a large grey untameable beard and his Afro grew out around a gleaming bald patch in the middle of his head. He puffed incessantly on a pipe clamped between his in-turned lips and with the fingers of his right hand, he counted the blue coral beads of the bracelet round his left wrist.

The double doors to the room opened. Ambrose looked over the rims of his glasses as Yellowman and Dr. Adeniyi Hope Babalola walked in. Babalola, the party's candidate, looked around at the men, the ones on the floor, the bags of naira notes, and the briefcase of dollar bills. His uncertain eyes settled on Ambrose. Nobody spoke.

The man on the floor counting the money picked the last bundle of dollars from the briefcase and flicked through the notes in seconds. He placed the rest of the money by his side and straightened his back.

'Is it all there?' Ambrose asked the black market money changer.

'Yes. You want to count?' the Hausa man asked, gesturing to the bags of naira.

'No. You may leave. Same time tomorrow, come with double the amount. Only big notes.'

The money changer and his colleagues shared the dollars amongst themselves, hid the money under their clothes, and left, leaving behind the bags of naira they had brought.

Ambrose stood up from his chair. He was a little over five feet tall. The other men stood also. He walked to Babalola and Yellowman.

'What is this?' Babalola asked.

'An emergency party meeting. Haven't you heard what happened?'

'Did we have anything to do with it?'

'Are you crazy?'

'But what's all this money for? Where is it from?'

'Mobilisation. You don't need to know where it's from.'

'With all due respect, when I agreed to run, I made it clear that it would have to be a clean campaign. What do we need mobilisation for? Who are we mobilising?'

'Everything has changed, my boy. For one, you need protection. They are saying you killed your opponent. You are staying with me from now on. Come with me.'

They walked out of the room into an adjoining parlour also full of party members, then into an unlit corridor with a window overlooking the front of the compound. The curtains were open, allowing moonlight to pour in through the glass.

'Before tonight,' Ambrose said, 'I had more chance of becoming the next president of America than you had of winning the election. You know it too. You are a divorcee. We have never elected a divorcee in Lagos. And you are from abroad. An outsider. But still I said I would support you. You know why? Because I have a vision.'

Yellowman walked behind them.

'You were just not eligible. You were not right enough or popular enough to rig the election for you. Yes, you heard me. I agreed that it would be a clean campaign, no rigging, because there was no point. No matter how much we spent, you were just not well known enough.' He stopped in the middle of the dark corridor, in front the window.

'You see, rigging is a necessity. If you don't rig, your opponent would still rig, so you have to rig just to counter their own rigging, and in the end, one person wins and the other goes to court to challenge the outcome of the election.'

'But you can only rig an election if the candidate is popular in the first place. Or at least more popular than the opponent. If you won against Douglas, may his soul rest in peace, the amount of people that would riot would be enough to convince any judge to declare a rerun without even looking at the evidence. You just wouldn't stand a chance. The plan was that by the next election you would have become a known name. We would have had to rig even if you were the people's popular choice. Do you think the opposition will just sit down and watch you get all the votes? They will do something, so we also have to do something, so that at the end of the day, their ojoro and our ojoro will cancel each other out and the real votes of the people would count. That is how democracy works.

'But all that has changed. Now we have a real chance at this thing. You can really be the next Governor of Lagos State.'

'You really think so?'

'I know so. This close to the election, they won't have time for primaries. They have to announce a candidate very soon.'

'Alhaji Hassan?'

'No. Douglas beat him in the primaries. It won't be somebody who already competed and lost in the party primaries. They have to choose someone new; someone who can claim the votes that would have gone to Douglas. Someone close to him. Someone popular.'

11

Abiodun pulled up behind a row of cars in front of Peace Lodge, Otunba Oluawo's mansion in Osborne Foreshore estate, in Ikoyi. The fence of the property extended the length of the street. There were cars on both sides of the road. Ojo suspected that it had something to do with the crashed plane – Otunba was the trump card behind the man's party. That the old man could spare the time to see Ojo during such a crisis increased Ojo's apprehension. Perhaps he would reveal Ojo and his daughter's divorce in front of all his political associates, thus ensuring Ojo became a total pariah.

There were extra guards at the gate that Ojo didn't recognise: police officers, army personnel, and thugs who openly carried unregistered shotguns and smoked their weed close to the law enforcement officers. A security guard bowed as he shook hands with Ojo and he let him through the foot gate.

Ojo walked slowly across the cobblestone compound towards the main building; there were seven buildings in total, with the main mansion taking centre stage at the end of a long driveway.

Standing in front of the door of the main house, Ojo considered turning round. Matilda had set him up and reported him to her father. The worst was done. Why was he here? To be told to behave himself? To be warned? To be fired as his daughter's husband the way Otunba fired politicians who offended him? Perhaps it was time he held his middle finger up to her and to her family. What had they done for him, anyway? The old man had never sent a contract his way, introduced him to any of his powerful allies, or for that matter taken him into his confidence. If he turned back now and left, what was the worst that could happen? He had three million dollars in a bank account in the US that Matilda didn't know about. He would survive without her family; only not in Nigeria.

His belly didn't feel better for considering walking away. He pressed the bell and waited.

A servant led him through a large parlour full of men dressed in bulbous agbadas in animated exchange. Politicians. He was right, there was a political meeting going on at Peace Lodge. Perhaps he could turn back today and explain that he didn't want to disturb the old man's political affairs.

The servant opened the door to Otunba's private parlour where Ojo had first met the man almost two decades earlier. He stopped. Otunba, sitting alone at the end of the room, stared directly at him from the middle of a sofa. On either side of him sat chiefs of the ruling party that Otunba had helped form. The men stopped talking when Ojo stepped in and turned to him. Ojo's belly felt even weaker and his heart began pounding. He took a step forward and a man stood, gathering the hem of his agbada over his shoulder. Ojo balked as the man approached him. It was Muhammad Kano, two-time governor of Taraba state and now a senator. He held out his hands to Ojo. 'Your Excellency,' he said, smiling as he shook Ojo's hands. The other men and women in the room got up too and walked up to Ojo, surrounding him, and taking turns to shake his hand, each of them addressing him as Your Excellency. Ojo looked past the politicians at Otunba, the only one still seated. The old kingmaker was smiling at his son-in-law.

12

'I will make you governor,' Otunba said, scanning his guests.

Ojo was next to him on the sofa. Servers were carting in food and drinks for the other politicians in the room who were standing or sitting in groups, chatting and drinking, eating and politicking.

Ojo kept his eyes on the old man as one would a coiled viper. He was confused. He had expected to feel the wrath of the kingmaker; instead he was being elevated to the echelons of power – or at least that was what was being offered.

'They said they didn't want Ishola or Michael,' Otunba said. 'They said I cannot nominate my own son. They forgot that I have one more son. Ishola is a senator; his brother is commissioner of works. Now you are going to be governor. I have said it.'

Ojo's hands were clasped over his knees, his body tilted towards the old man. He was not a politician; he wasn't even registered with any party – that dream had died with Matilda's brother mocking him. If he had more time to think, he would have pointed this out to Otunba, but the kingmaker had just held his son-in-law's hand up in front of all the big names in the party and declared, 'If this boy is fine enough for my daughter, he is fine enough for Lagos state,' and the assembled bigwigs had cheered and clapped.

'You heard about what happened to that boy?'

'That boy' was Douglas.

'Yes, sir. It's quite sad. It says a lot about the state of aviation...'

'It is not sad. It is unfortunate. Are you sad? Did you know him as a friend? Me that I knew him, I am not sad. Don't say sad. I warned the boy. I told him, 'They no longer want you,' what did he do? Did he listen? No. He started going on radio stations, inviting journalists, telling them this and that. That me, I gave him a list of people he must give contracts to. It is unfortunate, not sad. Say it: It is unfortunate.'

'It is unfortunate.'

'Yes. Your own case will not be unfortunate.'

'Amen.'

'It is not amen. You have to make sure of it yourself. Do you know why they killed that boy?'

'I thought it was a plane crash.'

'What kind of plane crash is that? How can a plane carrying you crash into your own house? It is not an accident. They planned it. Someone planned it. And do you know why?'

'No, sir.'

'I warned him. I said, 'the opposition have your skeletons; they will use it against you.' You know what he said to me? He said, 'Is it not right that we will rig the election?' Can you imagine?'

Ojo shook his head. Had Matilda not told her father about the picture on her phone and the stuff on the memory card? If she hadn't, what would happen when she did? Would this dream, that he was still trying to comprehend, suddenly be snatched from him? The feeling in the pit of his stomach returned. Would he also find himself a passenger in a plane about to crash?

Otunba continued. Ojo had missed some of what he said '...He is a stupid boy. When they brought him to me I said, 'Are we sure we want this boy?' They said he is modern. See what happened to him? Slaughtered like a fowl, and his wife too. His family wiped out like that. Only God knows whom he offended. Anyway, your own will not be like that.'

It was obvious who he offended. The Lion of Yorubaland. The kingmaker himself. The man once referred to by a Supreme Court judge as 'The only Nigerian you cannot take to court.'

'Amen,' Ojo said.

'Not amen. It is up to you. From now on, till the party officially announces you, you must not talk to the press. You and your wife. Let them speculate. We have leaked the news to our papers this night, but you must avoid any form of statement, do you understand? It has to come from the party.

'It is here in this parlour that the party chairman will come and meet you. I am going to make you the next governor of this state, but there is one thing you must first do for me. Can you do it?'

Ojo nodded. He braced himself.

'Do you have any skeletons?'

Surely he was referring to the memory card. What had Matilda told him? Had he seen the contents of the card himself? Was the copy of it safely stored on his phone, an example of his skeletons?

'Everybody has skeletons,' Otunba said. 'There is one thing I want you to know: right now, from this moment on, you do not have any friends. You don't have any family. Everyone you know will try to use you. Anyone who knows your secret will control you.

'I want you to go home and talk to your wife. Tell her that you are now referred to as His Excellency. It is me, Otunba, that has said it. I want you to go into your room or to any other quiet place, and I want you to get a pen and paper and write down every skeleton that you have so that we can deal with it. We must make sure that what destroyed that boy will not destroy you too.'

13

Her eyelids fluttered before they opened. There was a figure in front of her. It didn't surprise or scare her; it was as if she had already felt someone staring at her and that was what woke her up. Why was she sleeping? Who was the person standing in the doorway, piercing light shining from behind them?

Amaka brought a hand up to shield her eyes and the bed creaked. It wasn't her bed. She wasn't in her house.

The hazy figure turned and left. The door closed. Darkness. Amaka opened her eyes wide, trying to focus in the dark.

'She's awake o.'

It had to be the person in the door. It was a woman. Amaka sat up in the strange bed. It creaked. She strained to see. She began to make out shapes. The bed had no headboard or footboard. Boxes and bags lined the walls. There was a sofa with folded clothes on it. A dressing table had tubes and bottles and plastic jars and picture frames. On the wall, above the mirror, a vertical row of buttons glistened dully from an outfit on a hanger. The door opened. Light. It was a ceremonial police uniform. Its hat also hung from the nail in the wall. Ibrahim walked in. A woman stood in the doorway behind him, leaned her left shoulder against the frame and clasped her finger over her right hip.

'How do you feel?' Ibrahim said.

What was she doing in Ibrahim's home? In his bed. He

looked strange in a white singlet and blue sports pants with three stripes running down the sides.

'You were hit on the head,' he said. 'You should have been in bed.'

Amaka touched the back of her head where she felt the pain.

'What happened to the girl?'

'It was a man. A thief. They burnt him.'

He sat on the side of the bed. It creaked under his weight.

She'd thought the faint smell of smoke was from the bed. Now, in her head, she saw the burning body. The flames wrapped around it. The smell.

'No. There was a girl. What happened to her?'

'A girl? By the time I got there, it was all over. You are lucky. They were going to kill you too. You do not interfere in a mob action. When my boys got there, some women had surrounded you so they couldn't get to you.'

'Why didn't you take me to the hospital?'

'I did. You don't remember? We went to Wilmot Point. The doctor gave you something. He said there was a slight risk of concussion. You walked up the stairs here by yourself. You don't remember? Maybe you have to go back and see him in the morning.'

'But why didn't you take me home?'

'Have you forgotten? The plane crash. I told you. They have blocked all access to the entire area.'

'Oh. I remember you mentioned it. It was close to my house?'

'Yes. You know Chief Douglas?'

'The gubernatorial candidate?'

'Yes. His house. On Magbon Close. And it was his plane. He was in it.'

She looked at him.

'Yes. He was in the private jet that crashed into his own home. Crazy. People are saying it is the opposition. Already there are riots and...'

'You don't know what happened to the girl?'

'I already told you, there was no girl. I mean, there were lots of civilians there, and of course the women who protected you, but the boy had already been set on fire and we couldn't simply arrest all the onlookers.'

'There was a girl. They were going to burn her too.' She looked past him. 'Is that your wife?'

Ibrahim turned to the woman in the doorway. 'Yes.'

Amaka nodded at her. The woman pushed herself off the frame and crossed her hands over her chest.

'What time is it?' Amaka said.

Ibrahim searched his bare wrist for his watch.

'I'm not sure.' He turned to his wife. 'Abike, what time is it?'

She unfolded her hands, and folded them again.

'Where were you going, anyway?' Ibrahim said.

Amaka looked at him. He was staring directly into her eyes, his forehead creased with concern. She looked at his wife. Abike stared back, her face tight with loathing or anger or both. Amaka checked the time on her own watch. 11:30pm.

'Where's my phone?'

'I searched for it. I called it but it just kept ringing and my officers couldn't find it.'

'I need to find it. I filmed the killers' faces. And the girl. I got the girl as well. I got everything on video.'

'Amaka, the phone is gone. Where were you going?'

'My car?'

'We found it there. The key was in your skirt, but we couldn't find your bag. The door was open. Was your bag in the car?'

'Shit. My passport was in that bag.'

'Your international passport?'

'What other type of passport is there? And my laptop, too. And my other phone. Shit. I have to get my lines back.'

'You can do that in the morning, for now you really have to rest.'

'No, you don't understand. I have to get my lines back. The girls, they will be sending messages. I have to… Oh no.'

'What?'

'She slammed her palm onto the mattress. The bed creaked.

'What is it?'

'There was a memory card in the bag.'

'A flash drive?'

'No. A micro card. Fuck.'

'What is on the card?'

She looked at him, glanced at his wife, and then back at him.

'Where is my car?'

'It's downstairs. You should sleep. Are you hungry? Maybe you want to shower?'

'I'll be fine.'

'OK. I'll just leave you to rest now,' Ibrahim said. 'The doctor said you should sleep. I'll be just outside.'

He got up, paused to look at her, then turned to leave.

'Wait,' she said. 'Thank you.'

'You are welcome. Please, go to sleep. We'll talk in the morning.'

He walked past his wife. She walked up to Amaka.

'Ibrahim said they did not touch you,' Abike said.

Amaka was thinking of the lost memory card and didn't respond. Then she realised what Abike meant but decided it didn't call for a response.

'I'm sorry to be imposing on you,' Amaka said.

'You are not imposing. Ibrahim said you are welcome, so, that's all.'

'Abike,' Ibrahim called.

'We are in the parlour,' she said to Amaka.

Amaka nodded.

Abike lingered. She held her hand out, close to Amaka's face.

'Pass me my Bible under that pillow.'

Amaka looked behind her, raised the pillow wet with her sweat, and saw the red copy of a King James Bible. She was a Christian, married to a Muslim. Amaka handed the Bible to Abike who tucked it under her armpit.

'And the pillow.'

Abike waited as Amaka handed it to her, then she left and closed the door behind her.

Amaka sat staring at the door that Abike had left slightly ajar. She swung her feet off the bed and stepped on cold linoleum. She stood and searched around for her shoes, finding instead her car keys on a stool tucked under the dressing table. She found her shoes by the door, next to three pairs of men's shoes, polished to a mirror shine. She took one last look around the room.

Amaka stepped into the living room. There was a mattress on the floor in the middle of three red leather sofas that formed a U facing a console cabinet, against which were propped two flat-screen televisions side by side. On the mattress, Abike and Ibrahim were wrapped up in separate sheets with their backs to each other. Ibrahim stood up abruptly. He was shirtless, his chest covered in curly back hair. He reached for his singlet next to Abike's nightdress on one of the sofas.

'Amaka, where are you going?' he said.

Abike sat up on the mattress and pulled her sheet up to cover herself while with her other hands she picked up Ibrahim's cover cloth and held it up to him. He ignored her.

'I am very grateful to you for coming to help those people when I called you,' Amaka said, 'and I am grateful that you brought me here, but there is somewhere else I need to be. You said my car is downstairs?'

'Yes. But, you are not in a condition to drive. The doctor gave you an injection.'

'Probably just a mild sedative. How do I find the car?'

14

Ambrose stood in the middle of his floodlit compound and watched the gates open. Yellowman and Babalola were on either side of him; a dozen or so armed guards lingered around. The truck that had been rumbling on idle rolled into the compound filling the air with its diesel exhaust.

Two men climbed into the back of the truck while Ambrose and Babalola watched. It was loaded with sacks of 'Best Quality Golden Rice.' The two guards in the truck picked up a sack and passed it to two others waiting outside. The men placed the heavy sack on the ground in front of Ambrose and Babalola. They continued unloading the truck, taking more bags into the house.

Yellowman reached under his jacket and pulled out a sheathed dagger. He removed the blade and stooped down by the sack, and with one motion sliced it open. Grains of rice fell onto the pavement. He dipped a hand into the rice and pulled out a brand-new AK-47 assault rifle, without its magazine, holding the gun by the barrel. The weapon was the stockless variety. He stood up, and presented the gun to Ambrose.

Ambrose gestured to Babalola. 'Give the gun to Doc,' he said. 'Let him feel it'. Yellowman flicked a grain of rice off the body of the rifle, and, still holding it by the muzzle, handed the weapon to Babalola.

'What are these for?' Babalola asked. He took the weapon,

surprised at how light it was, and held it away from his body as if it posed an immediate danger.

'For the election. We are no longer playing games. We have to match them naira for naira, gun for gun, bullet for bullet.'

'Why are you letting me see this?' Babalola said.

'Because you have to know what it will take to get you into office. You are part of this; part of everything it takes to get you elected. Give the gun to Yellowman.'

Babalola held the weapon out to Yellowman, who removed a folded handkerchief from his pocket and flicked it open. With the cloth covering his palm, Yellowman gripped the top of the gun's barrel and walked away with it.

Babalola watched him leaving.

'Why did he do that?'

'Your prints are on the gun. In case you get any stupid ideas, or you are misled by anybody, that gun would be discovered next to a murdered member of the opposition.'

'That is blackmail.'

'Yes, it is. But is it not better than taking you to a shrine to swear an oath?'

'Prince, this is not what I signed up for.'

'No, it is not. But everything has changed now. You will become Governor of Lagos State, and guns and blackmail are all part of the machinery that will get you there.'

Another vehicle pulled up behind the gate and honked.

15

Amaka took a long drag on her cigarette, threw it to the concrete floor and ground it under her shoe. She searched and found a white button on the left side of the door and pressed it. A dull ding-dong sounded behind the door. Her head was level with the peephole. She moved away. She pressed the bell again, checked her watch, then turned around and looked over the sixth-floor balcony at the low-rise and high-rise buildings of 1004 Estate, home to 1004 households that had locked their doors and bedded down for the night. She looked down. Her Bora was just one of the hundreds of cars under the lamps of the car park. From the other side of the door she could hear footsteps approaching. Someone flicked a switch. Amaka looked down and away from the peephole.

'Who is that?' came a woman's voice from behind the door.

'Me,' Amaka said.

'Who?'

Amaka tried to disguise her voice. 'Me, babes.' Moments passed then she heard a key in the lock, followed bolts sliding.

The, slim, bespectacled young woman in the doorway wore a white silk housecoat that showed the curves of her breasts and her nipples beneath. Amaka looked up from the woman's cleavage to the confused face behind thick-rimmed glasses. The woman began to mouth 'Shit' and moved to shut the door.

Amaka wedged her feet in to stop it shutting. 'Naomi, please, I just want to talk,' she said.

'What are you doing here?' Naomi said. She kept her weight on the door.

'I need your help,' Amaka said.

'Go away. I already told you, I don't have anything to say to you. Go away or I'll call the police.'

'Call the police.'

Both women kept pushing against the door in a tense and unsteady impasse. A warm breeze blew down the corridor outside, wrapping around Amaka's ankles. A lone vehicle sped away in the distance on Ozumba Mbadiwe.

'I will shout thief,' the girl said.

'Malik is looking for me,' Amaka said. 'Someone told him about me; that I'm looking for him. Now he's looking for me.'

'It wasn't me.'

'I know it wasn't you, but I need your help. Please, Naomi, let me come in.'

'Just go away. After what you did, why should I help you?'

'I'm sorry about everything. Please let me in.'

'I don't believe you and I don't care. I already told you, I am not saying anything to you. You're going to get me in trouble.'

'He's going to kill me.'

Moments passed. The door opened and Amaka looked up at Naomi's heart-shaped face. Her thick and shaped eyebrows seemed to follow the curve of her prominent cheekbones. Her skin was smooth and shiny. Her large breasts were firm. Amaka had once described them to a male friend and he had asked her if she wanted to fuck the girl. Naomi slowly raised her hands to the housecoat, pulled the white silk over her breasts and stepped aside.

Amaka walked into the cool parlour. The walls of the duplex flat were white. White Venetian blinds hung over the windows. A white cowhide rug was spread over the white marble floor between two white sofas. In the largest of the many large white picture frames on the wall, Naomi was one of two girls standing, smiling, holding bouquets of flowers on either side of a seated woman with a tiara and a sash that said Miss Nigeria. Naomi's sash said 1st Runner-up.

Amaka and Naomi sat opposite one another and stared in silence, both of them recovering from their struggle with the door.

'What happened to you?' Naomi asked.

Amaka looked down at herself. Her clothes were rough and stained and only God knew what her hair was doing. 'I was robbed. I need your help. I need to find The Harem.'

'I already told you, I can't help you. Nobody knows how to get there. And besides, why would I help you?'

'Do you still work there?'

Naomi looked away.

'I know he pays you well, but you cannot keep doing this forever. What's your exit plan? You have a degree in economics, you're intelligent, you're beautiful…'

Naomi put her hand up. 'Yeah, yeah, yeah, I've heard it all before. Will you give me a job?'

'Naomi, what happened to Florentine can happen to you too.'

'I didn't even know the girl till you brought her here.'

'But she recognised you at the house and you saw what Ojo did to her there. She showed you the pictures on her phone. Right here, on this sofa. She showed you the pictures. Remember? The way he beat her. Almost killed her.'

Naomi clasped her hands between her knees and began to rock back and forth.

'Ojo meant to kill her,' Amaka continued. 'He almost did. He thought he had. And when he thought she was dead, Malik helped him dump her body on the road.'

'Maybe she stole from him.'

'That gives him permission to beat her up like that? To try to kill her?'

'I've already told you, I can't help you. I can't do anything. You'll get me into trouble.'

'Naomi, they tried to kill her, Ojo and Malik, and now they know I'm after them. I have to find The Harem. I'll protect you. I promise.'

'How? Look, I really don't know what you think I can do for you. First, you threaten to tell everyone that I'm a prostitute...'

'I only said it to make you talk. I would never have done it.'

'You called me a prostitute, a sex slave. Then you said I was suffering from Stockholm Syndrome.'

'I regret saying those things. I only said them because I was desperate to find The Harem.'

'Then you started following me all over Lagos.'

'I tailed you because I was hoping you would lead me to the house.'

'But I told you, the girl also told you, no one knows the way there. We meet at a guesthouse where they pick us up. And it's a different guesthouse every time and you don't even know where it's going to be until it's time for you to go. And yet you were tailing me all over Lagos. What if they found out? He would have thought I was working with you.'

Amaka hunched forward. 'Naomi, the last time we spoke you told me you wouldn't be doing this if you had a better option. I'm offering you one now. Help me find The Harem and you'll never have to do what you do ever again. I'll get you a job with my father. Abroad. He's an ambassador. I already spoke to him.'

'Your father is an ambassador?'

'Yes. I told him you're one of my workers at the charity and I want to help you start a career in the foreign service.'

'You're lying.'

'No I'm not. I'm his only child. He'll do anything for me. I'll call him and you can talk to him yourself. I protected Florentine, didn't I? I'll protect you too.'

They sat in silence. Naomi alternated between looking at Amaka and looking past her into space. She rocked back and forth on the sofa, twiddling her thumbs.

'How would we even find the place?' Naomi said. 'They will know someone is following us. I told you, the place is somewhere in the forest. For the last twenty minutes of the journey there are no other cars.'

'You can use your phone. You just have to send me a message with your GPS location when you are there. I can show you how to do it.'

'I know how to do it. But it won't work. They take our phones before they take us there and they only give them back when we return.'

'You can sneak it in.'

'They search us.'

'You can put it inside you.'

'Inside, how?'

'You know, inside.'

The women looked at each other. Naomi closed her eyes and began to shake her head. 'No.' She stood up, still shaking her head, and began to pace between the two sofas. 'No, no, no,' she repeated. 'Look, I already told you, I cannot help you. I do not want to have anything to do with this. Please, you have to leave now. And please, don't come here again. Leave me alone. Don't come back. Ever.'

'You saw those pictures on Florentine's phone,' Amaka said as she stood up. 'Think about that. It could be you one day. And one more thing; I will find The Harem, with or without you. And when I do, it would be better for you if you had helped me. I hope you understand. The offer with my father won't last forever.'

A white Range Rover Sport stopped on the drive in 1004 Estate. The brake lights of a Bora had come on in a row of parked cars. The man in the Range Rover adjusted the AC, selected a jazz track on the car stereo, and waited for the other car to pull out. His headlights caught the driver's face. It was a woman. She put her hand up to protect her eyes. As she reversed, the rear of her car came close to the front of his SUV before she engaged the forward gear and drove off. He watched as she turned along the row of parked cars, then when he couldn't make out her features any longer, he pulled into the space she had vacated.

He left the engine running and pressed the phone icon on the central console, scrolled through his phone book till he found 'Naomi Sexy'. As the call rang through the car's sixteen speakers, he leaned forward to look in the mirror. A light-complexioned face with a trimmed beard looked back at him in the darkness. He dusted a red speck off the shoulder of his black top, straightened the pen in his breast pocket, and sat back. He tapped his manicured fingers rhythmically on the steering wheel.

A female voice answered: 'Hello.'

'Are you ready? I'm downstairs,' he said.

'Give me five minutes,' Naomi said.

'Hurry up. I have to stop at Osborne Estate on the way.'

'OK. I won't be long.'

'Hey, who is the chick that drives a silver Bora in your building?'

'In my building?'

'Yes. She just drove away now. Dark, braids, pretty face.'

'What was she wearing?'

'A cream top, I think. You know her?'

'No.'

'Silver Bora. She was parked right in front of your building.'

'I don't know anyone that owns a Bora. I'm coming down now.'

Naomi placed the phone on her dressing table. Her hands were shaking. He saw her; he saw Amaka leaving 1004 but he didn't recognise her. He didn't know what she looked like, thank God. What if he'd realised it was her? Coming from her flat?

She placed her still-shaking hands on her knees and looked in the mirror. She had not had time to do her make-up since Amaka left. She removed her glasses and placed them down next to her contact lenses case; she picked it up, but rather than place the tiny lenses onto her eyeballs, she stared at her now out-of-focus reflection: Naomi, Miss Nigeria Runner-up.

The first time someone called her Naomi was in Queen's School in Ibadan. It was the literary and debating day, when they got to invite boys to the girls-only secondary school. She had fixed her hair like the supermodel Naomi Campbell's, and in place of her glasses, she had used a pair of disposable contact lenses her mum bought on vacation in London. A senior saw her and said she looked just like Campbell. Everyone agreed. She eventually saw it as well and it became her look – at least she decided it would be once she entered university. In the meantime the glasses returned, the Brazilian hair attachment came off, but the name stuck: Naomi. At first it was just a nickname and everyone knew her real name, Mayowa Idowu, but once she gained admission to study Economics at the University of Lagos and she began to introduce herself as Naomi, it became the only name most knew her by.

Outside the school uniform and regulation hairstyles of secondary school, her looks got her even more attention. Not only was she free to fix Brazilian and Peruvian hair just like the supermodel's, she could wear make-up, copying the images in Vogue and other magazines. She could also wear heels, and there was no senior to report her to anyone for wiggling her bum – mimicking the way she thought the real Naomi Campbell walked all the time in real life.

Then her friends convinced her to apply for the Miss Nigeria contest and without thinking she wrote down Naomi as her first name on the registration forms. But the organisers wanted identification. She explained how the name was not her real name and they understood, and they asked her to register again using her real name, but she wanted to keep her new name, so she applied for a quickie passport, paid a bribe, and it became official: First name Mayowa. Surname Idowu. Other names: Naomi.

She did not win. Her five-foot-nine frame and Naomi Campbell looks lost out to a five-foot-four, bleached-skinned, can't-speak-a-grammatically-correct-sentence Miss Lagos State – who was not even from Lagos. Everyone knew why Naomi lost, but when she heard it from her mother as well, it sounded more like an accusation than an explanation: 'Mayowa did not sleep with the judges.' Everyone knew it; the flabby-armed, dim-witted girl who won did so by sleeping with someone. Maybe not the judges, maybe not even the organisers. Maybe someone in the senate in Abuja, a boss who called the boss of the pageant and told him, 'My babe must be the winner.' Everyone knew Naomi should have won. But she didn't, and after a very short while, everyone knew who Miss Nigeria was, and no one remembered the runner-up.

A friend was keen to take Naomi to a juju man. The friend said that the juju man would place a curse on the winner to befall her with a scandal that would lose her the crown, or an illness that would end in death, so that Naomi would be given what was rightfully hers. But Naomi did not come from that kind of background. They did not do juju in her family.

Her mum was a civil servant who travelled the world attending training courses paid for by the government. Her father, likewise. The children went to good schools and spoke good English. The family lived in their official residence – a three-bedroom duplex in 1004, before the government sold the estate and the developers who bought it cheap turned the hitherto civil servant accommodation into expensive luxury homes.

The family moved out of Lagos, Naomi stayed behind for University. She entered the pageant and lost, but she had come so close, and for the weeks before and the weeks after, she had lived the world of beauty and luxury and pampering and wealth and had loved it. And one day, knowing fully well what it was, she accepted an invitation to a party in VI for visiting state governors and there she met Malik.

Was Florentine just like her? Was she also from a decent home? Did she also have good prospects? Could she also have done something different with her life than sucking off rich, fat men old enough to be her father?

Naomi could see the pictures on Florentine's phone that day the girl showed them to her. The bruises. The burst-open lips. The eyes swollen shut. It could have been her.

She pushed the edges of her nightgown off her shoulders and it fell over the stool. As she stood, she picked up her phone from the table, clicked the screen to check for messages, then held down the power button. She wetted her fingers, put them to the lips of her vagina and rubbed. She looked down at the dressing table. Her eyes settled on a tub of Vaseline. She turned and went to the bedside table, opened the drawer and returned to the mirror holding her phone in one hand and a tube of K-Y jelly and a condom in the other.

16

Amaka turned onto Oyinkan Abayomi Drive and her headlights illuminated a police van parked across the road. Two police officers armed with assault rifles shielded their eyes. She dipped the lights and waited for them to walk up to her car.

'Good evening, madam,' the officer by her window said. 'The road is blocked.'

'My name is Amaka Mbadiwe. I live here. Ambassador Mbadiwe's residence.'

'Can I see your identification?'

'Identification. My handbag was stolen today. The guards can identify me.'

'I see. We are not allowing any vehicles in or out till tomorrow.'

'Can I leave my car here and walk? I just want to pick up some stuff.'

'Madam, we are not allowing anybody to pass.'

Amaka pulled up in front of Bogobiri House on Maitama Sule Street. The road was dark as there were no streetlights. Cables from electricity and telephone poles criss-crossed above. Generators rumbled behind fences. The gate of the boutique hotel was shut. She left the car running and got out to knock. A sleepy night guard peered through the iron poles of the gate.

After Amaka asked about accommodation, he excused himself to fetch the night manager.

'Do you have any rooms available tonight?' Amaka asked the young man who looked like he'd been woken from sleep.

The guard began to open the gates at the night manager's bidding but Amaka stopped them. 'I just want to know if you have a room available,' she said.

'Yes ma, we do.'

'How much is it?'

'Twenty-eight thousand, ma.'

'OK. I'll be back.'

Amaka got into her car while the employees watched from the poles of the gate.

Amaka slowed down to turn onto Sanusi Fafunwa Street. As she did, a woman in a tight, black miniskirt and tube top, standing alone at the top of the road, tried to wave her down. On Sanusi Fafunwa Amaka drove past more women, standing alone or in twos, beckoning motorists looking to buy sex.

She came to a stretch with cars parked on both sides of the road. Here, in front of clubs, bars, casinos, and late-night shawarma spots, the women were concentrated and shared the road with hawkers of cigarettes, sweets, and condoms, and beggars soliciting only from the male customers going in or coming out of the many establishments.

Amaka pulled into an empty spot. A woman in bum-shorts and a studded bra squeezed between the Bora and the adjacent Range Rover and only turned back when she saw that it was a woman at the wheel.

Amaka ran her palms over her clothes before she walked towards Y-Not. The bouncer looked her over once, stared into her eyes for a few seconds then let her through. Amaka walked into the smoke-filled bar, stood at the doorway and looked around. She pushed her way through to the bar and sat facing the crowd. Most of the men inside where white, all the women were black and younger than the men, and they were younger than the women standing on the road outside, and better dressed, too. In time, as age eroded their youth, they too might end up on the sidewalk, beckoning to strange men in the night and hoping they did not wave down a killer and end up with their breasts cut off like the girl who'd been dumped in a gutter just yards from where other women now stood.

Amaka turned her back to the waiter and concentrated on the pool tables where a group of four white men were enjoying the attention of eight girls gathered round them at a table to watch a game. One of the men was chalking up while a tall, slender, light-skinned girl in a black slip-on dress lay half across the table aiming to take a shot. The man looked up and saw Amaka watching. He smiled and winked. Amaka winked back.

17

Malik got down and had walked past two other cars parked on the side of the road before he turned, pointed his key at the Range Rover with Naomi inside it, and pressed a button to activate the alarm.

At the entrance to Peace Lodge, he leaned close to a panel on the fence and spoke into the microphone. 'My name is Malik. Baba is expecting me.'

When he was still close to the wall, he removed a pen from the breast pocket of his black dashiki, twisted its cap until he heard a click, then replaced it, his actions hidden from the camera above the console.

On the other side of the fence a guard considered the tall, light-complexioned man on his monitor. A call had come from the main house letting the gate know that Otunba was expecting a Malik, but no title had preceded the name, no Chief, Prince, Senator, or even Honourable, so the guards had not known what to expect. The man standing outside could be a politician or an errand boy. He looked rich in his starched outfit with an embroidered emblem over the breast pocket. Even on the small, colour monitor, his skin looked like he was used to eating good food and living in an air-conditioned house. His beard, however, shimmering with pomade, made him seem more Lagos Big Boy than Abuja Big Man. The guard buzzed the foot gate open.

Two security guards were waiting for Malik when he stepped into the compound. One of them had a wand, the other held out a square, grey plastic tray. Three police officers holding AK-47s stood behind the guards and watched.

The wand beeped at Malik's trousers. Malik lowered his stretched-out arms to remove his two phones. He removed the keys to his Range Rover Sport from the other pocket, along with a wad of money in a gold clip. Everything went into the grey tray. Next, he removed his Hublot Fusion King Gold and gently placed the watch on top of the wallet already in the tray. He struggled with the clasp on his gold bracelet and the officer with the wand said, 'No need.'

The officer ran the wand down Malik's sides again and to his feet, down his back, over the insides of his legs, then along each hand, the wand beeping as it went over the gold bracelet. A black pen was visible in Malik's breast pocket. The officer waved the wand over it and it beeped. Malik removed the pen and was about to place it in the tray when the officer held out his hand for it. The officer tested its weight in his hand. He seemed fascinated by the floating star in the tip of its cap. 'Mont Blanc,' he said to the other officer, nodding, and returned the pen to Malik with a smile.

One of the waiting policeman asked Malik to follow him. They walked up to the main building, then turned right onto a pathway with trimmed edges on either side. They went past the building, turned along the footpath, past the wire fence of a lit-up lawn tennis court, past a row of white plastic pool chairs, and to the pool house on the other side of the large rectangular pool.

After fifteen minutes sitting alone in the pool house, Malik composed a message on his phone: 'I am at Otunba Oluawo's house. He asked me to come and see him. I don't know why.'

He selected several contacts in his address book, many of them with the prefixes, Senator, Honourable, Chief. He sent the message to all of them, watching his screen to see the messages get delivered.

From his armchair he could see the lit windows of the big house. He saw people walking past, stopping to talk, leaning against the window frame. It must have to do with the party's dead candidate. He could be waiting a long time. But why had Otunba reached out to him?

The policeman by the door, his rifle slung across his body, hands held behind his back, was probably there to keep him in place.

Malik had been introduced to Douglas once, at a party hosted by a senator, and he had seen him a couple of times after that at other parties, but they had never as much as said hello again after that first introduction. Douglas was not a real Lagosian. His life was really in America where he made his money selling subprime mortgages. He had returned to Nigeria only five years earlier to accept an appointment as Commissioner for Works and Housing, and in that capacity he made his name by allocating small parcels of land in the recovered areas of Lekki to groups of indigenes that then sold them on and became first-time millionaires. The people loved him. But what the hell did he have to do with Malik? Why had Otunba, whom Malik had never met, called him himself and asked him if he wouldn't mind coming to Peace Lodge immediately? Otunba Oluawo, who once kept a president of the federation waiting while he played table tennis with his grandson, and when he had time for the president, just wanted to tell him that he was invited to his only daughter's wedding, was keeping Malik waiting, but definitely not so as to invite him to something fun.

Malik kept his eyes on the policeman while he raised his hand to his chest pocket. The officer turned to face him. Malik dropped his hand away. 'Does he know I've arrived?' he asked.

'Sorry?' the officer said.

'Does baba know that I have arrived?'

'I think they called him when you arrived. Please be patient. He will see you soon.'

A back door of the mansion opened and a man appeared. Malik leaned forward, then stood. The policeman also stood to attention and Malik began to walk to the door.

'Please, remain here,' the officer said, holding out his hand.

Malik looked out the window at the old man getting closer. He looked shorter in real life than in the papers, slightly stooped, but at over eighty, it was impressive that he could still walk with such assured strides. He had no bodyguards with him. Well, it was his house, after all, but it still felt strange to see such a powerful man appear so vulnerable.

The policeman opened the glass door for Otunba.

'Malik, how are you?' Otunba said, extending his hand.

'I'm fine, sir,' Malik said, bowing as they shook hands. 'It is a great honour to meet you, sir.'

'Yes, yes. Sit down.'

Their armchairs faced each other.

'Leave us,' Otunba said to the policeman. The officer left, closed the door behind him, and walked to the other side of the pool where he stopped and turned to face the pool house.

With his hands on the armrests, Otunba began. 'I understand that my son-in-law visits your little club in the forest,' he said.

'Yes, sir,' Malik said.

'No. The answer is no.'

'Quite right, sir. No. I do not have a club in the forest.'

'Good. I was told your business is blackmail.'

Malik opened his mouth to talk. Otunba raised a hand to stop him.

'Do not deny anything. You let your customers arrange to meet the girls outside your club. They think they are cheating you but the girls are working for you. The girls arrange even younger girls and sometimes even boys for them. You videotape them doing all sorts with the little girls and boys and you use it to extort them but they think it is the girl doing it.

'They either pay the girls, or they tell you. When they do tell you, you tell them you will take care of it. The girl disappears, and you give them what you claim to be the only copy of the video and they fall into your debt. They think you have killed for them and they are not sure whether you have kept a copy of the video.

'Am I correct so far?'

Malik nodded.

'We know about your little games. You are a businessman and I am a politician. We both do what we have to do, I understand. Your business does not concern me, so you don't have to be afraid. But you must do what I ask you to do or else you will become my enemy right from this night. So, now that we understand each other, tell me now, what do you have on my son-in-law?'

18

The girl took her shot, potted the ball in the corner, looked up at her opponent and noticed he had not being watching. He was eyeing someone behind and licking his upper lip with the tip of his tongue. Still laying flat on the table, cue still in hand, she looked to see who it was.

Funke disturbed some balls on the cushion as she got up, then she tossed her cue stick onto the table, sending more balls in motion, and walked towards the bar.

Amaka turned in her stool and crossed her arms on the cold marble counter. When Funke climbed onto the empty stool next to her, she looked the other way.

'Aunty, what are you doing here?' Funke said, half-whispering. From the corner of her eyes she glanced over Amaka's clothes. 'What happened?'

'I was robbed,' Amaka said. 'How are you?'

'Oh God. What did they take?'

'My bag. The stuff inside it. Don't worry about me. Are you OK?'

'Yes. You mean, about him? Did it work?'

'Yes. Thank you, Funke.'

'When I didn't hear from you, I was afraid that maybe he knew I set him up.'

'No, he doesn't. Has he called you again?'

'No. Not since then. He sent a message that I am an ingrate. I just ignored him, like you said. Foolish man.'

'I'm so sorry I got you mixed up in all this.'

'Ah, no o, aunty. With everything you have done for me? And after what he did to that girl, I swear I will do anything to make sure he gets what he deserves. Evil man.'

'Thanks. If he calls you, tell him you're out of town. Stay away from him, and warn your friends, too.'

'Am I stupid? After you showed me those pictures. Maybe that is what he wanted to do to me too. You still won't tell me what you're planning to do with him?'

'It's better you don't know. For your own safety. Funke, I need your help.'

'What is it, aunty?'

'I need a smartphone, a new SIM card, 5K credit, and thirty thousand naira.'

'When?'

'Now.'

Funke stared at Amaka a while, then her face lit with purpose. 'I'm coming,' she said and she hopped off the stool.

Amaka watched Funke walk back to the pool table. Her former opponent was racking up the balls to play a new game with another girl. Funke walked up to two girls and spoke to them, and as the two walked away, Funke walked up to another group of girls.

Twenty minutes later Funke returned to the bar and sat next to Amaka. She had a Nokia phone and a charger, and a crumpled black cellophane bag wrapped around a little parcel. She placed the items on the bar top. The phone had a thin lateral crack curving across the screen, and the charger had a European plug. She opened the cellophane bag and brought out a bundle of notes in different denominations and handed them all to Amaka.

'Forty thousand,' she said.

'I only need thirty,' Amaka said.

'Don't worry,' Funke said. She reached into the bag and fetched a new SIM pack and several airtime scratch cards. She got the SIM card out and inserted it into the phone, and held down the button to switch on the device. 'Aunty, what are you drinking?' She asked.

While the waiter fetched Amaka a glass of neat Remy Martin VSOP, Funke began to tear open each scratch card packet, using her long red nail to scratch off the panel and review the code, and load the airtime credit onto the phone.

Amaka memorised the new phone number on the back of the SIM pack. Funke handed her the phone and she handed the SIM pack to the girl.

'This is the new number to use,' Amaka said. 'Tell the girls and tell them to tell their friends. The old number doesn't work anymore. At least not tonight.'

Funke nodded.

Amaka placed a hand on Funke's shoulder. 'Thank you again, Funke. For this and for everything else.'

Funke looked away as her eyes clouded over. She leaned forward and put her arms round Amaka. The two women hugged in silence while Wizkid serenaded the crowd around them.

19

Yet another car crawled past, searching for a place to park. It was the third since Malik left her alone in his car. The engine was off and the windows up, and he had taken his keys with him. He said he wouldn't be long but he'd been gone over thirty minutes. The residual coolness from the AC was gone and she was beginning to feel damp under her armpits.

She looked at the three soldiers a few metres away passing a joint among them. What if she tried to open the door and the alarm went off? She was in a pair of bum shorts and a tube top. Better to stay in the car and endure the growing heat.

Malik had only told her he had a quick business thing to attend to. She knew better than to ask him what, but from the large number of cars parked outside what looked like the largest compound in Osborne Estate, it had to be a party. It made sense. Some big shot was having a party and Malik was arranging girls for it. Was he planning to hand her over to someone here? Someone rich and important? Someone important enough not to have the time to make the trip to The Harem? Even though no one had ever suggested it, she was sure The Harem was not the only business he had going. The man dealt in sex, period. She had met him at one such party, and like this one, it was probably being thrown by a member of The Harem and they had contracted the pussy to him.

At first he had simply introduced himself as Malik, then he

was interested in her plan to study maritime law. He mentioned the University of Dundee before she said it. He seemed to know what he was talking about. They spent most of the evening together. He seemed to know everyone; the governors, the bodyguards, the businessmen, the young, pretty girls – his staff, maybe. But at the time she had just assumed he was a guest; a rich man like the other men, but a handsome one at that – and one with manners, who actually wanted to talk about other things than what he did, how much he was worth, how he was going to take care of her. He asked for her number, after they'd spoken for hours about things she could not even remember, and she gave it to him. When she had asked for his, he smiled and said he would call her tomorrow. He didn't try to take her back to his hotel room or his guesthouse or his home. No flirting, no suggestion that he wanted to sleep with her. It was confusing. He was confusing.

He did call her the next day as he promised, and he invited her to lunch at Double Four. After steak and wine, he took her to the Polo Club. It was the first time she ever entered the grounds of the club, and there, over more wine, he told her about this business he ran that could earn her millions in no time.

The soldiers up the road were excited over something. A joke, perhaps. One of them was bent over laughing. Another tried not to get his fingers burnt on the joint. They began moving away, walking towards the party. Naomi watched them disappear round the bend. She waited. She was alone. She looked back; no cars approaching. She looked ahead. Malik had been gone a while. Could he be returning soon? She checked both sides of the road again, her heart rate rising with her plan. She placed her fingers on the glove compartment and looked ahead. She pulled the lever. It was locked. Her hand snapped back to her lap and she checked the road again. Her hands were shaking and her heart was beating fast. It had become too hot in the car. She was looking straight ahead and she saw when he strode out of the gate onto the road. For the first time she realised she was afraid of him. She had always been afraid of him.

Malik opened the door and the inside of the car lit up. He had something in his hand. Naomi had to wait for him to close the door and place the object down between the two seats before she knew what it was: a metal detector – the type used at airports.

'Where did you get that?' she asked.

He held up the wand. The interior light had gone off. He switched it back on. Like a child showing off his new toy, he grinned as he said, 'I bought it. Just now. From a policeman.' He nodded towards the gate. 'They had a spare one. Guess how much I paid for it.'

Her mouth was dry. 'How much?'

'Guess?'

'Twenty thousand.'

'Fifty.' He was holding the wand up, inspecting it.

She had to appear normal. 'Do you even know how to use it?'

He looked around. His eyes fell on her bag in the footwell. He swept the wand over it. Beep, beep, beep. He swept it over his watch. He looked at her. Her large earrings looked metallic. She retreated as he raised the wand to her face. Beep.

'What are you going to do with it?' she asked. He ran the wand over the steering wheel then across the dashboard. Beep, beep, beep.

The guesthouse was in Ikeja. Outside, it was an unassuming bungalow, albeit one that sat in the middle of a one-acre compound. Inside, however, it was like all the other guesthouses: cold from 24-hour AC, good furniture, 42-inch flat-screen TV, a full bar, and a uniformed maid to welcome guests and stand over them. Naomi sat on an armchair and put her arms around herself. Goosebumps spread over her skin. As usual there were other girls. Two. The women exchanged nods and kept to themselves. Two police officers sat at the dining table eating pounded yam with their bare hands. In front of them, bottles of Guinness dripped condensation onto the table.

Two police officers meant two cars. They were expecting more girls: three would ride in the back of Malik's Range Rover with tinted windows; an officer would ride in front to make sure the car was not stopped at police checkpoints; in the back, the girls would be blindfolded. The first time, Naomi had been scared. She had trembled throughout the two-hour journey as she tried to build up the courage to snatch the blindfold off, open the door even with the car in motion, and jump out to safety. Fear had kept her glued to the seat till the car stopped moving, and doors opened, and she waited for the juju man who would strike her neck with a shimmering machete and use her head, dripping blood from the neck, in a money ritual. But that hadn't happened and instead she had been received by Sisi, Malik's business partner, and shown round the mansion in the middle of a forest. Two years on, and dozens of such late-night rides, Naomi, like other girls, was used to falling asleep till it was time for the blindfold to come off.

The doorbell rang and a maid went to welcome more guests. Dimeji, Malik's boy who recruited girls for The Harem from Unilag where he was a student, walked in ahead of two girls Naomi did not recognise. The new girls clutched their overnight bags against their bodies and looked about like fowl suspicious of new surroundings. It was their first time.

Dimeji joined Malik on the sofa where Malik was writing a message on his phone. They did a fist bump, then the younger man sat next to his boss and picked up the wand that was on the cushion between them. Malik looked at him and looked back at the text he was composing. Naomi watched. In no time Dimeji had figured out the device and was beeping his watch, his phone, his belt buckle.

It was time to leave. The police officers, fed and watered, reclaimed their rifles from the floor by the dining table, then stood, tummies bloated, behind Malik as he addressed the girls. Dimeji stood to the side with the handle of the wand in one hand, and the tip of the device resting in his other palm.

'You, you, and you, you're going with him,' Malik said. He had pointed at Naomi along with the two regulars. They would ride in Dimeji's car. 'You know the drill. Phones.' He held out his hand.

A girl stood up and handed over her phone. Another finished typing a message and sent it as she rose from the chair. She switched off the device just before she handed it to Malik who handed it to Dimeji. Naomi faked searching her duffel bag for her phone, then the too-tight pockets of her bum shorts.

'I think I left mine in the flat,' she said as she got up and continued placing her hands on non-existent pockets on her tube top and looking about on her seat.

Dimeji was sweeping the wand over the two girls who had handed over their phones. Beep. Bangles. Beep. Keys.

Malik looked into Naomi's eyes. His face showed nothing. She felt she had to say something.

'Maybe it's in your car,' she said.

He brought out his phone, dialled and placed the mobile to his ear, his eyes on Naomi.

Naomi tried to remember if she switched off the phone before putting it inside herself.

'It's switched off,' Malik said. 'We'll check in the car.

The other girls had walked out of the building ahead of her while Dimeji waited for her with the wand. She picked up her bag from the chair, and as she walked past Dimeji he held out his hand to stop her. Looking irritated, she raised her hand to deflect his.

'If you come near me, you pervert...' she said.

Dimeji looked at Malik. Malik wasn't watching them. Naomi continued out of the door, her heart pounding.

20

Amaka's room at Bogobiri House smelled familiar: old books, potpourri, and oil paintings. She closed her eyes and inhaled. The AC had been left on – by the night manager after she enquired about a vacant room, she imagined. Original paintings hung from all the walls, just like another room she had once stayed in at the hotel.

A metre-square Ndidi Emefiele hung above a carved mahogany desk. The greyscale painting was the side profile of a woman with a huge Afro, her head tilted upwards, with lines of shadow cast by Venetian blinds crossing her features at an angle. Amaka stared at the painting.

She had asked the night manager for some paper and a pen and he had pulled some A4 sheets from the printer behind the check-in desk, written down the Wi-Fi code for her, and handed her his own pen and the paper. She placed the items on the desk beneath the tranquil woman, then went in search of a socket for the phone charger.

Sitting on the edge of the bed, her phone plugged into a socket that had been used for the TV, she checked if she had received any text messages. None. It was late. The messages would have come in earlier. She thought of messages that would have been sent to the old number. She shook the creeping angst away. Now, she could only hope that those who needed her would get the new number.

She connected to the hotel's Wi-Fi, logged on to her email and searched. Satisfied that she had what she needed, she stood up and began shedding her clothes as she walked towards the bathroom.

Fifteen minutes later she returned from her shower wrapped in the hotel housecoat, sat in the chair at the desk beneath the painting, and picked up the pen.

In the centre of a sheet she wrote the name Malik and circled it. Around the circle she began writing other names and drawing lines from them to Malik.

'Ojo.' The relationship between him and Malik was at the centre of everything: The Harem. But Ojo would have to have figured out that she was the girl who seduced him at Soul Lounge. She said her name was Iyabo, and she'd agreed to spend the night with him in his hotel suite. He would have also had to deduce the reason she drugged him, went through his phone, and sent a picture to his wife. He would have had to realise it was because of what he and Malik did to Florentine.

'Gabriel.' Her childhood friend and the first person she phoned after Malik called and threatened her. As kids, Irene, his tall, slim, red-haired English mother, would sometimes pick the two of them up from school and Amaka would spend the afternoon playing at his house before Irene took her home later. It was only as an adult that Amaka realised that those days were planned by her parents who wanted precious time alone.

Amaka had been on her way to his house in Ikeja to drop off her car before leaving the country when she drove into the mob at Oshodi Market. The girl. The scenes from the market played back in her mind. She shook her head. Not now.

Just the other day she asked Gabriel if he knew Malik. Gabriel made his living selling expensive properties to wealthy Nigerians, he knew everyone worth knowing in Lagos; and those he did not know, he'd know someone who did. But when she asked if he knew any person called Malik, he insisted on knowing why she was asking, before telling her anything. In the end he didn't give her anything she could work with, instead warning her that there were dangerous people in Lagos she shouldn't be messing with. She drew a line connecting the two names.

'Florentine.' The girl that kind-hearted strangers had brought to Amaka's office, bruised, bleeding, and broken, beaten to within half an inch of her life. They had found her walking like a zombie along an express road, naked and unresponsive. She had barely survived the brutal battering from Ojo. Her luck was that when she passed out during the viscious attack, Ojo and Malik thought she was dead and they dumped her on the road. The bastards. Amaka drew a line connecting her to Malik.

She looked up and stared at the woman in the Ndidi Emefiele painting. She added Naomi to the list and drew a line connecting the former beauty queen to Malik. She looked up again, then added a last thought: 'Someone else.'

She got up, walked to the window, pen in hand, drew the curtain, and stared out. She returned to the desk and next to Gabriel's name, wrote: 'Doesn't know which Malik I'm looking for.' Beneath that she wrote: 'Won't put me at risk.' Then she crossed him out, tapped the pen on Naomi's name, making tiny dots on the paper. Against her name she wrote, 'Too scared,' then crossed her out. She tapped the pen on Florentine's name, got up, and paced the room, then returning to the desk she wrote: 'Said Malik hadn't paid her.' The pen hovered over Florentine. She added: 'Might have tried to get her money back.' She looked up at the ceiling, then she retraced the line connecting Florentine to Malik and wrote down the girl's phone number beside it. Her phone, charging in the corner, beeped twice: a message from a number she didn't recognise. It contained a car registration number and a name, 'Debo.'

She opened the email app, found a message she'd sent to herself, opened the attached Microsoft Excel document, then searched for the car registration number and composed a reply: 'Safe. But be careful. Might try to slip off the condom.'

She fell back onto the mattress and spread her hands over the sheets. It worked. The girls had the new number. And she could use a phone until she got a new laptop.

The phone began to ring but the rule was simple: messages only. Sometimes a new girl would call instead and Amaka would reply with a message explaining the rule. Only a handful of the girls who relied on her for the information she provided knew who she was and she wanted to keep it that way. She recognised the number, sat up and answered. 'Hi Funke.'

Amaka had memorised the phone number of the young girl who helped her lure Ojo into a honey trap: she always memorised important numbers.

'Aunty, where are you?' Funke whispered.

'I'm at a hotel. What's wrong? Where are you?'

'After you left the club, we came to a party in Banana Island. Aunty, some Lebanese men here are saying that he's going to be the next Governor of Lagos State.'

'Who?'

'Ojo. They said they've chosen him to replace Douglas. Aunty, I'm afraid. What if he finds out what we did?'

21

Dimeji made a sucking sound as he took a long drag. He held in the smoke and passed the joint to the police officer in the passenger seat next to him. All four windows were wound up, the music was loud, the AC turned on high, and he was driving fast.

Blindfolded, Naomi kept track of the sudden decelerations and the periods where the car slowed – something she used to do during the first few times she made the trip. Perhaps today she would know when they were on the express and she'd count the number of turns till they got there. If only she could hear the sounds outside, especially when they were stuck in traffic. Bus conductors calling out for passengers would help to plot a mental map. Once when she was riding with Malik, who also played music, but not as loud, she'd heard a conductor shouting 'Oworonshoki' but she couldn't be sure what direction they were travelling. Perhaps that was the purpose of the loud music: to make it even harder to tell where they were being taken. Malik had explained from the beginning, 'The Harem is a secret. You cannot talk about it to anyone. For your own safety it is better you do not know how to get there.' He never explained why it was dangerous for the girls to know the way. At first Naomi imagined it had something to do with deniability. Then when she thought more about it, she concluded, with a cold shiver, that he was alluding to the authorities finding out the place existed, an embassy of Sodom and Gomorrah in the forest of Nigeria, getting their hands on a list of the girls who 'worked there', and torturing them one by one for directions. But that was dangerous for him, not her, not the other girls. And at that point, many months ago, when there was a gaping inconsistency between what he said and what he might have meant, she stopped dwelling on it because to do so would be to admit the threat to her life he had made.

Marijuana smoke thinned in the cooled air. Dimeji was taking a break before lighting the next one. Naomi finally filled her lungs. She would feel the effect of the drug no matter how much she tried to avoid inhaling, but he wouldn't light another until they arrived. She was in the middle of the two girls. One of them was snoring; the other rested her head on Naomi's shoulder minutes after they left Ikeja. Naomi would have also slept, only to be woken up by a lack of motion, the absence of the engine sound and of loud music when they arrived. But she stayed awake, fought the fug clouding her mind, and struggled to concentrate on the journey and the phone inside of her, and on suppressing the need to pee.

As the weed began to take effect, she thought of what would happen if she forgot what was inside her and a client discovered it, thrusting his penis into her. Was that what happened to Florentine? Did a client bruise his dick on a phone she'd hidden in her pussy? Did Amaka make her do it? Is that why they tried to kill her? What was she thinking? She had to get rid of the phone as soon as they got to The Harem. It was safer for her not to know how they got there.

Keeping her thighs together and walking sideways, Naomi began to go up the stairs, one foot joining the other on one step; clench, then repeat. Malik was at the bottom with the new girls, watching her and about to stop her, she thought.

But he didn't. Midway, she stopped and looked at him. He was looking at her. She fought the haze; reminded herself that she was high. She had to be careful. She had to concentrate. She was being paranoid. She suddenly remembered that she still had the phone in her. How did she forget about it over just a step? The weed. Fuck.

'Yes,' she said. She heard her own voice as if it had been played back to her. Why did she have to shout it? He was looking at her, waiting for an explanation. Did he just ask how she was, or was it something else? Did he mention the way she was walking? Did he actually say anything?

'Dimeji was smoking again, abi?'

'Yes.' The haze lifted, giving her a window of clarity, but she knew it wouldn't last. 'I really need to wee.'

The lucidity was gone; no recollection of making it to the top of the stairs. She was sitting on a toilet bowl, bent forward, her shorts gathered around her ankles, her fingers deep inside her, trying to get higher up still. She couldn't feel it – the knot of the condom in which she had inserted the phone. She leaned her back onto the cistern and raised her bum above the toilet bowl, but rather than give her a deeper reach, the position caused her nails to scratch her. She was sweating. How long had she been in there? She was squatting on the floor in front of the toilet bowl. When did she get off the bowl? She pushed. The tips of her fingers touched it. She pinched the end of the condom and pulled.

A knock on the door was followed by a voice. Sisi. 'What are you doing in there?'

'I'm coming,' Naomi said. The knock, Sisi's voice, her own words, the sound of crickets outside the open window of the bathroom, all were sharp and crisp. The room brightened as well. Her thoughts cleared. She had the phone in her hand. Slimy and dangerous.

'You're not in this room today,' Sisi said from behind the door. 'I need it for some new girls.'

Naomi looked at the lock on the door then stood up, careful not to make any sound. Holding the phone, still safely protected in a knotted condom, she looked around. She had two options: stand on the edge of the bathtub, reach out the window and throw, or flush it down toilet. She pictured the compound and what lay below. She slid off her shoes and quietly placed them on the floor, and she climbed. The fence was too far from the building and too high. She weighed the phone in her hand and climbed back down.

Sisi knocked again, 'Naomi, did you hear me? I need this room for some new girls.'

'I'm coming,' Naomi said.

She listened. She hadn't heard Sisi walking away. Naomi gently placed the phone on top of the lid of the cistern, then, just as carefully, she lifted the ceramic top and slowly placed it across the toilet seat. She picked up the phone and put her hand into the cold water, dodging the parts of the flushing mechanism as she did so. After she replaced the lid, she tore off some toilet paper and wiped the top where she had placed the phone. She flushed and looked about the floor. Her panties and shorts were entwined next to a clothes basket.

22

Amaka was one of three guests at the small bar area of Bogobiri House that also served as the lobby and the restaurant. She had a bowl of fruit salad and a mug of coffee and was sitting facing the door so she saw Gabriel when he walked in. It was 7.45am. He must have driven fast. He had on a pair of worn, rumpled, khaki shorts and a light blue polo shirt that also needed ironing. Even with his bathroom slippers, his stubble, and his curly, greying hair, he still drew looks from the other women knife-and-forking their way through their continental breakfasts. Amaka was used to the effect that his light, mixed-race skin had on women. He often joked that she was only 'immune to his juju' because they'd known each other since when they used to run around in diapers.

He sat opposite Amaka and placed a brown envelope on the table. 'Are you going to tell me what the fuck is going on?' he said.

She sipped her coffee and looked at him above the rim. 'Good morning to you too,' she said.

'Amaka, you almost drove me mad with worry. You say someone threatened you, then end the call, and when I try to call you back your phone is off. I called the Commissioner of Police, you know?'

'Really?'

'Yeah. Really. I was worried. He called me back five minutes later. You were at a police inspector's house?'

'He told you that?'

'Yes. He said you tried to stop a lynching at Oshodi. What were you thinking? They could have killed you too, Amaka. He said the inspector rescued you. Inspector…'

'Ibrahim. And he did not rescue me.'

'Yeah, Ibrahim. I called the chap. I spoke to him.'

'You did?'

'Yeah. He said you left his place in the middle of the night. Amaka, what the hell is going on?'

'Is that the money?'

'Yes.' He slid the envelope over to her. 'What are you up to, Amaka?'

'Just taking care of stuff I should have taken care of sooner.'

'You are scaring me. Why is this Malik looking for you? Why were you looking for him in the first place? And who the hell is he, anyway?'

'It's nothing I can't handle. I need a favour.'

'No more favours till you tell me what's going on.'

'I need you to get me a meeting with someone,'

'Didn't you hear what I just said?'

She stared at him as she took a sip from her mug.

'Who?' he asked.

'Chief Ambrose Adepoju.'

'Prince. Not Chief. And why?'

'I need his help with something. Get me the meeting and I'll explain everything.'

It was a long walk from where Amaka parked and paid a young boy to watch her car to Oshodi market where she stopped and stood on the side of the road, amongst pedestrians and passengers waiting for buses in the congested traffic. There, between the passing cars, she could make out where the asphalt was stained from the fire. The air smelled of exhaust and fumes from burning refuse, but in it she could smell burning flesh. For the rest of her life she would smell burning flesh in smoke of any type.

The market was human chaos as usual; thousands of people cramped into one stretch of road, ramshackle stalls next to umbrella canopies and awnings caked in dirt, goods on mats on bare ground. A moving, heaving, noisy gathering of sellers and clients, pickpockets and kids paid to carry other people's shopping, white-robed prophets ringing bells and shouting their sermons, opportunists and traders, and among them also killers. The market was the subject of painters, many of whom captured the colourful madness from the narrow footbridge above. The market was due to be demolished, but in the mean-time it was business as usual and people even said the state government wouldn't dare carry out the threat. Oshodi was a dangerous place, they said, a place where riots start and spread through the state. A place where you could buy anything including human body parts was not a place to mess with.

Cars were passing over the spot where a body had been burning the day before and people were walking past it, trying to give each other space but still brushing against one another. It was as if it never happened - as if Amaka herself had not almost ended up consumed in the flames of their orgy of violence.

Women behind a stretch of baskets spilling over with tomatoes were standing closest to the spot. Amaka hadn't seen them yesterday – she couldn't have seen them through the thickness of the killer mob – but they must have been there, and the day before, and the month before. Now, sat on low stools behind their baskets, they called out to Amaka, each trying to convince her that their tomatoes were 'finer', 'sweeter', 'would make soup that your husband would love.' Amaka picked an old woman in mismatched Ankara iro and buba. She had not spoken the loudest or employed the most convincing embellishments, but the other women close to her looked like they were in their twenties while she looked like she was old enough to have children their age.

'Good evening, ma,' Amaka said.

The other market women shifted their attention to potential new clientele. The woman used a newspaper folded in two to stop flies landing on her tomatoes.

'Five for two hundred for you, my daughter,' the woman said.

Amaka stopped by her basket. 'Mama, I'm not buying today. Were you here yesterday?'

'Yesterday? I was here. I'm always here.'

'Did you see what happened here?'

'What is that?'

'The man they killed.'

The woman sighed heavily. 'We saw, my daughter. We all saw. May God forgive his sins.'

'Mama, there was a girl. They were going to do something to her as well. Did you see? Do you know what happened to her?'

'The girl? Who did you say you are again?'

'I was also here. I was trying to help the girl. They hit me on the head with something. Some women protected me from them until the police came.'

'Police? Are you a policewoman?'

'No, I'm not with the police. My name is Amaka. I am an ordinary civilian like you. I just want to know what happened to the girl.'

'The girl? Who is she to you?'

Amaka became aware of people standing around her. The other traders had come over, and with them stood men in blood-stained clothes. Amaka stood up.

A stout man in his fifties, wearing a pair of khaki shorts and a faded blue polo top, both pieces of clothing stained with brown smears of red, and holding a machete in one hand, asked the woman, 'Mama, kíni ó bi yín?' The lady explained that she was asking about the thief killed there yesterday.

The man said he hoped she hadn't told her anything. The woman shook her head and answered that she hadn't.

The man looked at Amaka while still speaking to the woman. He said Amaka was probably an undercover police detective or a journalist.

The woman raised her palms and reiterated that she hadn't said anything.

'Who are you? Wetin you find come?' the man asked Amaka.

More men pushed through to the middle of the arc that had now formed around Amaka and the old lady. Most of them were shirtless, their lean, hard muscles glistening under their sweat-oiled skin. A lot of them held machetes.

'Orukọ mi ni Amaka,' Amaka said.

'Ah, ó gbọ́ Yorùbá o,' someone exclaimed.

'Why are you disturbing this woman?' the stout man asked.

'I have explained to mama that I was here yesterday when it happened. I want to know what happened to the girl. She was almost killed along with the thief.'

'There was no girl. We did not see any girl. The police have already questioned us and we told them what I'm telling you, that we had nothing to do with it at all.'

More young men joined the crowd. Amaka and the old woman were enclosed.

'You did not have anything to do with what happened to the girl?'

'This is how you educated people behave, assuming that because we did not read as much as you, we have no sense in our heads. Why are you trying to put words into my mouth? Or, are you a lawyer? Did I mention any girl? I said we did not have anything to do with the area boys who set fire to the unfortunate boy.'

'You are right, I'm a lawyer, but I am not trying to put words into your mouth. I just want to find the girl.'

'Who are you to her?'

'I do not know her. I only want to know what happened to her. Like I told mama, I was here and I was trying to save her from the area boys when they descended upon me as well. I also want to find the people who helped me, who shielded and saved me from them.'

A young boy standing next to the man had been studying Amaka's face.

'She's the one that was struggling with the area boys,' he said.

One by one other people began to recognise her.

The stout man studied Amaka's face. 'It is you?' he asked, pointing with his machete.

'Yes. I was trying to save the girl,' Amaka said, staring past his machete into his eyes.

'Follow me,' he said.

The younger men got behind Amaka.

'Where are we going?' Amaka asked.

Someone pushed her from behind. 'Just follow us,' the young boy said when Amaka turned to look at him. His machete was in his hand by his side.

'What is happening? Where are you taking me?'

No one answered.

23

A thirteen-car convoy led and trailed by police vans with screaming sirens stopped in a line between the two rows of cars parked in front of Peace Lodge. Uniformed officers and stone-faced women and men in suits jumped out and looked around at the hitherto peaceful surroundings that their flashing lights and sirens had disturbed.

Soldiers in bulletproof vests and helmets, guns at the ready, spread out across the road, their backs to Peace Lodge, and scanned the road.

A woman in a black suit, her hand on the door handle of a black Mercedes S-Class in the middle of the convoy, looked around one last time, then pulled the door open. Other agents in suits gathered round the man who got out and they escorted him to the already open foot gate to Peace Lodge into which no cars, no matter how important the owner, were ever allowed to enter. Two police officers removed a large aluminium strong box from the boot of a black Land Cruiser in the convoy. The box received the same protection as the man that had preceded it.

In front of the open entrance to the mansion, Otunba Oluawo stood and waited to receive the VIP who was being led up the long driveway in the cocoon of bodyguards. To Oluawo's right, Ojo stood holding his hands behind his back, shoulder to shoulder with his close friend, Retired Navy

Commodore Shehu Yaya. On Otunba's left, stood a man in a black agbada, his eyes shielded by dark glasses; what remained visible of his face was stoic, and unsmiling. Other men and women flanked the four in the middle; they were dressed in expensive native outfits, with cowry beads around their wrists and necks. They were party bigwigs and Chiefs of the land.

The bodyguards and soldiers stood aside and a short man in a starched, sky blue dashiki and a red hat smiled, and with hands stretched out, walked up to Otunba.

'VP,' Otunba said, taking his hand. The vice president began to prostrate before Otunba, but Otunba put his hands out to stop him. 'Welcome home. Abuja is really treating you well. Look at your cheeks.'

'Baba, it is not so rosy in FCT. Molade is the only reason the cheeks have not deflated.'

'Are you sure she is the only one cooking for you in Aso Rock?' Otunba said with a smile on his face.

The two men laughed at their joke and the onlookers followed suit.

'I brought a message from Mr. President,' the vice president said.

'It can wait until we are inside. Have you met my son-in-law?'

'No, I haven't had the honour till today,' the vice president said, 'but I have heard a lot about him.'

Ojo bowed as he shook hands with the vice president. 'Good morning, sir,' he said.

'Good morning, Your Excellency' the vice president said.

'And Shehu, you know,' Otunba said.

The man in the black agbada who had been holding his hand out to shake the vice president's, stood with his arm still outstretched.

The vice president and Shehu embraced before slapping their hands together and snapping fingers.

'Old Navy,' the vice president said, 'I didn't know you were in our party.'

'Well, Ojo here is my close friend,' Shehu said.

'You mean, His Excellency,' the vice president said. All the men and the women smiled, except the man in the black agbada whose hand had been ignored and who Otunba had not bothered to introduce.

The strong box was placed on the floor in a bedroom and its bearers left. The vice president, his aide-de-camp, Otunba, Ojo, and Shehu remained.

'Open it,' Otunba said.

The agent stooped by the box and unlocked it. She opened the lid all the way back and stood back.

'How much?' Otunba asked.

'What you asked for,' the vice president said.

'In that case I take it your boss is happy with our candidate.'

'We cannot afford to lose Lagos,' the vice president said. 'He has faith in you to deliver the state.'

'And in my son-in-law?'

'He has absolute faith in your choice.'

'Good. We shall meet you downstairs to make the announcement.'

'What are we doing about the deputy governor?'

'What about him?'

'He didn't look happy just now. He already asked people to talk to the president.'

'And so?'

'He thinks he should be the candidate.'

'The party caucus has decided. I will deal with him if he proves stubborn. Go and wait for me downstairs.'

The vice president and his aide left.

'Ojo, bring one bundle,' Otunba said.

Ojo gathered his agbada and held it to his body, then bent

down and retrieved a cellophane-wrapped brick of hundred-dollar bills and handed it to Otunba who tore away the transparent wrapping. Some of the bundles fell on to the rest of the bricks in the box. He handed one bundle back to Ojo, and gave the rest to Shehu who began to arrange the money back in the box as neatly as he could.

'That is for the journalists,' Otunba said to Ojo who was holding the money in both hands awaiting instructions. 'They are having lunch in the big dining room. It is important they receive their money before they finish, but you must not be the one to give it to them. Tell Lasaki to put five hundred in one envelope each, then go to the dining room and greet them. Shake hands with each of them, ask them if they are enjoying their meal, if they need anything, if there is anything you can get for them, and if they are comfortable. Then when you leave, Lasaki will enter and give them their envelopes. Do not answer any questions if they ask you. Just smile and tell them to enjoy their meals first.'

Ojo put the money into his pocket and left. Shehu turned to leave with him.

'You wait,' Otunba said.

When Ojo had closed the door behind him, Otunba, looking down at the money, waved his hand over it.

'Alùjọnú bí owó ò sí,' he said. 'There is no spirit like money. There is enough here to buy private jets, entire estates in Osborne, and still have enough change for hundreds and hundreds of Mercedes cars. And if you stand in front of those things and look at them, you will not feel anything. But when you stand in front of money like this, if your heart is not strong enough you can run mad. That is because of the spirit that lives inside money. Money is power, and yet it is just paper.'

Shehu had been looking at Otunba the entire time. Otunba turned to him.

'You are his friend. He talks very well of you.'

'Thank you, sir.'

'You supply girls to your rich friends.'

'No, sir. I run a catering service. I supply ushers.'

'Call it whatever you want to call it. A man like you deserves more than the chicken change they pay you. Do you want inside or outside?'

'I don't follow, sir.'

'Inside is government position. Outside is government contractor. You know he's going to be the next governor and all this is mere formality. Our party cannot lose in this state; you have heard it from the VP - that is from the president himself. We have already won. When he enters the government house, what position do you want? Deputy governor is off the table, as are all the juicy commissions, but we can still find something for you. You know, here in Lagos state is the only place in Nigeria that you would find an Igbo man in the cabinet. You are from the north but we can still find you something. You follow now?'

'Yes, sir.'

'Don't give me your answer now. Go and think about it.'

'Thank you, sir.'

'There is one thing I want you to do for me. From now on, wherever he goes, you go. Whatever he hears, you hear. Whatever he sees, you see. You never leave his side. You understand?'

'I understand, sir.'

'Good. And this is between us.'

24

Blood-stained men with machetes surrounded Amaka and led her through the market. They marched her past suits and wedding gowns dangling from hangers, past heaps of second-hand women's underwear heaped on mats on the ground, past stalls of smoked fish, huge smoked rodents, and wood-shack shops selling car stereos. They marched straight through the crowd and people moved out of their path.

They arrived at a section where beasts and meat of different cuts were on display on wooden tables criss-crossed with knife marks and stained with blackened blood. The air smelt of butchered beef. Green bottle flies buzzed from table to table.

The men led Amaka behind the stalls and into a two-storey building with a doorless frame. They took her through a dark corridor that ran the length of the building to a paved backyard that sloped to one side. There, young men in shorts and rolled-up trousers used broomsticks and water from pails to wash coagulated blood into a gutter that was now foaming red. On the other side there were wooden benches smoothed with use, and metal poles with circular cement weights of varying thickness. The men stopped their work to look at Amaka.

Benches were brought out and Amaka was led to sit alone on one. The stout man sat on another, facing her, and the men gathered around.

'My name is Ajani,' the stout man said. 'I am the president of Oshodi Market Butchers' Association, chapter 111. You say you are the one who tried to save that girl?'

'Yes.'

'Do you know her?'

'No.'

'Why did you risk your life to save her?'

'She is a woman like me.'

'You mean you did not know her before?'

'No.'

'What were you doing there?'

'I was on my way somewhere when I saw what was happening. I was in my car.'

'OK. The women that surrounded you are from this market. When we got to the road, it was too late to save the boy. Nobody in this market had anything to do with it. Did you hear me?'

'I hear you,' Amaka said.

'Those area boys are always causing trouble for us. They have given Oshodi a bad name. Look at us; can you say any of us here we are criminals? In this market, we have Ebira people, Edo people, Igbo, Hausa, Yoruba. We even have people from Lomé, and we are all one: no difference among us, no fighting, no palaver. This market is our home. Why would we want any trouble here? But these boys, they keep making problems for us, and now, government that already wants to bulldozer our shops and chase us from this place will use this chance to drive us away, even though our hands are clean in this matter.

'You said you are a lawyer. Before now we have joined hands and contributed money to hire a lawyer to help us stop the government from destroying this market, but we did not know that the man we got is just a lousy somebody who drinks paraga early in the morning before coming to court. He has messed up the whole case for us. Government has given us a date that they will come here with bulldozers and demolish everything. What can you do to help us?'

Amaka took her time before responding. When she did, she spoke to the entire crowd, not just the stout man. 'I would be lying if I said there is anything I can do. The government cannot be stopped. You can only negotiate with them and hope they compensate you somehow. But if any one of you ever need a lawyer, just come to me and I will do everything I can.'

'There is nothing you can do about the eviction notice?' Ajani said.

'No.'

'Nothing at all?'

'Nothing at all. I would be lying if I said otherwise.'

'It is well. I understand. Thank you for your honesty.' He spoke to the men. 'Go and bring her.'

Amaka watched.

'Be patient,' Ajani said.

Two men returned with a young woman between them; the one she had tried to save from the mob. Amaka stood up. The men guided the woman to Amaka and sat her down on the bench. The woman stared straight ahead, her zombie-like gaze unwavering and focusing on nothing in particular. Amaka leaned forward so the woman could see her face. She waved her hand. The woman did not as much as blink or look at Amaka. Her eyes were red.

'She told us her name is Chioma,' Ajani said. 'She said that the boy they killed was not a thief. He is her brother. In this Lagos, all you have to do is shout thief, and the area boys will descend upon the person and beat him until he dies, and then they will burn him, even if he is not already dead. She has refused to go home since yesterday. She's afraid that the person who killed her brother will come and find her to kill her too.'

'The person who killed her brother?'

'Yes. She knows him. Let her tell you herself.'

25

A police van with its siren blaring drove ahead of Ojo's car. Police officers sat in the open back of the van with their guns pointed at motorists.

'Lagos is truly the only place in the world where you can go to bed a pauper and wake up a billionaire,' Ojo said. Shehu listened by his side in the back seat of the Mercedes. 'Look at me. Just yesterday I was no more than a joke to all those people, and today they are calling me Excellency. Imagine. Lagos na wa o.'

'You were not really a pauper though, to be honest.'

'No. But you get my point. In Lagos you can go from zero to hero in less time than it takes to…to... I don't know. You know what I mean.'

'A girl I know puts it differently. She says in Lagos you never know whose bed you'll wake up in. One morning you're on your tattered single mattress, plagued with lice, on the bare floor of your rat-infested face-me-I-face-you room, and the next day you're waking up on one-thousand-thread Egyptian cotton sheets in the Intercontinental Hotel next to some senator who's about to sign a five-million-dollar contract for you. My friend, you have woken up in the right bed this morning.'

Ojo stared out the window watching the low-rise towers of Dolphin Estate fly past. He heaved. 'Shehu, I have a problem.' He paused, then added, 'Do you remember the girl that was with me at Eko Hotel?'

'That pretty chick you picked from Soul Lounge?'

'She stole something from me.'

'That girl? What did she take?'

'The memory card from my phone.'

'She stole a memory card from you?'

'Yes.'

'What for? What's on it?'

Ojo looked at Shehu. He checked on the driver. 'Videos,' he whispered.

'Videos? What kind of videos?'

Ojo stared into his friend's eyes.

'Oh. I see,' Shehu said, nodding.

'No. It's worse. Some of the...' Ojo checked on Abiodun again. 'Some of the girls are young.'

'How young?'

'I don't know. Really young.'

'Eighteen? Nineteen?'

'Younger.'

'How young?'

'One girl said she was...twelve.'

'Bura ubanka. Twelve. Olabisi. Twelve. Why?'

Ojo looked out his window.

'If you want girls, I get you girls, but not kids, Bisi. Not kids. It is haram. And you recorded them. Why?'

'What can we do, Shehu?'

'We must find the girl.'

'I know. Baba said I should tell him any skeletons I have so he can take care of it. I should tell him about this, do you think?'

'No.'

'No?'

'No. Let me take care of it. This is...this is criminal. Twelve? Olabisi Ojo, twelve. Why?'

Ojo turned to look out the window. 'Please, help me make this go away.'

26

Amaka tried again to make eye contact with Chioma. 'My name is Amaka,' she said. 'I was there yesterday. Do you remember? I was trying to stop the men dragging you.'

Chioma looked at Amaka. She squinted, as if she was trying to remember, but after a few seconds she gave up and looked away.

'I am a lawyer, I...'

'Kingsley and his friends killed my brother,' Chioma said, still staring into space. Her voice was calm and emotionless.

'Who is Kingsley?'

'My ex-boyfriend.'

'Why did he... Why did he do it?'

'Because Matthew went to confront him at his house.'

'Matthew is your brother?'

'Yes. He was staying with me.'

'What was he confronting Kingsley for?'

'I did not know that Kingsley filmed us sleeping together. He sent the video to his friends after we stopped seeing each other. My brother saw it.'

'So your brother went to confront him about the video?'

'Yes.'

'Do you have a copy of the video?'

Chioma turned to look at Amaka. She held Amaka's gaze for a moment then she turned away. 'No.'

'I'm sorry I asked. I'm just trying to understand what happened. Why do you say Kingsley and his friends are responsible for it?'

'I saw them.'

'Where? Yesterday? They were there yesterday?'

Chioma nodded. Amaka reached out to hold her hand but she moved her arm away.

'I begged him not to do anything. I warned him that Kingsley is dangerous. I said he should wait for me to return from work so that both of us would go to my pastor for advice. He insisted that he was going to confront Kingsley so I begged to leave work early. On my way rushing to Kingsley's house, I saw the area boys chasing someone. One of our neighbours saw me. She was the one who told me that it was Matthew they were chasing.

'I ran after them. Kingsley and his boys were among the people beating Matthew. I wanted to remove the tyre they put around his neck but people wouldn't let me get close. I begged them but they did not listen. I told them he's not a thief but they did not listen. They accused me of being a thief, too. Then they set him on fire. Kingsley helped them. I saw him. We looked at each other.'

'If he was there and you saw him, you have to report it to the police,' Amaka said. 'I will go with you, as your lawyer.'

Chioma looked at Amaka. 'Kingsley is a policeman.'

27

The police escort had gone around the 7th roundabout on the Lekki-Epe Expressway when a motorcycle with a driver and a passenger swerved in front of Ojo's car, cutting the Mercedes off from the escort. Abiodun slammed on the brakes. Chief Ojo, not wearing his seatbelt, slammed against the driver's seat and partially fell into the footwell. Shehu unclasped his own seatbelt to help Ojo. Abiodun spread his fingers at the careless motorcycle driver then opened the door to step out onto the road. The passenger got off the bike. In his hands was an Uzi that had been concealed between his belly and the driver's back. He aimed at the windscreen before Abiodun had time to get out, and let out two short bursts of fire before climbing back on the bike. Hawkers and pedestrians on the side of the road ran away. The traffic warden at the junction fled. Motorcycles turned round and sped away. Cars reversed into the noses of other cars and a few drivers abandoned their vehicles altogether.

The motorcycle was speeding away in the distance towards Ajah. The officers in the escort van ran to Ojo's Mercedes and opened the back door. Shehu's body was on top of Ojo, pinning him down. Ojo was screaming 'Jesus, Jesus,' over and over. The officers grabbed both men and pulled them apart. Ojo resisted, kept his hands over his head and tried to bury himself in the footwell. 'Jesus, Jesus.'

The police officers stopped traffic at the roundabout, waving their guns about as if other assassins lurked among the motorists hiding beneath their windows. Pedestrians and people who had dared to come out of their cars were taking pictures with their phones. The police van reversed towards the Mercedes. Ojo, in the grip of two officers leading him to the van, turned to look at his car. The driver's side of the windshield was riddled with bullet holes. Abiodun was slumped sideways onto the passenger seat, a smear of blood left on his headrest, blood flowing from his body onto the central console.

28

Amaka reached back and opened the rear door. Two men with browned bloodstains on their shirts and trousers helped the girl with her face hidden under a long piece of Ankara cloth into the back seat. Chioma lay down flat and kept the cloth over her head. The men closed the door and watched as Amaka drove away.

The gateman stared at the covered body in the back of her car as Amaka drove into the compound. Gabriel and Eyitayo were waiting in front of the large patio of their white bungalow. The husband and wife helped Chioma out of the car and led her, arms over her shoulders, into their home.

Gabriel placed three shot glasses onto the dining table and poured brandy into each from a bottle of Hennessy XO. He held one of the glasses up to Amaka.

'I shouldn't,' she said, but she took the drink and downed it, grimacing as the liquor trickled down her throat. She had changed into a beige jumpsuit she borrowed from Eyitayo. They were about the same height, and Eyitayo was dark-skinned like Amaka. Gabriel liked to boast that she looked like Alek Wek. Amaka thought she was even more beautiful than the stunning supermodel.

Gabriel sat back down opposite her. Eyitayo was at the head

of the table between them, staring at Amaka, her mouth wide open.

Gabriel downed his drink then poured another. As if taking her cue from him, Eyitayo picked up her glass and downed it too. 'Oh my God, Amaka, they could have killed you,' she said.

'Yup,' Amaka said. 'But I'm alive, thanks to the market women.'

'And the poor girl. To see her brother killed like that,' Eyitayo said.

'Animals. Their leaders loot the treasury dry on a daily basis and they do nothing about it, but some poor chap is accused of lifting a wallet and they burn him alive.' Amaka held out her glass for Gabriel to refill. 'You should have seen them. They were excited. They were enjoying it – like it was a party or something. And rather than help, people were just watching and filming it.'

'This country,' Eyitayo said. She shuddered.

'I had it all on tape. I had them. If only I'd not lost the phone.'

'What are we going to do now? He can't be allowed to get away with it.'

'He won't. She doesn't want to go to the police.'

'Do you blame her? Her own boyfriend. Just imagine.'

'Ex. I'll get her to call him and I'll record the conversation. Hopefully he'll say something that will implicate him, then I'll have something to take to the police.' She checked the time on her watch. 'I've got to run. I'm really sorry to inconvenience you guys like this. I didn't know where else to take her.'

'Don't be silly. It's no problem. Gabriel said you spent the night in a hotel. Why didn't you come here?'

'It was late. I didn't want to bother you guys.'

'Nonsense. You're coming back tonight, right?'

'Yeah. I just have to sort out some things, get my mobile phone lines back, apply for a new passport, see some people, then I'll be back to get her. I just don't want her to be by herself.'

'That's not what I meant. You're not staying in a hotel tonight. And your god-daughter would be happy to see you.'

'Thanks, dear, but I should be able to return home tonight. They can't block the road forever.' Amaka turned to Gabriel. 'Did you get me the appointment?'

'You know, Amaka, only a few people in this country have the kind of connections, and command the kind of respect it takes to call up a person like Ambrose out of the blue and demand a meeting.'

'Tell me you're one such person.'

'I am. He'll see you this afternoon. He knows your father. That helped.'

Amaka stood up and downed the last of her brandy.

'Where are you going? I haven't even told you when or where.'

'I need to see someone in Ikoyi. When and where?'

'Four o'clock. VI. He said he'll text to let me know where he'll be. Is Guy the someone in Ikoyi?' Gabriel asked.

'Oh shit, thanks for reminding me.' Amaka said. 'No, it's not him. He returned to England yesterday. Shit.'

'What is it?'

'Just before the stuff at Oshodi, I sent him a message that Malik had found me. We haven't spoken since then. He would have been trying to call. Damn. I have to call him.'

'Guy is the oyinbo boy you brought to the Yoruba Tennis Club?' Eyitayo asked. Amaka nodded. 'Cute boy. And you dressed him up in your father's clothes. Everyone was looking at the two of you. You guys looked so good together. So much chemistry. Are you guys an item, or an item in the making?'

Amaka smiled. 'He's alright.'

'Is he coming back, or how do you people plan to do it? Long-distance relationships can be challenging.'

'Early days, but we'll see.'

'Gabriel likes him. He's rooting for him.' Gabriel shrugged. 'And who is Malik?'

'An irritant.' Amaka said. She held her borrowed phone and considered it. 'Can I call him on yours? I haven't retrieved my old lines yet and I want to keep this one for work alone.'

Both Eyitayo and Ibrahim unlocked their phones and held them out. She took Eyitayo's and dialled Guy's London number from memory. It rang for a while and she was about to hang up when someone answered.

'Hello lover boy,' she said. A female voice answered: 'Sorry, you must want Guy. He's in the shower. Do you want to leave a message or call back?'.

'I'll call back,' Amaka said and ended the call. She handed the phone back to Eyitayo.

'That was brief,' Eyitayo said.

'He's busy,' Amaka said. 'I must rush or traffic will catch me.' She started walking towards the door when Eyitayo's phone rang. She swung round. 'If it's him don't answer.'

Eyitayo answered. 'Hello? Guy? This is Eyitayo. Gabriel's wife. We met at the party. Hold on for Amaka.'

Amaka took the phone and turned her back to the couple. 'Amaka...' Guy said, sounding out of breath.

'Was that Mel?' she asked.

There was a long pause. 'Yes.'

'Your ex-girlfriend. Cool. Sorry to disturb you. Don't call back. This is Eyitayo's phone.' Amaka returned the phone to Eyitayo.

'Everything OK, hun?' Eyitayo asked.

'Yes. See you later.' Amaka walked towards the door.

'Amaka,' Gabriel said.

'What?'

'We had a deal, remember? I get you the appointment, you tell me what you're up to. I'm not sending you the details till you tell me.'

29

Hundreds of men had gathered on the road and in between the cars parked in front of Peace Lodge, waving shotguns and machetes. Some of them had liberated campaign posters of the deceased Douglas from walls and were holding them above their heads. Together they chanted a chorus in Yoruba, proclaiming that 'They killed our governor and we kept quiet; now that they have tried to kill another, we will not let it happen. We will kill their entire family including their dogs and cattle.'

Hours before, a police van had charged the crowd and forced its way through the thugs to make it to the gate. Afterwards, word spread that the van had brought Ojo back to Peace Lodge. The party's new candidate had indeed escaped the assassination plot. Police officers and soldiers did little to control the crowd; aside from a semicircle in front of the gate where the press had set up their cameras and military personnel behind them were holding people back.

The gate opened just enough for a man to squeeze through sideways. He surveyed the crowd, then tucked his head into the crack and spoke to people waiting inside the compound. The gates opened.

The crowd cheered at the sight of Otunba and Chief Ojo, escorted by a dozen other recognisable politicians and a dozen armed men; police and thugs.

Otunba held his hands up to silence the crowd, and like a

school principal in front of his assembly, the multitude quietened. Otunba addressed them loudly, pointing for emphasis.

'All those posters of Douglas, put them down. We are not going to vote for a dead candidate. They have killed him, but our new candidate is still alive.'

He held Ojo's hand up and the crowd cheered again.

The press adjusted their cameras and held their microphones in Otunba's direction.

'Put away those weapons. People are looking at us. And you, pressmen and women, make sure you record our supporters. See how many there are. Make sure you capture them. I do not want to see any poster of our late brother, Douglas. We have not printed posters of our new candidate, but you can take his pictures now and we will use your papers tomorrow as our posters.'

The crowd cheered.

Otunba took the microphone, scanned the crowd, then he cleared his throat and began.

'My fellow sons and daughters of Lagos, what kind of people attempt to kill two gubernatorial candidates in two days?'

Reporters jostled for space in front of Ambrose. He was standing outside his gate, flanked by elderly members of his party. Babalola watched from behind a window in an upstairs room - he couldn't hear what was being said, but the script had been agreed amongst the party inner caucus, as Ambrose called his most trusted colleagues.

As he spoke, gesticulating wildly, Ambrose's face was a mixture of anger and frustration, shots of saliva spraying from his mouth.

'Enough is enough. We cannot allow these people to turn Lagos state into a bloody battlefield because of their greed or lust for power. Are these the kind of people asking for your votes?

People who are killing each other just to become governor? If they can kill their own brothers, what would they do to you if elected? Yesterday, a plane crash, today, an assassination attempt. When would it stop? Who is next on their hit list? Our own candidate? Me? You, the electorate? They want to turn Lagos into war zone.'

A reporter held her voice recorder up to Ambrose. 'Otunba Balogun Oluawo has gone on record to accuse your party of being behind the murder of Chief Douglas and the attempted assassination of his son-in-law and new party candidate, Chief Olabisi Ojo…'

'And I am going on record to tell you that we are suing him for defamation today-today. We have instructed our lawyers. *I* am their victim. *You* are their victim. We are all their victims; victims of their lust for power. And we will not rest until we expose their faces. In fact, Dr Babalola has declared that the very first thing he will do once he's in office is to direct the police to carry out a proper investigation and get to the bottom of these dastardly acts and expose the faces of those responsible. We will not let them get away with turning Lagos into a bloodbath.'

30

Amaka leaned on the frame of the car door; one leg inside and the other outside. Gabriel stood on the other side of the door, shielding his eyes from the sun, waiting for her to talk, but he was met with silence. 'Come on, Amaka, what's going on?'

'You know Chief Olabisi Ojo?'

'Not much. Only that he's going to become the next Governor of Lagos State. Lucky chap. What does he have to do with you?'

'What if I tell you I sent a picture of me and him together to his wife?'

'What? You slept with him? No, Amaka. He's a slime ball.'

'No, I didn't sleep with him. Come on, Gabriel. And, I thought you said you didn't know much about him.'

'Yeah, but everyone knows he's a manshewo.'

'Manshewo?'

'Yes. Male ashewo.'

'You're crazy. Anyway, he's the reason I was looking for Malik.'

'OK. You're starting to scare me again.'

'I'm scared myself, and that's why I'm telling you this. In case anything happens to me.'

'You don't look scared, and don't say stuff like that. You're really freaking me out. I have a feeling I'm not going to like where this is going.'

'Ojo almost killed a girl at a place Malik owns. A secret sex club called The Harem.'

'What? Let me guess, you decided to take the law into your own hands, abi?'

'I met up with Ojo at his hotel. He thinks I'm called Iyabo. I spiked his drink.'

'You did what? Amaka. Damn.'

'I took a picture of us. My face didn't show in it. I sent it to his wife.'

'My God, Amaka.'

'There's more. I took a memory card from his phone.'

'What is on it?'

'Him having sex with kids.'

'No way. Fuck, Amaka. Fuck. Do you realise what you've done? He's going to do whatever it takes to find you and get that card back.'

'He already found me. Malik called me, remember.'

'Oh shit. Oh fuck. OK. I get it now. Ambrose is the leader of the opposition party. His candidate is the underdog who's going to run against Ojo. You're going to give them the memory card.'

'No. I lost it. It was in my bag.'

31

Otunba held a sheet of paper in his hand. He was in the middle of his sofa, the vice president sat to his left, Ojo was on his right.

Laying prostrate on the floor, his head close to Otunba's feet and his black agbada spread out on the carpet, the deputy governor wept.

About a dozen other politicians were in the room, senior members of the party, and with them, Shehu, watching with keen interest.

'I just want him to sign the undertaking that nothing will happen to my son-in-law,' Otunba said, holding up the paper in his hand. He refused to look at the sobbing man at his feet.

From the floor, the deputy governor pleaded, his voice strained with emotion as he directed his supplications to the vice president.

'I swear on the lives of my children, I had nothing to do with it. Please, help me beg baba.'

'Which of your children?' Otunba said. 'The bastard ones or the ones you were planning to take to government house with you?'

'Baba, I promise you, I did not have a hand in it. I have never been involved in such. Please, baba, hear my pleas. I will swear on anything you bring. Bible, Quran, Ògún, anything, Baba.'

'See? Someone that is ready to swear on anything, does that not prove that he does not believe in anything? What would be the value of his swearing? Just sign the undertaking.'

'But baba, how can I sign an undertaking that I would not harm his Excellency when I am not guilty? Please, beg baba for me.'

The vice president spoke. 'I had already boarded my jet when I heard. I was supposed to represent the president at a launching in Yola today; when I called him he had already heard as well.'

'I did not do it,' the deputy pleaded. 'Please help me beg Otunba. Your Excellency, I had no hand in it, sir,' he said to Ojo.

Otunba heaved himself to the edge of the sofa and looked down upon the deputy before him.

'You are not governor material. I have told you before. Even the deputy governorship that we offered you is mere political calculation; it is not like you can run for governor one day.

'You came here when I told you I was putting my son-in-law forward and you said no. To me, Otunba, you said no. Was I asking for your permission? Then when the party members confirmed our choice, you still had the temerity to come here today and be telling everyone that we have cheated you. You think they won't tell me? Who cheated you? And then this morning you stood at the announcement and you gathered your face like this, so that the whole world will know you are not happy with our candidate, abi?'

'No, baba, I did not gather my face anyhow. It was the sun that was in my eyes.'

'Oh. The sun was in your eyes? Why wasn't it in my own eyes?'

'Oh my God, help me God,' the deputy cried out. He buried his head into the carpet. His back shuddered.

The vice president joined Otunba on the edge of the sofa.

'Baba, please, let him just give his word. No need to sign anything. Mr. President already assured me that he would give us all the backing to find the culprits. Please, Baba, do this for me. Please.'

Otunba remained on the sofa as everyone left. Shehu was the only other person sitting. Ojo returned from walking the vice president to the door. He sat back next to his father-in-law.

'Come here,' Otunba said to Shehu. 'Stand there.'

Shehu stood in front of Otunba.

'You too,' Otunba said.

Ojo pushed himself off the sofa and stood next to Shehu.

'Now, tell me, why is someone trying to kill you?'

'You said it was the deputy governor,' Ojo said.

'Shut up. You must be a fool. Everybody knew he had nothing to do with it. Even Shehu knows it. I only used the situation to put him in his place. You must be really foolish to have believed he had something to do with it, in which case you really don't know who was trying to kill you, or you are not that foolish and you are only lying to me that you think it was him. Which one is it?'

'I don't know who did it, sir.'

'You don't know who did it? What about you, Shehu, who wants to kill your friend?'

'Personally, I don't think it was an assassination attempt,' Shehu said. The gunman had a clear shot and yet he only managed to take out the driver.'

'So you think it was a warning?'

'Most likely.'

'So, who is warning you?' Otunba asked Ojo. 'What are they warning you for?'

'Maybe it is the opposition,' Ojo said.

Otunba gave him a long look of disgust. 'I asked you to tell me about all your skeletons so we can resolve them before something like this happens. Now tell me, who is afraid of you becoming governor?

Ojo and Shehu looked at each other.

'What is it?' Otunba asked. 'The three of us will remain here until one of you tells me.'

'There is a girl,' Ojo said, still looking at Shehu. 'Her name is Iyabo.'

'Tell me everything,' Otunba said.

For ten minutes, Ojo spoke, uninterrupted.

Otunba stared into the distance between Shehu and Ojo and nodded continuously while his elbows rested on his knees and his chin on his clasped fingers.

'You were set up,' Otunba finally said, still staring straight ahead. 'You say you don't know how to find the girl. That is not good enough. You have to find her. She is dangerous. The picture she sent to Matilda is just to let you know that she means business when she contacts you. She probably took more. She will send them to the press, use them to blackmail you, or she will go to the opposition. After your announcement today, her price would have gone up, but we cannot afford to simply pay her.

'Find her, or find out how to find her and let me know. And bring me the picture on your wife's phone. She mentioned something like that. I thought it was nothing. Now I wish I had taken it seriously.

'The lesson I want you to learn from this is that actions always have consequences. It is your action, your carelessness, that has now cost the girl her life.'

32

Amaka pulled up at the side of the road in front of a shop with granite and marble headstones on display behind large floor-to-ceiling glass panes. Above the entrance, in the middle of the windows, a sign in gold script on black marble read: B. Adeniran & Sons. Solemn Undertakers.

Amaka looked around, checked the address in a text message and looked around again. She dialled a number and scanned the shops on the other side of the road.

Ibrahim knocked on Amaka's window, making her jump in her seat. She ended the unanswered call to him and wound the window down. 'You scared me,' she said.

'I'm sorry. How are you?' Ibrahim said.

'What are you doing here? Did someone die?' she asked.

He looked at the shop. 'I've always wanted to get a headstone for my father's grave. I came to make enquiries.'

'Oh, I'm sorry.'

'Oh no, he died seven years ago. I just never got to it.'

'I see. Where is your car?'

'I sent my driver to go and fill the tank. Have you filled your tank?'

'No. What for?'

'We're expecting riots. There's been some sporadic outbursts that we have managed to contain, but once the politicians have had time to arm their thugs, we expect full-blown civil disorder. They might even declare a state of emergency.'

'Over the plane crash?'

'You've not heard? They tried to kill his replacement. The party already selected a new candidate. Chief Olabisi Ojo. There was an attempt on his life today.'

'Really. He survived?'

'Yes. You should not be driving about today. What was so urgent that it couldn't wait for me to get back to the station?'

'I want to report a crime.'

Shehu, a cigarette smouldering in his hand, watched a single dry leaf floating on the glistening swimming pool water. Ojo stood next to him by the empty pool house, in the shadow of the towering main house. Apart from toilets and private bedrooms, this was the only place in Peace Lodge where they could be alone. Politicians and their thugs had taken over the building.

'I was afraid you would mention the memory card,' Shehu said.

He had checked once, but Ojo looked back at the pool house to make sure there was nobody there who could hear them.

Almost whispering, he said, 'Do you think I should have?'

'Hell no. Nobody apart from you and I can know about that.'

'What if she sends it to the press? Or hands it to the opposition?'

'Well, that is why I must find her before your father-in-law or anyone else does.'

'How will you find her?'

'I know where you met her and I know what she looks

like. I still have access to resources I can call upon – the kind of people who find people. I will find her.'

'Then what?'

'Then we find out what she wants, who else has seen the videos, and who she's working for.'

'You think she's working for someone? Maybe the opposition?'

'How can it be the opposition? Did they know Douglas's plane was going to fly into his house and take him out?'

'What if the opposition killed him?'

'So they took Douglas out, and at the same time they sent some girl to steal a memory card from you because they knew Otunba was going to handpick you to be the replacement?'

'You're right. I'm not thinking straight. I'm stressed out, Shehu. Maybe I should tell Otunba.'

'Look, ol' boy, those videos in anyone's hands are enough to make them your puppetmaster for life. Or even to send you to jail. Do you understand? Nobody, not even Otunba, can see those videos. Let me find the girl and neutralise the threat.'

'Do you mean you will...?' He waited for Shehu to complete his thought.

A man with a leaf skimmer walked out and approached the pool. He bowed at them, plunged his net into the shimmering water and dragged it across the surface.

'I will do nothing more than your father-in-law would do,' Shehu said. 'Only, with me, no one else would get to know about the videos.'

'Thank you, Shehu. Thank you so much.'

'Get in,' Amaka said. She reached over and opened the door for Ibrahim.

'What crime?' Ibrahim asked as he sat next to her. He searched for the lever to adjust the seat. 'Are you talking about the lynching at Oshodi? The girl you said you saw?'

'No. I found her by the way.'

'Really? Is she alright?'

'Yes. The boy they killed was her brother.'

'Kai!'

'She recognised one of the men who took part in the lynching.'

'That is good. Bring her to the station to make a statement. Where is she now?'

'She's still in shock. I'll bring her to the station when she's stable. Listen, a few months ago some people brought a girl to The Street Samaritans. They found her naked and barely conscious on Lagos Ibadan expressway. She had been beaten up.'

'A prostitute?'

'No. She's one of many girls kept as sex slaves in a building somewhere in the middle of the forest between Lagos and Ibadan.'

Ibrahim turned his body to face her.

'She told you this?'

'Yes.'

'And you believe her?'

'Yes. From the sounds of it, it might even be a baby factory. They continuously rape the girls to get them pregnant and sell their babies.'

'The girl escaped from this place?'

'Not so much escaped as she was dumped. They thought she was dead; that's why they dumped her on the express.'

'My God.'

'I've been trying to find the place. She was blindfolded when she was taken there. She described it as a big building in a large compound surrounded by forest. I searched Google Maps. There are hundreds of such isolated buildings all over the place. I went to the Ministries of Lands and Housing in Lagos,

Ogun, and Ibadan. She told me the name of the owner of the place. Malik. I was hoping to find the name on a certificate of occupancy or land title deeds.'

'Malik, what?'

'I don't know.'

'You should have come to me. Where is the girl now?'

'That's the problem. After she recovered, we helped her relocate out of Lagos. I've not been able to get through to her phone since yesterday. I tried her number several times and sent messages. Her phone was still off as of this morning and she hasn't replied to any of my messages. She would have let me know if she changed her number.'

'You think something happened to her?'

'I hope not. Maybe she's not responding because it's not my number that she has. I'm worried, though. Malik called me on my phone. He knows I am looking for him. He threatened me. The only way he could have learnt about me and also gotten my number is from her. He might have found her.'

Ibrahim stared at the dashboard for a while. 'There is really nothing I can do right now. You can't contact the girl, you don't know how to find the building, and you don't even know who Malik is.'

'If I find out who he is, will you be able to do something?'

'I don't know. I need the girl's statement. Find her and we'll take it from there. For now, all I can say is that you should be careful.'

33

Tall trees formed a dense canopy above, and tangled vegetation covered the ground below. Two shirtless men dug with shovels as sweat rolled off their bare backs and mosquitoes hovered around them. Three feet down they reached the body. The men set their shovels aside and cleared the earth with their hands. The corpse had begun to bloat beneath the pink polo top and blue jeans. The men searched in the soil, one on each side of the uncovered grave. The one at the feet exposed an inch of pink plastic near the girl's legs. He stood up with the girl's phone in his hands, brushed it with his fingers, then wiped it on his trousers. When they buried her, they had tossed her belongings in with her: phone, bag, and shoes.

The man wiped his face using his forearm, blinked sweat off his eyelids, and swatted at a mosquito that buzzed near his face. He turned the phone over in his hand and held the 'on' button with his thumb. The screen lit up. He waited till he could see the icons, then holding down the same button he switched the phone off again and put it into his pocket.

They began to cover up the body.

Malik leaned forward in the tall burgundy seat behind his desk. The leather upholstery squeaked. Two air conditioners hummed, keeping the large room at a constant 17 degrees. A closed, space-grey Apple laptop was the only item on the red leather surface of the wooden desk. Sisi, tall, and with gym-toned muscles and immobile breasts bought in Brazil, was standing next to Malik in a see-through black camisole and a pair of black short pants. On the other side, two middle-aged Russian men sat drinking coffee from teacups that looked small in their thick, bejewelled fingers. Both men had noses that had been broken more than once. They had gold chains under their white shirts, visible around their tanned necks. Behind them, standing in a row, twelve Ukrainians girls shifted from leg to leg, looked straight ahead at the people conversing at the desk, listening for words they could recognise.

'How long do I have them for?' Malik asked. His eyes moved from girl to girl, from face to feet and feet to face.

The man on the right held up three fingers. 'Three weeks. Only three weeks. Then I come and I take them.' His accent was thick.

'And medicals?'

'All certificates, I give already to Sisi.'

Malik looked at Sisi. She nodded.

'Tell them to take off their clothes.'

The man turned and spoke in Russian. Some of the girls had already begun undressing.

'I need something from you, Dmitry. Something special,' Malik said.

'Very young girl?'

'No. A tranny. You know what that is?'

'Da. Transvestite. Girl with...' he signified a penis with his finger over his crotch.

'Yes. Can you get one?'

'One? I get you many. You tell me, I bring.'

'Just one. He... She must look like a woman.'

'They sexy even more than real woman.'

'I want someone who looks young, good breasts, good

body, voice like a girl. I want to see her pictures before you bring her.'

'No problem. When you want tranny?'

'As soon as possible.'

Someone knocked on the door behind the girls. They all looked. The door opened. Naomi, in a red bra, red pants, red high heels and black stockings with suspenders, entered the room. She walked through the middle of the girls. She had a brown envelope in her hand. She handed it to Malik.

Malik tore open the envelope and looked inside. He turned it over and a phone with a pink cover dropped onto his desk. He picked up the device between his thumb and index finger and turned it over, inspecting it closely, then looked up. Naomi was looking at the phone. 'What?' Malik said.

Naomi shook her head. 'Nothing. Nothing is wrong.'

'I didn't ask you if anything is wrong.'

'I'm sorry.'

34

A man in a white sailor's uniform held out his hand to Amaka. He had come down from the yacht to help her on board. She ignored his offer, gripped the railing with one hand, and looked down at the metal mesh beneath her feet as she stepped onto the steep gangway leading to the vessel. It was anchored at the private moorings of the exclusive Aquamarine Boat Club of The Civic Centre on Ozumba Mbadiwe Avenue. Written in gold on the side of the mega yacht was Ẹja nlá: Big fish.

She took care not to let her heels slip into the tiny holes in the flooring beneath her feet. On either side, the plastic debris of Lagos Lagoon swelled with the water and slapped against the concrete.

An albino man waited for her on board. He asked her to follow him, then led her through a door into a living area with white leather seats set against oak-panelled walls with porthole windows. A staircase rose to the upper floor.

The man went up first. They stepped into a meeting. The room had white walls, a mirrored ceiling, and the floor was covered in a deep pile cream rug. A group of Chinese men in suits occupied two of the fixed-in-place white sofas. In another, Amaka recognised the heir apparent of the Mourtadas. It clicked; the yacht belonged to the billionaire Lebanese family. On another sofa she recognised Ambrose sitting alone, the shortest of all the men there.

'This way, please,' the albino said, holding his hand out

towards the glass door. The men continued talking. Amaka pushed the door open and stepped out onto the deck. She looked at the hot tub at the far end, then up at the nautically-inspired Civic Centre building before casting a glance at the other boats moored alongside Ẹja nlá. Finally, she looked out across the lagoon to Oyinkan Abayomi Drive. Her home was behind trees lining the lagoon. When she walked through, the men had continued talking as if they didn't see her. Now she sat and faced them. They stood up. Amaka watched. Ambrose motioned for them to sit down, said something, then turned and walked towards the door with the albino man in tow.

He walked on to the deck, squinted at the sun and approached Amaka. He was shorter than she expected.

'You are Amaka?' he said, but he did not try to shake hands. The albino stood behind him, his eyes hidden behind the reflective lenses of his glasses.

'Yes,' Amaka said, standing up. 'Thank you for seeing me.'

'Yes, yes. As you can see, I'm very busy. What do you need from me?' He checked his watch.

'I have information on Chief Olabisi Ojo. In return, I want to become a member of your party.'

He looked up. 'What kind of information?'

She looked at the albino.

'Quick,' he said. 'I have to return to my meeting.' He checked the time again.

'Videos that can destroy him.'

'Where are the videos?'

'On a memory card I got from his phone.'

'Do you have it here with you?' He held out his palm.

'No.'

'Bring it to my house tonight. Ask Gabriel for the address.'

He turned and returned to the meeting. The men stood up again as he entered the room. The albino stayed behind on the deck, holding out his hand to see her off.

35

The sun was beginning to set when Ambrose walked down the gangway from Ẹja nlá. Yellowman followed behind, and Babalola, in a sky blue agbada that billowed in the wind, waited at the bottom.

'Doc, we have scored a joker,' Ambrose said as he stepped off the gangway. He began walking towards the car park, Ambrose alongside him. 'Manna has fallen from heaven right into our laps.'

'The Mourtadas are supporting us?'

'They will always support whatever I do. It's not them. I have found a wife for you.'

Babalola stopped. Ambrose had walked a couple of steps before he paused and looked back. 'Come on,' he said, gesturing with his hand. 'I have found you the perfect partner. The woman who would help you win the election.'

'Prince, what are you talking about?'

'Do you know Ambassador Mbadiwe?'

'Yes.'

'His daughter came to see me today. A name like that on our ticket and we have won.'

'Prince, we did not discuss this.'

Ambrose stopped walking and grabbed Babalola's agbada.

'What you do in the privacy of your own room is none of my business,' he said, 'even if you do it with another man. I know everything about you. Everything. Do you understand? This girl will be by your side till you enter government house. It is non-negotiable.' He let go of Babalola and started walking away, then stopped and turned around.

'And one more thing. That boy that follows you everywhere, I don't want to see him again. I give you twenty-four hours to get him out of the country.'

Otunba Oluawo walked alone past his swimming pool and into the pool house. A reflection of the sinking sun shone as an orange line, thicker and brighter in the middle, across the glass wall. Inside, a short man in blue jeans, floral short-sleeved shirt, and a black trilby hat was waiting in an armchair.

'Area, how are you?' Otunba said. 'You took care of everything?'

'Baba,' Area said. He started to shimmy out of the chair but Otunba raised a hand to let him know it was OK to remain seated.

'They said the boy survived till he reached the hospital,' Otunba said.

'He must be strong, or his juju is strong,' Area said. 'He chopped six bullets.'

'Were you there?'

'No.'

'Who did you use?'

'Sky and Mutiu.'

'Good. Ex-soldiers are always better. I need them to do another job. A girl. I don't have her details yet but tell them to be on standby. And this time it has to look like a robbery. Or even an accident. In fact, I prefer that. I want it to look like an accident.'

'Baba, I only trust those boys with shooting.'

'OK. Robbery is fine.'

'Baba, please don't be annoyed with me for asking you

questions, but the boys are asking me why we carried out action on one of our own people. They are wondering what the driver did to you?'

'He saw things he shouldn't have seen.'

'And the girl?'

'She's one of the things he shouldn't have seen.'

36

'Whose phone is that?' Sisi asked.

'Somebody who is about to make me very rich,' Malik said.

The Russians and the Ukrainian girls had left and Malik and Sisi were alone in the office. Malik opened a couple of drawers on his desk and found a packet of wet wipes. He pulled one out and began to clean the phone.

'Does she have a name?' Sisi asked.

'What makes you think it's a she?'

'Pink. Doh.'

She sat in a one of the chairs opposite.

'Oh, yes.'

Malik held the phone up. The pink cover had little hearts etched into it. He peeled off the cover and tossed it into a bin behind his desk. The phone's white case looked new.

'I'm guessing the owner isn't getting their phone back?' Sisi said.

'Nope.'

'What are you up to, Malik?'

'Nothing that concerns you.'

'Who is the tranny for?'

'A client.'

'He asked for a tranny?'

'Not exactly. But we are getting him one.'

'What if he isn't into that?'

'It doesn't matter.'

'Malik. We agreed. No more of this. No more blackmail. Whose phone is that?'

'Someone who no longer needs it. You have asked enough questions. If you don't want to know the answers, don't ask.'

'Should I be worried?'

'Only if you get in my way.'

'Malik. You scare me when you talk like that.'

'Good.'

'Good?'

'Yes. Good. Because that fear will keep you out of trouble.'

'Malik, I can't go on like this.'

'Makes two of us. You want to know who the tranny is for? I'll tell you. Ojo. Yes. Chief Olabisi-idiot-Ojo. The fool is going to become Governor of Lagos State. Did you know that? That moron would become a governor. That fool. A governor. This is my chance. Whoever controls him controls Lagos and that person is going to be me. I deserve it. I lost a good girl because of him.'

'Is that the girl's phone? The one he attacked?'

'The one he killed.'

'What are you going to do with the phone?'

'It has nothing to do with you. What concerns you is to get him in bed with the tranny when she arrives. I'll handle the rest.'

'Blackmail. So we're back to this.'

'We never stopped. We just didn't have a catch big enough.'

37

Ambrose walked ahead of Amaka down the dark, unlit corridor in his mansion. Yellowman walked behind them. Ambrose stopped in the middle of the corridor where moonlight poured in through a window overlooking the front yard. He turned to Amaka. 'Did you bring it?' he said.

Amaka looked at Yellowman. Light from the window cut across his body from the shoulders down. In the shadow, his neck and face were a pale grey. He held his hands behind his back where he stood a couple of metres away but still within earshot. She looked at Ambrose. 'Can we be alone?' she said.

Ambrose gestured to Yellowman and the tall figure withdrew into the shadow. Amaka waited to hear the door shut, then she turned to Ambrose.

'I have a confession to make. I don't have the memory card but he doesn't know that. You just have to tell him exactly what I described to you and he'll be convinced you've seen the videos. He'll have no choice but to withdraw his candidacy. I can deal with him as a civilian, but if he becomes governor, he'll be too powerful and he'll have immunity.'

'Immunity does not mean he cannot be investigated. Gani Fawehinmi vs Inspector General of Police. 2002.'

'You're a lawyer?'

'No. I am a politician. But I know the law when it affects me. How did you lose the memory card?'

'My handbag was stolen at Oshodi. It was in it.'

'I see.' He looked larger in the darkness. He leant on the window ledge and crossed his arms. 'In that case, the information is useless. What if he calls my bluff? What if there is no video? I mean, I know the man is a dog, but the things you described are unbelievable even from me.' Amaka was about to talk. He put up his hand. 'And what if we want him to run? Have you considered that?'

He turned to the window. Outside, beyond the compound's fence, empty plots of fenced-off land stretched out next to rows of houses in different stages of construction.

'Look,' he said. 'Everything you see belongs to me. Buildings, land, roads, everything. But one small boy can come and become governor and say that government has revoked my allocation and just like that I lose it all. That is power. All this land you see, the land on which this house is built, it is all allocation. This is how I have made my money, from government allocation, and I do not want to lose it. This is called stake. This is my stake. What is your stake in this? You say you don't want him to be governor. You say because he's a bad person; he does bad things to little girls. But I'm not convinced. There must be more to this. This is personal.

'You say you can't tell me how you got your hands on the things on his phone, but now that he's running for governor you want to use the evidence to destroy him. I think you're afraid that any time he thinks of his governorship bid, he thinks of you as well. You stole from him and now he wants back what you took.

'Protection, I think that is what you really want. Am I correct?' He peered into her eyes above the rim of his glasses. 'My answer is yes. You can join our party. Now, normally we would take you to a shrine where you will swear before a babalawo, but that wouldn't work on you because you, you know it is all bullshit. The second option is to get your hands dirty. That is what you will have to do.

'You will be one of my moneybag men. You see, rigging is a leaky business. For every million you spend, only a few thousand gets to the intended recipients. That is why we lost the last election; our own people were stealing the money meant to buy us votes. You will personally handle the dispersal of funds. You will carry the bribe to the INEC officials who can either accept it or hand you over to SSS if they've already been bought by the opposition. Can you do this, knowing who your father is?

'But even that only buys you membership. For what you really want, for my protection, you have to do something else for me.'

38

The crickets chirped from all directions. The moon was full beneath thick clouds, and a breeze blew warm air.

Ojo and Shehu stood by Otunba's stretch limousine, which was idling in the middle of six other cars, armed men behind their darkened windows. The old man was alone in the back seat, his window down and his arm over the door as he spoke to the two men standing with hands behind their backs.

'Shehu, are you staying here tonight?' Otunba asked. 'You can send someone to go and bring your things from your house.'

'No, sir. But thank you for the invitation. Alhaja is expecting me home tonight.'

'They can bring her here too. This is the safest place you can both be right now.'

'I'm sure I'll be alright, sir.'

'You'll be alright?'

'Yes, sir.'

'And what about you, Olabisi? Are you staying here?'

'I will ask Matilda, sir.'

'You will ask Matilda. All right. Both of you be here by seven am. We have a lot of work to do tomorrow.' Otunba retreated into the dark interior of the limousine and the three-inch-thick bulletproof glass window slid up.

The gates opened and the cars rolled out of the compound.

Shehu and Ojo remained standing under the dark sky, the sound of the crickets louder now that the cars had left.

'Can you imagine him asking you to stay here as if you are a child,' Ojo said.

'He was only concerned for our safety,' Shehu said.

'No, Shehu. It is about control. See how we were standing like schoolboys reporting to the headmaster. He knows what he's doing. That is what he expects would continue to happen when I become governor.'

'You expect different?'

'Forget it. You know what, Shehu, I want to take you somewhere really special.'

'I'm not sure it's a good idea to go anywhere again this evening.'

'Are you afraid?'

'Of your father-in-law?'

'Of assassins.'

'I'm more afraid of Otunba than I am of assassins, believe me. And you should be too.'

'It's all going to change soon. Very soon, it will all be different.'

Shehu sighed.

'This place I'm taking you to, you have never seen anything like it before. If anyone told you a place like this exists in Nigeria you will say it is a lie. My friend, you are in for a treat tonight. Your eyes will see wonders and miracles.'

'I'm not sure I like the sound of that.'

39

Two men wearing chef's uniforms were tending to a goat roasting atop a spit, their sweaty, oily faces glistening in the leaping orange flames they tried to tame. Beside them another cook was turning skewers of suya on a charcoal grill. Smoke, laden with the aroma of spice and roasted meat, blew across the pool. Malik, his face hidden behind a white mask with holes for the eyes and nostrils, his white agbada plastered against his body by the night breeze, stood with a group of men in similar masks. The five Chinese men, an American, and two Nigerians had all paid their first five million naira annual membership fee and Malik was taking them through their induction, telling them about specific girls, boasting of orgies in the pool, reminding them of the special rooms for special experiences.

Across the pool in a white bikini, sprawled on a sun lounger, Naomi watched Malik. He gesticulated, shook with laughter, slapped someone's back, looked around and nodded at her. On either side of her, also in bikinis and laying on sun loungers, were the half-Nigerian, half-Lebanese twins from Kano. They also watched Malik and the new clients.

The back door of the mansion opened. Sisi stepped out in a black, flowing, see-through slip. From across the pool, Naomi could see she wore nothing underneath. Ashewo, she thought. Prostitute. Sisi had a champagne flute in one hand and a smouldering cigar in the other. She sashayed in her high heels, and behind her the Ukrainian girls followed, all in bikinis, their creamy white skins untouched by the sun.

Naomi waved a buzzing mosquito from her right ear. Sisi led the girls to the men and Malik stepped aside to reveal his new staff. The American raised his glass of beer to the girls, for some reason the Chinese men clapped. The girls stood in an awkward row, each of them maintaining a pose as if they were in front of pageant judges.

Naomi shook her head. They didn't even speak English. How would they communicate with the men? Malik encouraged the girls to talk with the clients. 'Pretend you're on a date,' he would say. How were these girls going to *date* their clients when they didn't even speak English? And Sisi, the bitch, the whore of whores who sucked Malik's dick even when he was not there, had given her room to the Ukrainian girls. All the girls had their own rooms, rooms that they used when it was their rotation at The Harem. Often, Naomi would arrive at the mansion and find that a pillow was missing, or a chair had been moved, or a wine glass had been left on the bathroom sink, and she would wonder whose room *her room* had been when she was away.

'Look at them, they look like ghosts,' one of the twins said. 'Ghosts that have HIV.' The other twin agreed: 'These ones look like they have full blown.'

Naomi thought the girls looked like models. Perhaps they were models back home. *Had been* models back home.

The wind picked up. The smell of suya and roasted goat came in wafts of smoke that stung the eyes. One by one, the masked men left with the girls. Sisi took the tall white man's hand and led him out of the group and round the pool. They passed the spit and the barbecue and continued walking.

The twins sat up in their sun loungers and both adjusted

their breasts and hair in the same movement. Naomi remained on her back.

Sisi stood over the three; the tall American loomed by her side.

'Ladies,' Sisi said. She looked at the twins in turn and the pair stood, smiling and pushing their chests out and into the hands of the waiting client. They entwined their arms in his, each on either side of him, and led him away. Sisi, sipping from her champagne flute watched them go, then looked down at Naomi, and without a word she walked away, her cigar smoke trailing behind her.

Naomi watched Malik snap fingers with one of the remaining black men. The girls that were still there stood in place till Sisi walked past them, waved, and they followed her into the mansion.

The wind picked up. Smoke blew thick from the spit and the barbecue. Malik led the men towards the building, turning to look at Naomi before he stepped inside. She nodded back but he had already turned away and entered the house.

Alone by the poolside, Naomi watched the cooks struggle with the smoke and look up to the sky, expecting rain. The air already smelt of wet soil.

Sisi did not come out for her. Nobody did. She did not know when she dozed off, but when she woke up it was because a drop of rain had fallen onto her eyelid. The cooks were gone, the spit and the barbecue emptied, and the night had grown darker. Another drop fell onto her belly. Moments later more tiny cold drops fell onto her. Beyond the tall fence, the forest rustled and branches waved in the wind. Naomi stood up from the pool chair.

Inside the building, the foyer was empty. Naomi went to the window and looked out onto the car park. The rain was roaring now. Six cars were parked outside. Malik's Range

Rover was in its usual spot, close to the gate and next to Sisi's red Audi TT. He was always around before the clients arrived, and left before them - unless one was spending the night, which didn't happen often. Dimeji had left after dropping her and the two girls. Naomi suspected Malik didn't like him being there. Good riddance.

Malik came down the stairs and opened the front door. The wind howled, wrapping his agbada against his body. He hunched his shoulders and dashed out. The wind slammed the door shut behind him. She listened for his car, her heart already racing.

Naomi walked along the corridor. She stopped in front of her room and held the cold, polished chrome handle but she didn't turn it. She placed her ear against the door, the handle still in her grip, then she lifted her head away. She began to turn the handle.

'What are you doing there?'

Naomi turned round. Sisi was at the other end of the corridor. She had just come down from her apartment on the second floor. She walked towards Naomi. 'I told you you're staying with the twins, didn't I?'

'Yes, you did,' Naomi said.

'What are you doing here, then?' Sisi was without her cigar and her champagne flute. She placed her hands on her hips and waited for an answer.

'I forgot,' Naomi said. She began to walk past Sisi but Sisi caught her by the hand and stopped her.

'You forgot?' Sisi said. 'And that is why you were listening? I saw you.'

'I lost an earring. I wanted to check inside.'

Sisi looked at her ears. Naomi wasn't wearing earrings. 'Malik just called me to say he's coming back,' she said.

'Why?' Naomi asked, then she thought she asked too quickly. But why was he returning, and why was Sisi telling her?

'He's expecting someone very important. I want you to go and freshen up and wait for me to come and get you.'

'OK.'

As Naomi walked away, her heart beating fast, something occurred to her. Sisi had a phone. Even if she couldn't get to hers, if the water had somehow gotten into the condom and destroyed the device, if she could just get her hands on Sisi's phone she could still send the location of The Harem to Amaka.

40

Otunba passed the armed policeman at the gate of the three-storey pink building in Magodo where his convoy had stopped. The house, like the rest on the street, had been built to take up all the available space in its compound. Either side of the building, there was only a metre from the fence. A navy blue BMW and a gold Jaguar saloon were parked side by side. The front door had been left open. Another policeman standing guard saluted.

Otunba walked across a large parlour busy with servants in white uniforms ferrying trays from a door that kept swinging open and shut. They carried the food up a marble staircase while others hurried down with empty trays. The room smelt of jollof rice and fried chicken, beer and egusi soup. Otunba went up the staircase. The servants bowed as Otunba passed them. They plastered their bodies against the wall and held their trays high above their heads to give him even more space. His hand trailed over the polished banister and he nodded as he passed each servant. At the top he dipped his hand into his pocket and held out a fist of cash to a man standing at attention. 'Thank you, sir,' the man said, bowing.

'Share it with the rest,' Otunba said.

The landing had sofas pushed against three walls that each had a door leading from them. The fourth wall had double doors in the middle and picture frames everywhere else. Laughter and loud talking came from the room behind the double doors. Otunba crossed the floor and opened them. Smoke and cool air washed over his face. Around a large dining table in the middle of the room, people were seated with playing cards in their hands. Some had cigarettes wedged between their fingers, others smoked cigars. A thin man with a slim face and a white Afro was smoking a pipe, and the only woman at the table – slim, older, her grey hair combed back – was smoking a joint. On the table, cards, poker chips, and bundles of dollars took centre stage among ashtrays, glasses, and bottles of beer, wine, brandy, and champagne.

At the far end of the table, Ambrose looked up from his cards that he was guarding with his other hand. He was the only person not smoking. His eyes locked with Otunba Oluawo's. He reached for his champagne flute and raised the glass to his lips.

41

The gateman watched Amaka as she paced the compound, smoking. She stubbed out her cigarette, but instead of going up the steps and into Eyitayo and Gabriel's bungalow, she lit another and continued to pace.

Gabriel was clearing dishes from the dining table when Amaka entered. 'You just missed dinner,' he said.

She had two boxes with her, a new iPad and a new phone. She set them on the table, sat down and slumped backwards in the chair.

'How did it go?' Gabriel asked.

'I'm exhausted, Gabriel,' she said. 'I just want to go to bed. Where is Chioma?'

'She had dinner with us. Eyitayo just took her in.'

'*In* where? She's coming with me.'

'Amaka, we think you should stay with us till this thing is resolved.'

'This thing? What thing? And what do you mean we?'

'Eyitayo and I. I told her everything. We think it's safer for you to stay with us till you can leave the country.'

'Leave the country? For what? I'm not going anywhere. I'm going to stay and I'm going to get that bastard who killed Chioma's brother, and I'm going to get Ojo and Malik. Ojo will not be governor of this state, whatever it takes.'

'Even your life?'

'Please, Gabriel, I can't do this now.' She stood up.

Eyitayo walked into the living room. She stopped at the doorway and looked at both of them. 'What's the problem?' she asked.

'She wants to go home tonight,' Gabriel said.

Eyitayo walked over to Amaka, put her arms over her shoulder, and tried to lead her to a sofa. 'She's already asleep,' she said. 'I gave her a pill.'

'Thanks,' Amaka said. She eased herself out of Eyitayo's arms, 'but I really have to go home. Look at me. I can't keep borrowing your things.'

'Am I complaining?'

'It's not just that. Look, guys, I just really need to be in my own space so I can think.'

'Amaka, they already threatened you. Do you honestly think they will stop at anything to stop you publishing those videos you took?' Eyitayo said.

'Gabriel shouldn't have told you about that.'

'Well he did, and I'm glad he did, because if he is ready to let you leave this house tonight, I'm not. Until you can leave the country, you're staying here. It's safer. Nobody will know where you are.'

'My house is the safest place I can be right now. I've got armed police guards, remember?'

'Shh,' Gabriel said.

Eyitayo looked at him. 'What?'

'Quiet.' He cocked his ear. They all listened.

'Who's she talking to?' Eyitayo said.

'Oh no,' Amaka said. 'It's him.'

'God will punish you for what you did, Kingsley,' Chioma wailed into the phone. Tears streamed down her cheeks. 'You will never know peace in your life.'

Amaka grabbed the phone from her hand. It was wet with her tears. She ended the call and tossed the mobile onto the bed. Chioma crumpled into her arms.

Gabriel and Eyitayo watched from the door. 'I didn't know she had a phone,' Eyitayo said. She looked apologetic. Gabriel put his arm around his wife.

'I'm taking her home,' Amaka said. Chioma sobbed into her chest.

42

It had stopped raining. The wiper blades of the bulletproof Range Rover squeaked against the windshield. The driver switched off the engine and Shehu stepped out. Gravel shifted beneath the thin leather soles of his shoes. Other cars were parked around the large compound. All wet. Floodlights hid the forest beyond the tall fence. Shehu looked to his right from where he could hear the faint hum of a soundproof generator. Everywhere else the only sound was of crickets. In front loomed the huge, unpainted house.

Between two pillars that stretched the height of the two-storey building, and beneath the light above the front door of the mansion, a man stood in a black agbada, his face hidden behind a white mask and his hands clasped in front of his body.

Ojo walked up to the building while Shehu and the police officers watched. Underneath the light above the doorway, Ojo and the masked man spoke before the man entered the house and closed the door behind him. Ojo turned and beckoned to Shehu.

Shehu stood in front of Ojo on the gravel, just before the raised marble platform in front of the door. He looked at the police officers; their necks were arched, taking in the house.

'What is this place, Olabisi?' Shehu asked.

'You'll see,' Ojo said, grinning. 'We have to wear masks before we can enter. He's gone to get them for us.'

'I'm not wearing any fucking mask.'

When Malik returned, he had two masks in his hands: a pink one, the face of a pig ending at the snout, and a red one, a half face that looked like a snarling devil with a long nose that bent downwards. He handed the pig to Ojo and the devil to Shehu.

The three men stepped in through the doorway into the foyer. A row of girls in lingerie stood waiting for them; Sisi stood in front.

Malik turned to Shehu. 'Sisi will look after you while I discuss some business with him.'

The girls stepped forward smiling and surrounded Shehu. Their arms went up his chest, down the side of his legs, and across his back but he resisted their gentle nudge to move him towards the stairs. 'Nope,' he said. He peeled the arms off his body. 'I go wherever he goes.'

The girls looked at Malik. Malik held the chin of his mask to adjust it then he nodded to the side. The girls walked towards the door in the direction he had indicated. 'That's fine,' he said. 'You will also like what I have planned for him.'

'I am alive today,' Ojo said. 'If I die tomorrow, I am OK. But as for today, I am alive.'

He was naked except for his mask. His arms were over the shoulders of two white girls on either side of him in the hot tub. He looked at each of them in turn. They continued to stroke his wet chest.

On the other side, the water bubbled around Shehu's chest as he watched Ojo and the girls.

'Old Navy, don't be shy,' Ojo said.

The head of a third girl rose out of the water. She wiped her face and smiled at Ojo as she filled her lungs. He put his hand on her head and pushed her back under. He closed his eyes and threw his head back.

'Oh yeah. Oh yeah. Yeah. Yeah.'

'Do not do something nasty in the water,' Shehu said.

Ojo opened his eyes. He looked at Shehu.

The submerged girl was coming up. Ojo put his hand on her head and held her down.

'You shouldn't be coming to these kinds of places,' Shehu said.

'Why?'

Ojo held the girl down in the water.

'You are going to be governor.'

'So? As governor I shouldn't enjoy myself?'

'As governor you shouldn't expose yourself.'

'All the girls are tested.'

'Politically.'

'Oh.'

The girl slid her head away from Ojo's hand, broke the surface in a flash and gulped for air. Shehu used the back of a knuckle to wipe away a drop of water that had found his eyelid through an eyehole of his mask. The girl continued gasping for air. She said something to Ojo in Ukrainian, then she splashed water at him. Ojo slapped her with the back of his free hand. She fell backwards into the water and into Shehu.

In his office, hunching over his laptop, his white mask on the table, Malik watched Shehu put his arms around the girl. Malik stood up, picked up his mask and left the room.

Sisi knocked and then opened the door. 'Everything to your satisfaction, boys?' she said.

Ojo turned in the water to look at her. She put her hands

on his shoulders from behind and slid them down his chest. She played with his nipple between her thumbs and forefingers and whispered into his ear. Ojo smiled. He stood, his failing erection hidden beneath the flab of his huge belly. Sisi and one of the girls helped him out and he picked up a towel and wrapped it round his waist.

'See you soon,' he said to Shehu. A grin spread across his face.

'I'll have him back in no time,' Sisi said, winking. With her arm on his back, she led Ojo out of the room.

Sisi kept her hand over Ojo's closed eyes. 'Don't look till you hear the door close,' she said. She unwrapped the towel from his waist and took it with her.

The door closed and Ojo opened his eyes. It was pitch black in the silent room. 'Hello?' he said. He spread his hands until he touched something cold and hard. His hands snapped back to his body. The chain rattled.

The lights went on. Malik was standing alone by the wall on the other end of the room. Between them, long, shiny chains dangled from hooks in the ceiling. The walls were covered in padded white leather. There were no windows and the floor was tiled black and white.

Ojo put his hands over his crotch. 'Where are the twins?' he asked.

'There are no twins.'

'What is going on?'

'You are in deep trouble. Florentine is alive.'

'What?'

'The girl you tried to kill. She's not dead.'

'But, you said she was dead.'

'I was wrong. She's alive. And she contacted me.'

'How can this be?'

'It be.'

'Malik, you are trying to blackmail me.'

'No. And neither is she. She just wanted some money I owe her.'

'Malik, are you lying to me? How did she survive?'

'Some people picked her up. They took her to a place called Street Samaritans.'

'A hospital?'

'No. A charity. The woman who runs it, she's the trouble you have.'

'Why?'

'Because Florentine told her what you did and the woman swore to do something about it. She's not going to go to the police. She's going to take matters into her own hands. That's what she promised Florentine. And now that you're running for governor, she can really, really hurt you. Unless something is done about her.'

'How can I do something about someone I don't know? Who is she?'

'Her name is Amaka. She needs to disappear. If she contacts you, do not try to negotiate. Do not meet her, do not talk to her. Any contact you have with her, she will use to harm you.'

'What about Florentine?'

'I will take care of her.'

'Where is she?'

'I don't know yet. She won't tell me. She's afraid after what you did to her, but I'll find her and I'll take care of her. For you.'

'How do I know she's alive?'

'You still have her number?'

'Yes.'

'Call her.'

43

'Who invited this old baba?' Ambrose said from his seat.

Those who hadn't noticed Otunba followed Ambrose's gaze to the old man in the doorway. Two men moved their seats apart so that an additional seat could fit at the table. Otunba sat and the servant holding his chair asked if he wanted anything to drink. Otunba waved the man away.

'Who is trying to kill your candidate?' Ambrose asked and everybody laughed, including Otunba.

'Don't mind the boy,' Otunba said. He removed a brown envelope from his pocket and pulled out two bundles of hundred-dollar bills. 'What is happening? Your people are not yet rioting.'

'Your people have to start.'

'We started yesterday. It died when your people didn't arrive.' Otunba accepted a stack of chips.

'We were there. Your boys had sophisticated weapons. If we engaged, it would have been bloody for us. Your guys would have gotten too excited.'

The lady spoke. 'Boys, you know the rules, no business at the table.'

'No riot, no emergency security vote,' Otunba said. 'No emergency security vote, no money.'

'You mean Abuja hasn't sent money by now?'

'Boys,' the lady snapped.

44

'I know who the girl is,' Ojo said. His hair left a wet path on the headrest in the back of the Range Rover as he turned towards Shehu.

'Which girl?' Shehu asked.

'The girl at Eko hotel. The one that took my memory card. Iyabo.'

Shehu leaned forward. 'Park here,' he said to the driver.

The driver looked at Ojo in the mirror. Ojo nodded. The driver stopped the car on the long narrow road in the middle of the forest. The police escort also stopped, then reversed to be close to the SUV. Two officers jumped from the van with their weapons. The Harem was now out of sight beyond a bend in the road. Ojo motioned to the officers to remain where they were as he and Shehu got out. Together they walked back a distance in the sandy strips between the floundering grass. The clouds had cleared from the full moon. Under the stars, the forest grey and noisy around them, Ojo talked and Shehu listened.

When Ojo had finished talking, Shehu pointed in the direction from which they had come. 'This happened in there?' he asked.

'Yes. But it was an accident.'

'Oh Lord.'

'I didn't mean to.'

'How badly did you beat her?'

'We thought she was dead.'

'Oh Lord. Olabisi. Oh Lord.'

'It was Malik's idea to dump her body on the road.'

'And now he just told you she's still alive?'

'Yes.'

'And you believe him?'

'She sent me this message.'

Shehu took Ojo's phone and read the message: 'I'm sorry for what happened. Please let bygones be bygones. - Flo.'

'When did she send this?'

'Just now. Before we left.'

'Did you talk to her?'

'No. She didn't answer my call so I sent her a message that she should call me back and she replied with this. Malik said she's afraid.'

'What is her name?'

'Florentine.'

'Does she always sign her name off like this when she texts you?' Shehu looked at the message on Ojo's phone.

'Yes.'

'And she told this Amaka lady everything?'

'Yes. Malik said so.'

'And now you think Amaka is Iyabo.'

'Yes. Malik said she's a lawyer. Iyabo also said she's a lawyer. It is the same person, Shehu. It makes sense. She set me up because of Florentine. I knew there was something suspicious about the girl.'

'And yet you still invited her to your hotel suite. Where is Florentine now?'

'Malik said he would take care of her for me.'

'Take care of her for you. Brother, you do not want anyone other than me to take care of anything or anybody for you, do you understand? Not Malik, not them,' he pointed at the police officers, 'not your father-in-law. Especially not your father-in-law. This doesn't go beyond here. Tell Malik to do nothing to the girl. Let him arrange for me to meet her. Did you tell him about the hotel? About Iyabo?'

'No.'

'Did you?'

'No. I'm not stupid.'

'Good.'

'What if they're working together with Malik?'

'Now you're thinking.'

'I think I should just tell Otunba. He can sort this thing out faster than us.'

'Once you tell him, you become his slave. Is that what you want, to become his slave? I will take care of this. Call Malik now and tell him to arrange for me and Florentine to meet.'

45

A thin man with thick, curly hair on his exposed forearms gathered the chips on the table to himself.

Otunba and Ambrose both got up and left the room. On the landing they waited while a servant left, then they sat in the sofa furthest from the room they'd come from.

'I heard the VP came to see you,' Ambrose said. 'And before he left Abuja, a bullion van was seen at his house.'

'And so?'

'You said your governor has not received any emergency security vote.'

'Where are the riots?'

'It cannot come from our camp. It is your camp that lost a candidate and almost lost another. Did you have anything to do with that?'

'Make an attempt on my own son-in-law?'

'It was not an attempt on your son-in-law. He would be dead.'

'They will release Douglas's body to his family tomorrow.'

'They were able to retrieve his body?'

'It is a mess. What remains of it. They will take the coffin to his ancestral home at Isale Eko.'

'In the heart of our grassroots base.'

'Precisely.'

'We don't want any losses. Tell your boys, no killings. We

don't want Abuja to declare a state of emergency.'

'And about the emergency security vote, when it comes, the governor still gets his usual two thirds.'

'Why?'

'It is his last term. He's working for his retirement.'

'He's greedy.'

'We split the rest.'

'Fair enough.'

'After this Douglas thing,' Otunba said, 'I'm hearing that your candidate feels he has a chance.'

'Who said so?'

'Call him to order. Nothing has changed. Same deal as before.'

'Is it true that his girlfriend's husband was flying the plane?' Ambrose asked.

'Yes. The boy killed them all.'

'What a shame.'

'Yes. Anyway. It's less than six weeks to elections. We will start campaigns after the burial. No need for any trouble after that. The security vote should have arrived by then and you would have received your share.'

'Good. We have a new party member. The daughter of Ambassador Mbadiwe. Amaka. Amaka Mbadiwe. She has to be on the safe list.'

'I don't know her.'

'Your son-in-law does. That is why she is on the safe list. She's untouchable. Let him know that.'

'Like I said, I don't know her.'

'It doesn't matter. She is one of ours. She is a no-go area.'

'I have heard.'

46

Insects flew in circles round fluorescent tubes hanging in rows from the ceiling. Below, the congregation wailed and sang and clapped and jerked in holy frenzy. In front, on a raised stage covered in red carpet, the pastor, in a white suit, white shirt, white shoes and a red tie, was sweating from the hairline of his jerry-curled head as he ran from corner to corner screaming into his microphone and spraying spittle onto the faces of the most ardent followers who were kneeling at the foot of the altar.

In the first row, swaying to the choir's song, Area stood with his hands up, his eyes closed, and his face to the heavens as he repeated the proclamations the man of God commanded: 'All my enemies, somersault and die.' All around, the chorus, 'Die, die, die,' reverberated through the church.

Area felt a tingle against his leg. He fetched his phone and checked the caller display, then pushed his way past the kneeling, standing, jumping worshippers in his row, and jogged down the aisle for the exit, a hundred metres away.

Catching his breath outside the main auditorium of Faith and Fire Miracles Ministries, stars above, warm breeze blowing, he looked at the screen and saw the seconds counting.

'Baba,' he said.

'Her name is Amaka.'

'The girl?'

'Yes. Amaka Mbadiwe. Ambassador Mbadiwe's daughter. Do it tonight. She lives in her father's official residence in Ikoyi. The ambassador is not around, but there will be police officers guarding the place. Take as many boys as you need. Kill everybody. Take jewellery, TVs, things like that. I'm at an important meeting. I will wait until you call me to say it has been done. OK?'

'OK.'

Otunba returned to the landing from a door by the sofa. He winced and rubbed his stomach as he closed the door behind him.

Ambrose watched him settle back onto the sofa.

'Are you alright?' he asked.

'Something is disturbing my system,' Otunba said. 'I think I've flushed it out.'

'Have you?'

'We shall see.' He rubbed his stomach again. 'We shall see.'

Ambrose exchanged his remaining chips for cash. He'd not done well. He stood from the table and walked around shaking hands. Otunba was the last person he bade goodbye.

'You're leaving so soon?' Otunba asked.

'If we are to have a riot by tomorrow, I have to start working tonight,' Ambrose said.

Yellowman held the car door open for Ambrose before he walked around the car and got in next to his boss.

'From now on, Amaka is your number one priority,' Ambrose said. The car pulled out onto the road.

'Didn't you tell him she's on the safe list?' Yellowman asked.

'I did. He said he doesn't know who she is. He will make it look like an accident.'

'You want me to bring her in?'

'No. I want her to see what he's capable of. But you must be there so that we don't lose her. You, personally. Not anyone else. Round the clock. From this night on, her safety is your responsibility.'

'What if he doesn't make a move?'

'Then we will do it for him. Just like he did with his own son-in-law.'

47

Amaka raised her leg from the warm soapy water and placed her heel on top of the chrome tap. She inhaled vapour from the peppermint bath oil. Her eyes tingled. She raised her hand, skimmed the surface with her palm, and watched the water lapping against her skin in the dim light of a candle burning on the lid of the toilet bowl.

Her phone rang – the new one with her old number. She dried her hand on a towel on the rack, then leaned over the side of the bathtub. The caller display showed: Guy Collins. Her hand hovered over the device. She laid back into the water, stared at the ceiling, and let the phone continue ringing till it stopped. She became aware of her elevated breathing rate. She took deep breaths through her nose and exhaled through her mouth. She felt the vapour in her chest.

The phone beeped twice. She stayed in the water a while then she dried her hand and picked it up. She had a new voicemail. She lay back in the water and listened to Guy's voice.

'Hi Amaka. Eyitayo said you got your phone back. Amaka, the other day, when I got back to London and I saw your message that Malik had found you, I tried to call you back. I thought I should've never left Lagos. All I wanted to do was to fly right back to Nigeria. And I almost did. I was going to get a ticket when I called you again, and this time a man answered. People were shouting, screaming in the background. He said they'd killed someone, and they were beating you too. I begged him to help. He said there was nothing he could do. Then, he told me it was all over and he hung up.

'When he said that, it was the most awful feeling I've ever had. I didn't know what to do or who to call or what to think. Mel's father lives in Nigeria. I called her and I told her what had happened. I asked if her dad could help; if he could do something in Lagos. Call someone, go to the police, anything. All the while I thought it was too late. I thought Malik had got you.

'Mel said she'd call her dad. She suggested I come over in case he needed to talk to me. I was in such a state, Amaka. I couldn't be alone. I took a taxi to hers from the airport. We stayed up late waiting to hear back from her father and talking about what had happened. I slept on the sofa.

'Amaka, I was only at Mel's place because I'd reached out to her for help. Nothing happened between us. Nothing could have happened between us. When I thought I'd lost you, it was the most horrible feeling I've ever known, and it made me realise that, even though we've only known each other a short while, I'm in love with you. Amaka, I love you. And if you think there's a chance that maybe you feel the same way about me, please call me. If you don't, I'll understand. I'm just relieved you're OK.'

She continued to stare at the shifting patterns on the ceiling, and then slid into the bathtub, fully submerging her head in the water.

48

A Range Rover pulled up in front of the gate and sounded its horn. Behind it was a Mercedes saloon, and behind that, another Range Rover.

A man in a khaki uniform opened a foot gate and shielded his eyes from the headlights. The driver honked again. The gateman walked to the SUV while behind him, holding his AK-47 high above his head, a policeman yawned and stretched in the frame of the foot gate.

The rear window of the Mercedes rolled down. A single gunshot lit up the interior of the car and the rifle dropped from the hands of the policeman in the foot gate. He grabbed his belly, folded forward, and fell, head first onto the concrete pavement.

'Put your hands down,' Area said to the gateman, who was staring at the pistol aimed at his head. The gateman lowered his hands to his sides and stood rigid.

Men with automatic pistols climbed out of the cars and made for the foot gate. The first four jumped over the dead officer. The last two carried the body into the compound.

'Is Amaka in the house?' Area asked the gateman. The man shook his head.

'Why are you lying to me?' Area said.

'I no dey lie, sir. Na only me and the officer dey for house.'

'Any other officer dey inside?'

'No, sir.'

A single shot rang from within the compound. The gateman flinched and grimaced. Area shook his head at him.

The gates opened. Two dead bodies on top of each other in an X shape lay in front of a car covered in a tarpaulin. Area nodded to the gateman to enter the compound. The cars drove in and the men closed the gates behind them.

Amaka's head broke the surface of the water. She wiped her face, sat up in the bathtub and listened. She reached for the towel on the rack and dried her face and ears. 'Hello?' she said. No answer. She waited. She sat back in the bathtub and closed her eyes. The water would soon start getting cold.

His heart racing, a pistol pressed into his back, the gateman walked along the unlit corridor. Moonlight from a window illuminated his path while behind him, four armed men and Area followed, their footsteps silent on the rug.

The gateman stopped at a door and looked at Area. The little gangster's black trilby was tilted to the left. The pistol dangling by his side looked too big for his little hand.

Area pointed at the door. The gateman nodded. Area waved. The man was led aside, the gun still planted in his back. Two men stood either side of the door and pointed their pistols at it. Area stepped back. Holding his pistol in both hands, he levelled the weapon at the door and nodded. One of the men knocked on the door.

49

Yellowman pulled up under a mango tree by the Lagoon. Illuminated windows dotted the night sky across the water that was dark and still in the night, and across the road the mansions of Oyinkan Abayomi Drive slumbered peacefully behind tall fences topped with electrified wires.

He focused on the black gate two buildings away. The windows of the house behind the fence were dark and the floodlights in the compound were on. He imagined Amaka sleeping. The police officers attached to her ambassador father were oblivious to the danger she was in; oblivious of the man sent to protect her from it, sitting outside in a car, chewing bitter kola nuts to stay awake, ready to take a life to preserve hers.

He split another kola nut in his palms and placed one half on the passenger seat, next to his Uzi and two spare clips. He bit a chunk off the remaining half and his eyes caught a glimmer in the mirror.

Crouching by the fence, one of Area's men watched through the gap between the fence and the gate, his pistol raised. He strained to see the face of the person in the car that had parked across the road right in front of the building.

Two headlights appeared in the distance behind Yellowman. He kept his eyes on the mirror and picked up his weapon. Watching the car approaching from behind, he cocked the submachine gun in his lap.

The police patrol vehicle slowed as it got closer. The officers inside looked at Yellowman's car. Muzzles of AK-47s peeped out of their windows. Yellowman watched them. They wouldn't see through his tinted glass. The patrol car continued before stopping a few metres away by the black gate. Keeping his eyes on the car, Yellowman lifted the Uzi from his lap and tucked it under his chair. He did the same with the spare clips from the passenger seat. The police van idled in the middle of the road, emitting dark smoke from its exhaust pipe. Yellowman lifted his shirt and pulled out a Glock 42, pulled back the slide, and tucked the pistol underneath his legs.

The police van stayed in the middle of the road. The engine revved. Black smoke shot out of the exhaust. The engine revved again and the van started moving forward.

Yellowman watched till it had disappeared out of sight. He wound down his window and listened to the diesel engine turn right onto Bourdillon Road, then looked at the house again. Something glinted on the ground in front of the gate.

He tucked his pistol under his shirt and retrieved the Uzi and spare clips. He put a clip into each pocket of his jacket, then checked both ends of the road. He got out of his car, held the weapon under his jacket, and crossed the road.

He kept his eyes on the gate as he crouched down to pick up an empty shell from the ground, and sniff it. He put it into his pocket and searched around him. His eyes fell on a spot in front of the gate. He walked over, crouched again, and touched it. It was wet. He rubbed his fingers together and sniffed them. He pulled out his Uzi and aimed it at the gate, backed up towards his car, got inside without taking his eyes off the gate, and started the engine.

The lookout behind the gate lowered his pistol. He kept close to the ground as he crept towards the house.

50

Amaka's eyes darted towards the door.

'Who's that?' she said.

The handle turned and it began to open. She sat up in the water, reached for the towel and covered herself. 'Who's that?'

Eyitayo entered the bathroom. She was in a blue kimono and she had a bottle of wine and two glasses in her hands. 'It's just me,' she said, using her bum to shut the door behind her. Amaka returned the towel to the rack and sank back into the bathtub.

'Here,' Eyitayo said. She handed a glass to Amaka and filled it, then moved the candle from the toilet lid onto the edge of the washbasin and sat.

Another knock on the door.

'Go away,' Eyitayo said. 'Girls talk.'

'Can I open the door?' Gabriel said.

'No. She's naked.'

'Shebi, it is bubble bath. I won't see anything.'

'No it is not bubble bath and that's not the point.'

'OK. I'll open it and just sit against the wall out here. So we can all talk.'

'And who told you we want to talk to you?'

Gabriel opened the door. His eyes were covered with one hand, a bottle of Remy Martin wedged under his armpit, and a cup in the other hand.

'Hey!' Eyitayo said.

'Sorry, sorry,' he said. He left the door wide open and sat outside on the ground, his back against the wall next to the door.

'Just say the word and I'll send him to bed,' Eyitayo said to Amaka.

'He's alright. We'll let him play,' Amaka said.

'He can stay up late?'

'Yeah. He can stay up late. Just today.'

'OK. But only today.'

'Amaka,' Gabriel said, 'when last did you hear this?'

'Hear what?'

'Hold on.'

Moments later the long instrumental intro to Fela Kuti's *Trouble Sleep Yanga Wake Am* began playing from the sound system in the living room. 'It's the most chilled out song I've ever heard,' Gabriel said, humming along with the saxophone.

'Guy called,' Eyitayo said. 'I'm sorry, I told him you got your phone back.'

'I know,' Amaka said. 'He called me. It's alright.'

'Are you guys going to be OK?'

'There is no 'you guys'.'

'He really likes you,' Gabriel said from outside.

'Shut up, nobody asked you,' Eyitayo said.

'Just saying,' Gabriel said.

'I'm really sorry about Chioma,' Eyitayo said.

'Don't be. It's not your fault. I should have told her what I was planning.'

'He's not going to implicate himself over the phone now, is he?'

'I doubt it. I really wish I'd not lost that phone. I had them. All those bastards, I recorded their faces. I'm sure I got his face as well.'

Amaka held her glass out for Eyitayo to refill it, then sat up. Eyitayo backed away to avoid being splashed.

'Why didn't I think of that before?' Amaka said. 'I know what to do.'

51

Area opened a drawer in Amaka's bedroom. It was full of underwear. He put his hand inside, felt around and held up a brown thong. He rolled the silk pants into a ball and put it into his pocket. He looked around the room then he hopped onto the bed. He crawled to the top, lay on his back, and crossed his hands under his head on the pillow.

The gateman stood in the open-door frame. From behind, a man pressed a pistol into his back. Another man was getting undressed, pushing his tight jeans down his legs, his shirt already on the ground by his feet.

'What time is she coming back?' Area asked the gateman.

'Oga, I don't know.'

'I am not your oga. Did she tell you where she was going?'

'No, sir. She just left yesterday.'

'Since then she has not returned?'

'No, sir.'

'Stop calling me sir. I am not your oga.'

'Yes sir.'

'And stop lying to me.'

'I swear to God, I am not lying to you sir.'

Area nodded at the man behind the gateman. The thug raised his weapon and hit the back of the man's neck with the gun. The gateman yelled and fell to his knees. The other man at the door was down to his underpants. He bent down and picked up the black trousers he had taken from one of the dead police officers and he held it up by waistband. The belt was still in the loops. Behind him the lookout entered the room.

'Why did you leave your post?' Area asked.

'That one they call Yellowman, him park moto outside, come begin dey search ground. He just leave now.'

52

The doorbell started ringing again. Amaka turned over in bed and moaned into her pillow. She couldn't understand why Eyitayo or Gabriel wouldn't get the door. The ringing continued. She groaned as she got up, still dizzy from all the wine they'd had. She couldn't focus.

The living room lights were off; it was still dark outside, raining and cold. Naked under the T-shirt Gabriel had lent her, she stretched out her hands to find her way to the door. As she opened it, she made a mental note to tell Eyitayo and Gabriel not to leave the key in the lock. Just then she realised she hadn't asked who it was, but it was too late, they were already pushing the door open.

She froze. The door missed her face by an inch. Cold wind plastered the T-shirt against her body, and there, standing in the dark on the porch, his hair wet against his face, was Guy.

She gasped. 'What are you doing here?' she asked.

He stepped inside, dripping onto the carpet, wiping his face.

'When did you return?'

He stared at her.

'Look, Guy, you shouldn't have come. We both know this can't work. You live in England and I live in Nigeria. Everything happened too quickly and…'

He turned and spoke to someone outside. 'She's here. You can come in now.'

As if materialising out of the darkness, Mel walked in through the open door.

'What? You brought your ex-girlfriend back with you to Nigeria? To me? Why?'

His phone began to ring again.

Amaka woke up. It was dark. She could hear the rain outside. The air conditioner was humming and the room had become too cold. She was on her back. She rolled onto her side and saw the screen on her phone fade to darkness.

She reached across to the bedside table where she had left her mother's Rolex Datejust. It was just after 6am; she must have passed out the moment her head touched the pillow.

Her phones had been charging next to the watch. She picked up each one in turn, clicking to lighten the screen. On her personal line she had seven missed calls. She sat up and unlocked the phone. She also had an unread message.

She unplugged the phone and sat on the edge of the bed. The missed calls were all from the same number. She hadn't saved the contact, but she recognised it. It was Ambrose. She checked the time of the calls. The earliest was 1.30am; the last was the one that woke her up.

She stayed a while on the edge of the bed with the phone in her hand, then she shook her head. The unread message. It was from Florentine.

'Aunty I am in Lagos for a church festival. I have received all your messages. I can come and meet you later if you still want to see me.'

Amaka stood up and read the message again, then she scrolled up to read her own previous messages that Florentine had not replied to, but they were missing on the new phone. She clicked out of the messaging app, sat back on the edge of the bed, stared at the carpet, and tried to think.

53

Someone knocked on the door while Amaka was standing behind it.

'Whoa, you're already dressed,' Gabriel said. She was in new clothes borrowed from Eyitayo. He was in a housecoat and had an iPad in his hand.

'I've got to get somewhere quick,' she said. 'What's wrong?'

He held the iPad out to her. 'Someone beat you to it,' he said.

She took the tablet from him and recognised the header of the gossip blog. She didn't bother with the story beneath the pictures. The first image was of Ojo laying on a bed, a naked woman on top of him. The second picture was also of him, on a settee, naked, a girl straddling him. The third was similar to the second: same room, same sofa, two additional girls waiting their turns by the sides of the chair. She glanced at the fourth then scrolled up.

'That's me,' Amaka said, her finger on the first picture.

'What?' Gabriel looked at the screen.

'That's me.'

Gabriel took the iPad.

'That's you?'

'Yes.'

He looked at her chest then back at the screen.

'Stop it,' she said.

'Sorry. Did you send it to her?' he asked.

'Did I send a picture of my naked boobs to Gloria Mbanefo? Of course not. I don't even know her.'

'So, how did she get it? I know. Maybe the person who stole your bag?'

'No. But they're clever, whoever sent this to Gloria Mbanefo.'

'I'm not following, Amaka.'

She took the iPad from him.

'That is me.' She pointed at the first picture. 'Whoever did this is a genius.' She scrolled to the fourth picture. 'I don't know who that is, but she was not in the room. See what they did? It's the same picture I sent to his wife but they've Photoshopped this girl into it. I bet they'll release the original pictures from which these other pictures were composed and they'll easily discredit any further pictures of him that surface.'

'Wow. You're right. That is some really clever shit.'

'So it has begun.'

'They aren't playing. This is some serious gangsta chess shit. Maybe it wasn't a good idea to get into bed with this guy. I don't mean literally. Even though you did get in bed with him.'

'I know what you mean. And it's never a good idea to get into bed with a Nigerian man.'

'Harsh.'

'But true.'

'What now?'

'They've fired their first salvo. They did this in anticipation of my next move.'

'What is your next move?'

'Better you don't know. Let's just say, I'm going to rig the Lagos State elections.'

54

On tiptoes, Amaka and Gabriel approached Chioma's bedroom. The sound of singing could be heard from behind the closed door. Amaka turned the handle and slowly opened it. Chioma was on her knees on the side of the bed, her back to the door, singing into the sheets. Her head was buried, her elbows deep into the bedding and her hands clasped in prayer. Her shoulders shook visibly. She raised her hands and her face to the heavens and began a heart-stirring rendition of *Amazing Grace*. The high notes shuddered in her powerful voice as she swayed from side to side, spreading her sorrow across the ceiling, across the room, across the building.

The sun shone in Amaka's face as she drove to Oshodi market. There were fewer cars than usual. On her way down she had passed parked police vans with officers loitering around them as if they were bored waiting for the riots to start. Their presence seemed to be keeping the riots at bay, and fear of riots was keeping traffic away. She could transverse Lagos freely - in a way that was usually only possible in the dead of night. But now Amaka had the safety of daylight.

She parked on the side of the road and resisted looking at the spot where the fire had curled around Chioma's brother. She walked into the market, past rows of stalls already laid out, till she got to the butchers' section and fat flies buzzed around her face. She walked between stalls, behind them, and into the two-storey building that the butchers had taken her to.

Young men with blood smeared on their exposed torsos watched as she walked to the building. The butchers followed a short distance behind. She walked through the open doorway and down the corridor that led out back.

In the backyard, shirtless young men in shorts and rolled-up trousers were lifting weights, doing squats and bench presses, or assisting others, the sweat they worked up making their lean, muscular bodies glisten in the sun. They put down their barbells – improvised from metal rods and moulded cement discs – and gathered around Amaka.

'I'm looking for Ajani, your president,' she said. 'He told me I should come and see him if I need anything.'

'We remember you,' said one young man. 'Baba Ajani is not in the market today. What do you want?'

'I need your help to catch the men who killed the brother of the girl you saved yesterday. I saw a lot of people using their phones to record what happened. Perhaps they captured the faces of the people responsible. The police can print the faces in the newspapers and declare them wanted. Nothing will happen to any of you. Nobody will know whose phone I got the pictures from. Baba Ajani told me how none of you had a hand in what happened. He told me how you tried to stop them. How you and the market women saved Chioma and me as well. Please, help me catch them. She could have been your sister. He could have been your brother. If you took any pictures or recorded any videos yesterday, I need them.'

The butchers watched her in silence. Their mates from the stalls had filled the corridor and spilled out onto the backyard as well. Then the young man who had spoken took his hand out of his pocket and looked at his phone. He clicked a few buttons. All around, other men began retrieving their phones and clicking. Then they started to step forward, one at a time, holding up their phones so she could see the pictures they had taken and videos they had recorded.

55

Amaka put her phone on speaker, placed it on her lap and looked in the mirror as she pulled out.

'Hello Ibrahim,' she said, 'I have evidence that a policeman was responsible for the lynching yesterday at Oshodi.'

'I'm at your house,' Ibrahim said. 'Where are you?'

'I'm not at home.'

'I know. How soon can you get here?'

Amaka didn't recognise the policeman who opened the gate when she honked. As she drove in, she saw him peering out onto the road. She pulled up alongside a black Range Rover with tinted windows parked in front of her father's old Rolls Royce. She couldn't see Matthew the gateman and the front door had been left open. Ibrahim's car was not in the compound.

She watched the policeman in the mirror as he shut the gates. She was sure she had never seen him before. She kept an eye on him as she unlocked her phone, then she became aware of somebody by the passenger door. The man bent down to the window. She dropped the phone and her hands flew to the steering wheel and the ignition. She had started to turn the key when Ibrahim walked out of the front door.

'I'm sorry I startled you,' the man said.

Amaka got out of her car.

The man was in his twenties. He had a gleaming shaved head and a full beard. He was slender and wore a purple polo top tucked into faded, tight blue jeans. He stared into Amaka's eyes.

'Who are you?' Amaka asked.

'Alex.' He held out his hand. He had at least three bracelets on his wrist, leather, wooden beads, and colourful fabric.

'Alex, what?'

'Just Alex.'

She did not take his hand. 'You don't have a surname?'

'He's with a branch of the DSS,' Ibrahim said.

'What are you doing in my house?' Amaka said facing Ibrahim. She noticed that Alex was watching her.

'Where were you last night?' Ibrahim asked.

'I don't see how that is any of your business, and you haven't answered my question.'

'I'm sorry. Last night we received an anonymous tip that your house was being raided. I wasn't on shift then. They sent a patrol van. Our men spoke to the security guard.'

'What did he look like?'

'I don't know. I came here first thing today after they updated me. Nobody was here when I arrived. The gate and the front door were both open.'

'Had the house been burgled?'

'Yes.'

'What did they take?' Amaka walked towards the door.

Ibrahim and Alex followed her into the living room. She looked around. The TV was missing from the credenza. Nothing else looked out of place.

'What happened to the guards?'

'Ibrahim thinks they robbed you and absconded,' Alex said.

Amaka looked back from the bottom of the staircase. 'They will never rob us.' She began to climb. The men followed.

'I agree with you,' Alex said.

'And why are you here again?' Amaka asked on the landing.

'Ibrahim was afraid something had happened to you. He contacted the Foreign Ministry. They sent me.'

'You could have called,' Amaka said to Ibrahim. 'I got my phone lines back.'

The door to her parents' bedroom was open. She stood in the doorway and looked inside. Someone had pulled out the drawers of her mother's dressing table.

'May I?' Alex said. He eased past her into the bedroom. 'What kind of robbers will leave that behind?' He pointed at her father's double-barrelled shotgun resting against the wall by the bed. 'And this,' he waved his hand over the dressing table. 'It's too neat. Also, they didn't take the TV in the library. The trouble of taking it down the stairs was too much for them?'

Amaka left the doorway and went to her own bedroom. The contents of her drawers were on the bed. The wardrobes were open, clothes and hangers on the ground, shoes, bags and boxes strewn everywhere.

'They took their time here,' Alex said. 'Do you know what they were searching for?'

Amaka walked around the bed, her eyes not missing anything.

'Who is Malik?' Alex said.

Amaka shot him a look.

'I asked Ibrahim if anyone would want to harm you. He told me everything you told him.'

'I didn't know where you were,' Ibrahim said.

'It's OK,' Amaka said. 'You don't think this was just a robbery?' she asked Alex.

'No.' Alex said. 'Ordinary thieves won't attack a well-guarded house. And they would not leave a gun behind, unless they had superior firearms. It also looks like the driveway has been washed. I suspect to get rid of blood. I believe the guards are dead.'

'If they're dead, where are the bodies?' Ibrahim asked.

'I believe they took the bodies to make it look like an inside job.' He pushed his hand into the tight pocket of his jeans. When he brought out his hand he had two empty shells in his palm. 'I found one downstairs and in your room.'

'When did you find those?' Ibrahim asked.

'One was under your car. I collected it after your driver left. The other one was in one of her shoes. You missed it. This was not a robbery. This was an assassination attempt.' He turned to Amaka. 'Ibrahim said you've never met this man and you've been trying to locate his building. What more can you tell me about him?'

'I know how to find him,' Amaka said.

'How?'

'The girl he left for dead on the express, the reason I'm after him, her phone has been off and she hasn't been returning my calls. Last night she sent me a message. She wants to meet.'

56

On one of four flat-screen monitors in his bedroom, Malik watched retired Navy Commodore Shehu Yaya walk through the gate into the compound of his duplex in Gbagada. The guard closed the gate behind Shehu and for a moment both men stood close to each other in the one-metre space between the closed gate and the nose of Malik's white Range Rover, neither talking nor moving.

Malik watched the two men in their little impasse, then he stood, picked up a kimono housecoat from a papasan chair and threw it over his naked body.

The bulletproof front door opened and Shehu swung round. Malik was in the doorway in his kimono, his legs, arms, and chest covered in thick black curly hair. A black pistol dangled from his right hand. In his other he held two phones, one white, one grey. 'How did you find my place?' he said.

'Come on,' Shehu said. 'You and I both know that Ojo is not the smartest man in Lagos.'

'Even then, he knows better than to give out my home address.'

'Does he? Like he shouldn't have brought me to your little sex house last night? You give him too much credit and it's not fair to him.'

'If anyone other than Ojo had brought you, I would not have allowed you enter The Harem last night.'

'But we both know our friend is about to become the third most powerful person in Lagos.'

'The third?'

'Oh yes. He would never wield as much power as the man who puts him there. And combined, they would never be as powerful as the man who knows what it took to get him there.'

Malik nodded at the guard who was standing aside, unsure what to do.

'Come in,' Malik said.

A deep-pile cream rug covered every inch of the floor. A solitary beige armchair sat in front of a 52-inch flat-screen TV on a stand in the middle of the room. There was a single white leather-bound chair at a glass dining table large enough for six chairs. Opposite the stairs, there was a mirror-panelled bar with two stools.

'What would you like?' Malik said walking behind the bar and placing his pistol and the two phones on it. From underneath he fetched two shot glasses and a half-finished bottle of Cognac and placed them on the top.

'Louis XIII,' Shehu said. He stood a metre from the bar. 'I would normally say no to alcohol this early, but it's not every day you get a sip of a half a million naira brandy.'

'Cognac.'

'I have never known the difference.'

'Do you mind?' Malik said. He fetched a glass ashtray and a cigar from behind the bar, placed the ashtray on the top and held the cigar between his fingers.

'Please, go ahead,' Shehu said. He searched his pockets and brought out his packet of Consulates, put a cigarette to his lips and searched his pockets for his lighter.

'You organise girls for your friends in the force,' Malik said.

Shehu looked up.

'When they drove you from the Navy you became a pimp. I know who you are. The Harem must have made you jealous.'

'Jealous?' Shehu smiled. He shook his head and placed his hands on the bar.

Malik picked up the pistol and pointed it at Shehu's face.

Shehu stood still. He stared into Malik's eyes. Seconds passed. Malik squeezed the trigger. Click. Shehu flinched. An orange flame burnt upwards from the muzzle of the lighter-gun. A moment passed. The tiny flame danced between the two men, the constant hiss of the gas lighter the only sound in the room, then Shehu leaned forward and dragged the flame into his cigarette. Smoke rose between them.

'Why are you here?' Malik asked.

'The girl. Florentine. You told him she's alive.'

'Yes.'

'Is she?'

Malik removed the unlit cigar from his lips. The end was still sealed. He looked behind the bar and got his gold-plated cigar cutter.

'Is she?' Shehu repeated.

'Why?'

'Because if she is, and you are hoping to use her as some sort of insurance or leverage, that complicates things for me.'

'So what if I'm using her as a bargaining chip?'

'When I was a young boy of about twelve, my father told me something that has guided me ever since. He said, if you must have an enemy, have a wise man as your enemy, because a stupid enemy would do something stupid that would harm you and harm himself.'

'She's not the only one.'

'Yes, I know. You told him about another girl looking for him.'

'She's the dangerous one. She's a lawyer. Her father is an ambassador.'

'I am taking care of her.'

'How?'

'How else?'

'Have you ever taken care of anyone?'

'Are you joking? I'm a military man. I saw active service in Bakassi. Do you think one silly girl in Lagos would be any problem for me?'

'He asked me to take care of her.'

'When?'

'Last night.'

'See what I mean? He'll make a big mess of what should be handled quietly, and then when the caca hits the fan, he'll call in his father-in-law and we will both end up in the bottom of Lagos Lagoon. *That* is why I'm here. To clear up this mess before it gets to the old man.'

'What do you suggest we do?'

'Let me have the girl you have, and let me take care of the other one.'

'Then you have all the hands.'

'This is not about hands, my dear friend. It's about staying alive.'

57

'Amaka,' Ibrahim said, 'you cannot meet the girl. It's a trap.'

'Of course it's a trap,' Amaka said. 'She's probably dead. She most likely contacted Malik to get the money he owed her and he lured her in. After leaving her to die like that, when she returned, he would have had no choice. Stupid girl. She's probably floating in the lagoon or rotting in a shallow grave somewhere.'

'Take it easy, Amaka,' Ibrahim said.

Her eyes had glazed over, even as her face had hardened with anger. 'I'm fine,' she said. 'I was hoping we could play along and set a trap for him too.'

'It's risky,' Ibrahim said.

'You're a police officer. You can figure it out. It might be the only chance to find him.'

'Then what? What would I arrest him for? There is no evidence to suggest he's connected to this. And what if it all goes bad? You're basically suggesting that we use you as bait.'

'Yes.'

'Amaka, this is not a game. They…'

'Don't fucking tell me it's not a game. Do I look like I'm playing? He dumped her on the fucking road. A human being. He thought she was dead. Arrest him for that. He runs a brothel. Arrest him for that. He threatened me – he said he would kill me. Arrest him for that. Just fucking arrest him. Are you going to wait until I'm dead before you have a reason?'

'Calm down,' Alex said.

'Don't tell me to calm down. Don't tell me to do anything unless you're going to tell him to fucking get with the programme and catch this bastard.'

'If I may,' Alex said, 'I disagree with you, Ibrahim. I believe the two are related. Someone threatened her, and subsequently her house is raided. Until we know exactly what happened here last night, we have to investigate all angles, including this. Even if just to eliminate it.'

'It would be dangerous,' Ibrahim said.

'It *would* be dangerous,' Alex said, 'but it's doable. She will wear a vest. We will choose the location.'

'Are you joking?' Ibrahim said.

'What about my office?' Amaka asked.

'That could work,' Alex said. 'We can place officers inside and outside, but I doubt he would agree to that. In any case, he thinks you think you are talking to the girl, so we must play along. It would only be natural that you ask the girl to come to your office.'

'Are you seriously considering this?' Ibrahim said. 'We could be dealing with a very dangerous person.'

'Yes, he's a dangerous person,' Alex said, 'but we know he's planning an ambush, so we have the advantage of ambushing him first.'

'What if he expects you to expect it's an ambush?' Ibrahim said.

Amaka threw up her hands. 'What if he's Lex Luthor? This is our first chance to catch him. If we don't, he'll get me sooner or later. And even worse than that, he'll still have all those girls in his harem.'

'How can that be worse than you dead?' Ibrahim said.

'I am one person.'

She began to type into her phone.
'What are you doing?' he asked.
She pressed send.
'I just asked to meet at my office today.'

58

The white phone rattled on the glass bar top. Malik picked up the dead girl's mobile, swiped the screen and read the message.

'I don't fucking know the address,' he muttered at the screen.

'What's that?' Shehu asked.

'Nothing. Just some business.' He placed his cigar into the ashtray and swiped through the messages Amaka and Florentine had exchanged in the past. He hissed.

'Do we have an agreement?' Shehu asked.

Malik sent a message on the white phone, placed it face down on the counter, picked up his cigar and took a drag. He puffed a circle upwards and watched it twirl and float away. He extended his right hand over the counter. Shehu ignored it.

'I'll take care of the Amaka girl and this should all be over,' Shehu said.

'Why don't I find her and talk to her?' Malik said.

'He asked me.'

'He asked me too.'

'Ok. Here's the deal. Whoever gets her first, we both talk to her. Deal?'

'Deal.'

'And that means I talk to your girl too.'

'Sure,' Malik said, his hand still extended. Finally, both men shook.

Malik let out a puff of smoke that expanded and lingered between them, for a moment hiding their faces from each other. As the smoke cleared, he said: 'It is me they should all be afraid of. I am the thing that swallowed the thing that swallowed the elephant.'

59

Amaka's phone beeped in her hand. 'He replied,' she said. She read the message out loud: 'I don't want people to see me. I can take a taxi to meet you somewhere so that we can talk in your car.'

'Good,' Alex said. 'He doesn't seem to suspect anything.'

'What if it's really the girl?' Ibrahim said.

'She's dead,' Amaka said without looking up. She made a call and waited.

'Who are you calling?' Ibrahim asked.

'Confirming she's dead.' She stayed on the phone. Ibrahim and Alex watched.

'Is it ringing?' Ibrahim asked.

Amaka put up a finger to shush him. 'Hello? Hello? Florentine, can you hear me? Hello? Florentine, I can't hear you but if you can hear me, listen carefully. You must not contact Malik or Ojo under any circumstance. I will explain when we see each other.' She ended the call.

'He's also reading the messages wondering if I suspect anything. It would be odd if I didn't try to call her.' Her phone beeped with a message.

Amaka read the message first. 'It's him,' she said. She read it out: 'I could hear you but you could not hear me because my mouthpiece is broken. I will take a ferry to Fiki Marina Boat Club on Ozumba at 3 today. Let us meet there.'

'Well played,' Alex said.

'Fiki Marina,' Ibrahim said. 'When robbers raid banks on VI, they escape through the lagoon.'

'So that's why he chose to meet there,' Alex said. 'Someone will be waiting for her. Once she's spotted, they'll open fire. A boat will be waiting for them.'

'I'm really not too comfortable with this, Amaka,' Ibrahim said.

'You don't have to be,' Alex said. 'I was sent to investigate what happened here. This is part of my investigation. You were told to give me any assistance I may require. I'm just doing my job and you are just following orders.'

60

Two men got out of the Peugeot 504 station wagon and crossed the untarred road in Oniru Estate. Identical bungalows lined both sides of the street. A black goat crossed the road, its kid strutting on little legs behind it. Further down, young children kicked up sand as they chased after an orange rubber ball.

The two men returned bundling a slim, young, albino woman who was in her pants and bra. She struggled against their grip. One of the men had his hand over her mouth and the other around her body. The other man tried to keep hold of her ankles but a leg came free and she kicked. He dodged and caught her leg again. From the front seat, Area opened the back door of the station wagon. The men bundled the woman into the car and sat her down. She froze at the sight of Area's pistol aimed at her head.

'You couldn't get her something to cover herself?' Area said.

The two men looked at each other. One of them let go of the woman's hand and got out of the car. He crossed the road back to the bungalow.

'You are Yellowman's sister?' Area asked.

The woman did not answer.

'You don't remember me? They call me Area. Me and your brother used to play football in Maroko. You were little like this then. You have really grown. See your breasts.' He reached over the seat and cradled a breast in his small hand.

She spat in his face. He wiped it off with the back of his hand, then he slapped her with the same hand.

'I don't want anything with you. This is just business and even your brother will understand. After me and him conclude our deal, I will release you to him and that will be all. In the meantime, you have to learn how to behave yourself and respect your elders.

'When I give you my phone now, I want you to call him and tell him to come and meet us at the usual place at Tarkwa Bay to discuss business. OK?'

61

Naomi lay awake next to the twins who were still sleeping. She stayed on her back in the king-sized bed and she stared into the mirror that covered the ceiling. This was the first time she had slept in *their* room. They had taken their client, the tall white man, into this very room. They always worked together - it was what the clients wanted, and it always made Naomi wonder how it made them feel.

Instead of Malik's 'someone very important,' Sisi had brought a Chinese man to Naomi. The short man's black mask reminded her of Kato, the superhero sidekick, and since they were not allowed to know their client's names in The Harem, she named him Kato. It always helped to give her clients names. She even had imaginary, parallel conversations with them in which they meet somewhere other than The Harem. It was always she who initiated those conversations, and she always started by introducing herself: 'Hi, I'm Naomi. *The* Naomi.'

Throughout the back massage Kato asked for, Naomi kept thinking of her phone tied into a condom, submerged in water in the cistern in her room that the white girls now had. What if one of them tried to flush and checked inside to see why the toilet wasn't flushing?

The twin on the right pulled the duvet she shared with Naomi to herself, exposing Naomi to the chill of the air conditioner. Naomi pulled it back. If only she could get her phone back. Sisi had a phone but it would be impossible to get her hands on it. She kept staring at herself in the mirror above. She closed her eyes, took a deep breath and she lifted the duvet off her naked body.

Nobody in The Harem was up before midday, which was when Malik arrived. Even the workers, the few men in the boys' quarters behind, never came to the building before then, and when they did it was only when they had been summoned by Sisi to move furniture, repair something, or tidy one of the speciality rooms or communal areas. The girls were responsible for the rooms they used and the large kitchen where they cooked their own meals.

Naomi fetched a T-shirt from her bag and pulled it over her body. She put on her glasses and opened the door, taking care not to make a sound.

The corridor was quiet and dark. She walked on tiptoes to her room where the white girls were and she opened the door. Four girls were in the bed. Another four were on the floor on duvets they had spread on the cold marble. Naomi stepped over the girls to get to the bathroom but it was shut. She looked under the door. No light. She turned the handle and opened the door. She looked behind her. The girls had not stirred. Her heart was racing. She stepped into the bathroom and closed the door behind her.

The girls had arranged their toiletries all around the sink and on top of the ceramic lid of the cistern. She began to pick objects off of it one by one and place them on the ground by the bathtub until all the perfume bottles, deodorants, cleansers, and wet wipes were lined up on the bath mat.

When she stood upright her back ached. She placed her hands on either side of the lid and lifted but it scratched against the cistern and she stopped. She listened, then continued. She placed the lid on the mat next to the toiletries and dipped her hand into the water. It was icy cold. She felt around with her fingers and touched the phone, removed it, and held it up to the dull light from the window. It didn't look like water had gotten inside.

'What is that?'

Naomi turned round, holding up the phone inside a condom. Sisi was standing in the doorway in her black slip, hands on her hips.

62

One of Area's men reached into the fibreglass boat to help Area climb out. All six men that had returned from Tarkwa Bay walked to their waiting Peugeot. The driver had left the engine running. They dusted sand from the bottoms of their trousers before getting in, and the last man placed a heavy sports bag in the boot; the barrel of a M16 rifle that was too long for the bag poked out from one end.

In silence they drove on the Lekki-Epe Expressway towards Victoria Island. There were hardly any cars on the road.

Police riot vehicles were parked at the tollgate. Officers in riot gear stood between lanes just outside the toll booths, holding their guns in both hands against their bulletproof vests and peering into cars as they drove through raised barriers. A white Honda was parked along the same side as the riot vans. Five young men with their hands raised above their heads were standing by their vehicle while an officer searched in their pockets and another poked around inside their car.

'Just keep moving,' Area said to the driver. 'Slow down but don't stop.'

The Peugeot rolled through the barrier. An officer with his mesh visor raised over his helmet and his finger on the trigger of his weapon looked into the car. Area, in the front seat next to the driver, looked up at the man. Their eyes met, then the officer looked into the back as the car continued moving.

The Peugeot carried on to Ikoyi, to Dolphin Estate. It stopped in front of 39B Eti-Osa Street. Office of the Street Samaritans.

63

A yellow taxi that was missing all its rear lights, coughed and spluttered black smoke as the driver revved the engine to stop it from dying while the ageing car idled on Ozumba Mbadiwe in front of the gates to Fiki Marina. Ibrahim waited to collect his change before he got out. At the station he had changed into a pair of blue jeans and a black polo top he kept in a drawer in his desk. Once out of the car he stood on the side of the road, his back to the jetty, and tried not to inhale fumes from the taxi as it drove off.

He pulled his sunglasses from the V in his unbuttoned polo-top. Across the road a giant yellow banner hung from the side of one of the towers of Eko Court. To the left, almost overhead, was the flyover to Ikoyi-Akin Adesola Street that everyone called Falomo Bridge. To the right, the smell of the fish market. When he was sixteen he lived with his aunty in Port Harcourt. She was a fish farmer and he was there to learn the trade. After six months of handling fish all day he decided to join the police.

He pulled a cigarette from his pack, put it between his lips and cupped his lighter over his mouth. As he did, he turned to the marina. The tops of boats parked on trailers were visible over the fence. A few metres along it, a beggar in brown rags that looked heavy from accumulated dirt sat across the gutter, his bottom on one side and his feet on the other, straddling stagnant green water below. An aluminium bowl lay by his side and his stick rested across his lap.

A beggar was a strange sight on Ozumba Mbadiwe. Stranger still was a blind one without a seeing child announcing the beggar's affliction to the hearts of passers-by. Ibrahim walked over to him.

The beggar's black boots were covered in mud, his eyes hidden behind dark glasses that had white scratches in the middle; the plastic lenses too dark for anyone to see the state of the eyes behind them. Written in capital letters on the brown cardboard hanging from his neck were the words: MAY YOU NOT BE BLIND LIKE ME. His begging bowl was empty.

His eyes on the beggar, Ibrahim removed his wallet and pulled out a one thousand naira note. He held the money in front of the beggar who had not reacted to his presence. The beggar did not reach out for the charity.

Ibrahim stooped. He checked both sides of the road, then, still holding out the note he said, 'You should have heard me in front of you.'

The beggar remained still.

'Next time,' Ibrahim said, 'say something when someone is in front of you trying to give you money.'

The beggar nodded.

'Now, take the money,' Ibrahim said.

The beggar held out his cupped hands straight and steady.

'Good,' Ibrahim said. He put the money in the beggar's hand. 'I want that back after the operation,' he said, then he stood up and checked both sides of the road again before walking towards the gates into Fiki Marina.

64

Amaka opened up the engine of her Bora and drove in a straight line right in the middle of Ozumba Mbadiwe. Alex had told her to drive fast.

Her phone buzzed. With one hand on the steering wheel she picked up the phone from her lap, looked at the screen, and pressed down on the brake pedal.

She stopped the car at the side of the road. The two new messages were from 'Naomi-Harem.' She opened the first. It was a little map with a red pin in the middle of it. The second read: 'You are right. Florentine is dead. Come quickly.'

A car pulled up behind her. Amaka looked in the mirror. It was a military van. The door opened and two female soldiers in camouflage gear and helmets, holding their rifles with their fingers on the triggers, walked towards her.

'Madam, any problem?' an officer asked.

The soldier's young face was tiny beneath her net-covered green helmet. She could have been in her twenties – or younger. Amaka smiled at her. She did not smile back.

'There's no problem,' Amaka said.

'Where are you going today?'

The young soldier looked into the empty seats of the car in turn as she spoke.

'Is it because of the riots?' Amaka said. 'I'm going to Fiki Marina.'

The soldier finished her inspection of the inside of the car then their eyes met.

'Why did you stop here?' she asked.

Amaka still had her phone in her hand. 'I had to take a call. You shouldn't drive and use the phone.' She smiled.

'Have you finished?' the soldier asked.

'Yes.'

'OK. Move along,' she said.

Amaka watched in the mirror as they returned to their car. The van pulled out. Soldiers in battle gear in the back looked at her as they drove past. She watched till the barrels of their rifles no longer pointed at her.

She called Ibrahim. 'I have the location of The Harem,' she said.

'How? Where are you?'

'Almost there.' Her phone beeped with another call. 'I'll call you back,' she said and took the incoming call.

It was Eyitayo. 'Chioma wants to talk to you,' she said.

'Tell her you can't reach me,' Amaka said.

'Yes, that's correct. Yes, she's here with me,' Eyitayo said.

Amaka bit her lip. 'Is she OK?' she asked.

'Yemisi is fine. She's been asking for her godmother. She wants to tell you something. Anyway, I didn't know you were driving. Don't let LASTMA catch you using the phone.'

'Thanks, Eyitayo,' Amaka said. 'Please, look after her till I get back. Tell her I'm taking care of everything.'

'OK, I understand. What is that? You'll bring suya from Polo Club when you return? Oh, thank you. That would be nice.'

'Is that your price? You are cheap.'

'OK, bye. Be safe, hon.'

'Thanks Eyitayo.'

65

From his seat under one of the octagonal gazebos, a warm, untouched bottle of Star on the table in front of him, Ibrahim watched river taxis come and go, passengers alighting onto wooden docks next to anchored boats, and staff helping them out of their orange lifejackets. At the next gazebo, close to the bar overlooking the lagoon, a group of noisy passengers already in lifejackets were talking their way through doughnuts, meat pies, scotch eggs, and bottles of mineral water. Among them was a woman. She rolled up a large map, tucked it into her black backpack and placed the bag on the ground near their table. It was to her that a member of staff who had come to enquire about their journey had spoken, but one of the men in her party answered loudly enough for Ibrahim and others to hear: 'We are still waiting for our friend.'

Ibrahim checked the time on his watch before placing his phone on the table. The same white speedboat with four men inside had just returned, this time heading east. He had timed their passage. In exactly five minutes their engine would roar past again.

Ibrahim held up his hand and waved. Amaka peered at him over her sunshades. At the table she took off the glasses.

'Where is Alex?' Amaka said looking around. 'What's the plan?'

'We wait.' There was some time to go before 3 o'clock.

'I know where The Harem is,' Amaka said.

'You said so. How?'

Amaka unlocked her phone, opened up the message from Naomi, and showed it to Ibrahim. 'That's the location.'

Ibrahim read the message under the map.

'Who is this?'

'Someone who works at The Harem. She knew Florentine. I went to see her last night after leaving your place. She smuggled her phone there.'

'Yesterday?'

'Yes. I'd tried to get her to do it before, but she was afraid of what Malik would do to her if she got caught.'

'And now she's suddenly happy to help?'

'I know you're thinking it's too good to be true, but I spoke to her. I looked into her eyes. She was at breaking point. She wants out.'

'What changed between when you first spoke to her and now? You don't think this is a trap?'

'I asked myself the same thing. But if he has already set one trap for me, why would he bother with another? See what she wrote. She just confirmed Florentine is dead. That's what she found out that made her change her mind.'

He tapped on the map to expand it. 'This location is closer to Ibadan than Lagos.'

'Yes. And it's way, way off the express, just like Florentine described. I've got my tablet. We can check it out on Google Maps.'

'One thing at a time,' Ibrahim said.

The woman sitting with the men at the next gazebo had been looking at Ibrahim and Amaka from time to time. She reached down and pulled out her rolled-up map from her bag, tapped the man sitting next to her on his back as she stood up, then walked towards Amaka and Ibrahim. She stood in front of their table with the map stretched out in her hand.

'Can you help me with a location?' she asked.

Ibrahim moved his untouched bottle of Star out of the way and the woman spread the world map out on the table. Her finger was bent over the Horn of Africa.

'Amaka, look here,' Ibrahim said, his finger on the middle of the Pacific Ocean.

'This is police superintendent Fatima Alao,' he said. 'Don't look up; they might be watching us. Leave your car keys on the table and come with me.'

Amaka looked at the woman who was still staring at the map.

'Where are we going?' Amaka asked.

'For a boat ride. Fatima is trained in defensive driving. When they make contact, she will pretend to receive the call, in case they're watching. Once we spot them we'll move in to apprehend them and she'll manoeuvre out of harm's way.'

'There won't be a call,' Amaka said, 'Florentine is dead, remember? It'll be a message.'

Fatima spoke without looking up. 'That won't be a problem.' Her voice was soft. She had dark skin like Amaka; they were about the same height – perhaps Amaka was taller.

Amaka looked at Ibrahim.

'Keys, on table,' he said. 'Please.'

66

Ibrahim stood up and held his hand out for Amaka. He led her past the gazebos, past the outdoor bar, down the jetty and the moored boats, to a grey boat with NNS 455 painted on its bow. It was larger than most of the other boats including the Fiki Express boat taxis.

Ibrahim got on board at the stern. Holding the railing, he stretched his hand out to Amaka but she ignored it and climbed aboard the way he had. Ibrahim opened the cabin door and stood aside. Amaka bent down and looked into the belly of the vessel. Even from the deck she could hear the whirring of computer fans. She descended the steep, narrow steps into the cabin. There were four men inside. Two had their backs to her. They were hunched over laptops on a shelf that ran along one wall. Between them there was a foot-wide, white drone on top of a black, heavy-duty box.

Alex was at the back, sitting on a narrow bed. He nodded at Amaka. Next to him was a man in a brown Ankara, arms folded across his chest, giving a toothy grin. Amaka recognised him even out of uniform. It was Sergeant Hot-Temper. She looked for his weapon. An old AK-47 with a folded metal stock was resting on the floor of the cabin and leaning against his thigh.

'Madam, you are welcome,' Hot-Temper said.

Amaka nodded. She moved aside so Ibrahim could climb in. Ibrahim slapped the shoulder of one of the men causing him to cry out in pain. He turned in his swivel stool. His laptop was displaying a grainy image of a road. His left hand was bandaged and in a sling.

Amaka gasped. 'Captain…' She tried to remember the name of the secret service agent to whom she probably owed her life.

'Mshelia,' he said. 'But please, call me Bala. You are now a guest of the Nigerian Navy. Please, sit.'

Amaka looked around. The only place was on the bed with Hot-Temper and Alex. She remained standing. 'Your arm,' she said.

'Yes,' Mshelia replied. 'I should be in bed, but I hear you've been digging up more trouble for us.'

'I'm really sorry about all this,' Amaka said.

'Nah. Don't say that. We're just doing our job. Ibrahim and our young friend here have filled me in. I wish we had more time to prepare, but we will get the idiot if he strikes.'

Amaka looked at the image on his computer. 'Is that…?'

He swung round to face the laptop. 'Yes. Ozumba. And it's live. CCTV. You didn't know we have CCTV in Lagos, did you?'

Amaka shook her head.

'We like to keep it that way; it makes the criminals lazier. And once he contacts you, we will deploy this baby.' He looked at the drone. 'Gboyega here will pilot it and we will get a live feed right in here.'

Ibrahim answered his phone and left the cabin.

'That one, he likes you,' Mshelia said.

Amaka nodded, looking around again for a place to sit.

'Madam,' Hot-Temper said, standing up, his head almost touching the roof of the cabin. 'Come and sit here. I want to go and smoke.'

She smiled at him and sat next to Alex.

'Abeg, jus' no touch my gun o,' Hot-Temper said, grinning as he left the small cabin.

'What about the oyinbo?' Mshelia said. 'Guy Collins. He also likes you, you know? If not for him you wouldn't be here. I mean, well, we were on to the bastards and we would have caught him, but Guy played his part. How is he?'

'He has returned to England. What time is it?'

'And by, 'what time is it?' you really mean, 'I don't want to talk about that.' I get it.' He smiled. She smiled back. 'So, I need to ask you, do you look for trouble or does trouble look for you? First, Malik threatens you, then you almost get yourself killed trying to stop a lynching - very brazen, but not recommended. Then your house is raided. My young colleague here is convinced it was an attempt on your life.

'Before I lose count, how many lives is that so far? Not to mention all the shenanigans with Amadi. It's like your life is on drugs right now. On hyper gear. Even a cat doesn't have that many lives in Nigeria o.'

'I know, I know. And I'm a good girl o. You won't believe it, but if you put butter in my mouth, it won't melt, lai-lai. It's not like I'm the one looking for all this trouble...'

'But trouble keeps seeking you out. Mm. When trouble sleep, yanga go wake am.'

'Something like that.'

'But your own trouble is for good reasons, if that is even correct to say.'

'You know what they say, there is no rest for the righteous.'

Ibrahim climbed down the steps, his face creased with worry.

'What is it?' Amaka asked.

'I sent officers to your office. Just a precaution. They've just reported a shoot-out.'

Amaka shot to her feet. 'My staff,' she said.

'They're OK. We engaged them before they gained entry into the building. They managed to escape. They were heavily armed. I've sent out a signal for their vehicle.'

'Do you think it's the same people who attacked my house?' Amaka said.

'It's possible. They sustained injuries. Every officer on duty in Lagos today is on the lookout for them.'

'You didn't tell me you sent men to her office,' Alex said.

'That's where I sent my car after you came up with your theory. I told them to go there and wait till they see her. Then I told them to remain there, just in case you were right.'

'You could have compromised my mission,' Alex said.

'Your mission? Without me there would be no mission. I saved the lives of everyone in that office. I could only spare two people – my driver and a sergeant. Maybe if all the officers here had been there instead of here, carrying out your crazy plan, we would have apprehended them.'

'It's my mission and I should have been informed.'

'Erm, boys,' Mshelia said, 'you're on my boat. My boat, my mission.' He smiled at them, but their eyes remained locked on to one another.

'I'm just saying, he should have told me about it.' Alex said.

'I don't need your permission.' Ibrahim said.

Gboyega raised his hand. 'There's something happening,' he said.

They all turned to his screen. It was scrolling with text.

'Tango One reported an okada with a female passenger,' Gboyega said. 'Tango Two also confirmed. Heading east. Now, Tango Three has reported sighting the same Okada with the same passenger, returning.'

Ibrahim checked his watch. 'It's too early,' he said. 'Tango Four should have eyes on them.' He unclipped a radio from under his shirt.

Gboyega was typing when the screen scrolled up; he stopped as they all read the new message from Tango Two: 'Female passenger alighted in front of Roundhouse. Driver on the move.'

Ibrahim spoke into his radio. 'Tango Two, maintain your position. Tango One, pursue and pick up the driver.' He turned to Gboyega. 'And no one has reported any suspicious movements?'

'Nope. Nothing.'

'Any activity from the boat?'

Gboyega scanned his screen. 'Nothing from Tango Five,' he said. 'Tango Two says subject is standing on the road using her phone.'

Amaka's phone vibrated. She read the message then she held the screen up to Ibrahim and Alex so they could read it too: 'I am at Fiki Marina. Where are you?'

67

'Could it be Florentine?' Ibrahim said. 'Could she be alive?'

He checked the time. 'It's only two o'clock. She said three, abi?'

'Yes,' Amaka said.

'And she said she would take a ferry to Fiki Marina. Or was it that she would take a Ferry *from* Fiki Marina?'

Amaka began to scroll through her messages. Her phone beeped as another came through. She read it out. 'Are you close? I'm standing outside Fiki Marina.'

'What should I say?' she asked.

'Let's bring her in,' Alex said.

Ibrahim pulled out his mobile phone. 'Fatima, female subject just made contact in front of Roundhouse. We are doing plan B.'

'I'm deploying the drone,' Mshelia said.

Gboyega picked up the aircraft and its controller and headed above deck. Ibrahim spoke into his radio. 'We are going with plan B. I repeat, plan B. We have a lone female subject in front of Roundhouse. Fat girl moving into position.'

'And we are live,' Mshelia said. He moved away from his monitor so Ibrahim and Amaka could see the aerial view on his screen. Alex joined them. The camera swept over the lagoon, the marina and the moored boats, the vessels within the muddy compound of Fiki Marina, and the cars parked along the wall.

The drone steadied. It showed Fatima walking to Amaka's Bora and getting into it. A girl was standing on the other side of the fence, a few metres away from Tango Four who was watching her through scratched dark glasses from where he pretended to beg for alms.

'Is that her?' Mshelia asked.

Amaka peered at the screen. Looking at the girl from above, all she could tell was that she had black hair, wore a purple top, and had a red bag.

'I can't see her face,' she said.

'Send her a message,' said Ibrahim. 'Say exactly this: Meet me inside the car park.'

Amaka sent the message. On Mshelia's screen they all watched the girl reading the message on her phone. She looked about her for the gate, then began walking. On the other side of the fence they watched Fatima straightening the wheels of the Bora as she rolled towards the gate. Behind the car, the other undercover officers she had shared a table with were fanning out, their hands inside the rucksacks they carried.

The drone followed the girl.

She looked up, as if into the lens, and continued walking. Her hands flew up and she fell backwards. The image on the screen shook. Inside the boat, everyone ducked at the sound of machine-gun fire from outside.

The undercover officers inside Fiki Marina ran for cover behind cars and boats as shots pelted the ground around them. Amaka's Bora stopped moving. The gunfire was concentrated on the car, punching holes through the bonnet, through the windshield, through the roof.

Mshelia screamed at the screen. 'What the fuck is happening?'

The camera swept over large swaths of road and water before steadying on four figures standing on the bridge, firing automatic rifles. As they used up magazines, they reloaded and continued raining bullets upon the immobile Bora.

68

The shooters crossed onto the other lane on the bridge and got into a waiting black Lexus SUV. The car drove at speed towards Ikoyi while the men continued shooting from open windows. The few motorists they encountered pulled over fast.

Sergeant Hot-Temper ran below deck grunting 'Dan banza' over and over again, and grabbed his gun. He didn't bother waiting for instructions from his superior as he dashed back up the steps. Ibrahim pulled the pistol from his belt and followed the sergeant. At the door he turned round. 'Stay here,' he said, pointing the gun at Amaka, then he was gone.

Alex clasped his hands over his head as he stared at the screen, his mouth open and his eyes bulging with disbelief.

'This is fucked up,' Mshelia said, shaking his head at his screen. The drone hovered over the bullet-riddled Bora. The undercover officers were standing around the car; some of them had their backs to it, their weapons drawn.

'She won't make it,' Mshelia said. 'Even if she was wearing a vest, she's gone. This is so fucked up.' He turned to Amaka. She was breathing fast. 'You know this was an illegal operation?' he said. 'This.' He waved at the equipment. 'We didn't get clearance for any of this, and now an officer is dead. This is really fucked up.'

'I'm sorry,' Amaka said.

'For what? You didn't kill her.'

'That should have been me.'

'Lucky for you it wasn't. Who exactly is this man; this Malik who is supposed to have set this up? Those guys on the bridge, they were not ordinary criminals. The way they handled their guns; the way they leaned in to shoot – they are trained. They are military. Or ex-military. Who the fuck is this guy?'

On the jetty, Ibrahim and Hot-Temper ran past civilians cowering on the ground, fingers clasped over the backs of their heads. At the car park all four doors of the Bora were open. A woman was inside, feeling for a pulse on Fatima's neck. She got out of the car; her fingers, arms, and the top of her shirt were smeared with her colleague's blood. She looked at Ibrahim and shook her head.

Ibrahim looked into the car. Fatima's body was covered in blood and glass. She had been reaching for her pistol on the passenger seat. His radio crackled. He held it to his ear. 'Tell me,' he said.

The officers nearby also heard the message: 'We've found their car. It's on Alfred Rewane Road. Near Aromire. They're not moving. Officers approaching now.'

The undercover cops gathered round Ibrahim to listen.

'The vehicle is empty.'

'Fuck!'

69

Ibrahim climbed into the Navy boat. Amaka was sitting on the bed with her hands on her knees. Gboyega was putting the drone back into its box. Alex was standing in the corner by the bed.

'Why didn't you follow the car?' Ibrahim said to Gboyega. His pistol was still in his hand.

Mshelia spoke: 'Range.'

'They escaped,' Ibrahim said. 'They abandoned their car on Alfred Rewane and they escaped.'

'What of the girl? The one texting Amaka?'

'Arrested. Her ID says Elizabeth Babalola. They're taking her to the station now. I'll find out if she knows anything.'

'Fatima?' Amaka said.

'Dead. Show me that message with the location.'

'Amaka told me about that,' Mshelia said. 'Some girl suddenly sends the location of The Harem. It sounds like another trap.'

'Maybe, maybe not,' Ibrahim said, 'but unless they have a battalion there, I'm going. They just killed my officer.'

'It's on my screen,' Mshelia said. He moved aside so Ibrahim could see his laptop. 'What do you see?'

Ibrahim moved closer. 'A big house in the middle of nowhere. Just like Amaka said.'

'Yes, but look at the road. They'll see us coming a mile away.'

'If they think they got Amaka they won't be expecting us.'

'Yes, but still you'll need more than a few police officers

to carry out such an operation. You don't know what they've got in there. Those guys shooting from the bridge, they were military. If there are more of them, if they've got equipment, all it takes is one RPG.'

'Like I said, unless they have a battalion there, I am taking that house. If we dismount here,' he pointed at the screen, 'go through the forest here, we take the building from all sides. Surprise them.'

'How high do you think that perimeter fence is?' Mshelia said. He squinted at the screen. 'And is that barbed wire? We can't just go and storm a building we know nothing about. What do we know they've got in there?'

'You don't need to be a part of it if you don't want to. It is my officer they killed and I am going to get them.'

Mshelia stood up. 'Ibrahim, you're not thinking. For God's sake, you cannot let emotions rule you now.'

'What do you want me to do? Let them get away? Will you tell Fatima's family what happened to her?'

Gboyega was standing rigid, watching the two men square up to each other. Amaka remained still on the bed; Alex did not speak a word.

Mshelia sighed. 'Everyone has been put on riot patrol right now. At best I can get two men. Four max. And some equipment.'

Ibrahim turned to Alex. 'You. Can you handle a gun?'

Alex nodded.

'That's five,' Ibrahim said.

'There could be blowback,' Mshelia said. 'Basically, we're going to be mounting another illegal operation. We need to come up with a reason for carrying out an operation in Oyo State and it'd better be good.'

'This is all my fault,' Amaka said.

Ibrahim shook his head. 'No. It's mine.'

'The only guilty parties are the ones who killed Fatima,' Mshelia said. 'And we're going to get them.'

70

With one arm around the driver, the wind in his face, the passenger on the speeding motorcycle shouted into his phone. 'Chief, the information is good. We have successfully delivered the message.' With just one hand he slid open the back of the phone, and removed the battery, letting both components fall into the road. He felt inside for the SIM card and put it in his mouth. He threw the rest of the phone away and spat out the chewed up SIM.

Otunba stood up from the sofa, followed immediately by Ojo.

'You want to follow me to the toilet?' Otunba said to his son-in-law. Ojo smiled and remained standing while Otunba walked away with his phone in his hand.

He went into an empty bedroom and closed the door behind him, looked out of the window onto the pool as he waited for someone to answer, then said: 'Your information was good.'

Malik dropped the towel onto his bed and sat down on the mattress. His body was still wet from his shower. He listened. He waited. Otunba didn't speak. 'She showed up?' Malik said.

'I believe so,' Otunba replied.

Malik closed his eyes. A smile spread across his face. He waited for the older man to talk, but again Otunba said nothing.

'She's taken care of?' Malik said.

'What do you want?' Otunba asked.

'Sir, what do I want?'

'Yes.'

'Like, how, sir?'

'What do you want from me?'

'In return? Nothing, sir. You asked me to tell you what I know about Ojo, that's all I did, sir.'

Otunba drew his finger across the glass and looked at it.

'If you don't want anything,' he said, 'that means you think you already have something.'

'Sir, I don't...'

'Shut up and listen to me. Whatever you think you have, whatever you are planning to do with it, you will not live long enough to regret your actions if you go ahead. You will leave Lagos today. You will stay away till after the election. You will not contact me, or my son-in-law, or anybody, till you hear from me. Then, when I say it is OK, you will return to Lagos and you and I will talk.'

Otunba put his phone in his pocket and walked out of the bedroom.

Malik placed his hands on his hips and looked down at the bed. He stood still for a few moments, then he scrolled through his contacts and placed a call.

'Who is this?' a woman's voice said.

Malik ended the call. He gritted his teeth. His hands curled into fists and he hurled the phone at his bed. It bounced once on the mattress and settled onto the wet towel.

Ojo stood as Otunba returned to the parlour and sat on the sofa. Members of the Market Women's Association who had come to assure the kingmaker of their support for his son-in-law were talking amongst themselves. Otunba looked around. 'Where is your friend? Where is Shehu?'

Ojo looked around the room as if he expected to find Shehu sitting or standing amongst the women. 'He said he has some personal things to deal with at home,' he said.

'He said so?' Otunba looked into Ojo's eyes as if he expected a better answer; as if there was something wrong with the one Ojo had given.

71

Shehu answered the call from the driver's seat of his wife's Toyota Prius parked up the road from Malik's house. 'Ol' boy,' he said. 'What's up?'

'Where are you?' Ojo said.

'Waiting for you know who. Why?'

'Otunba was asking after you. He wanted to know where you were.'

'What did you tell him?'

'I said you went home to deal with something.'

'Did he ask what?'

'No.'

'If he does, just tell him I didn't say.'

'Have you spoken to him?'

'Yeah. He's not going to give up the girl.'

'So they're really working together?'

'It's possible. If she's alive.'

'What about Amaka?'

'I'm getting close.'

'How close?'

'Very close.'

'OK. Shehu, I'm really very grateful that you're doing this for me. I mean it. Thank you, my brother.'

'No problem, brother. Just stay calm and let me handle things. And one more thing.'

'What?'

'Malik said you also asked him to take care of Amaka. You really have to let me handle this.'

'I'm sorry, Shehu.'

'You've got to trust me, man. I'm the only person you can trust. Always remember that.'

72

In the dark, damp cell that smelt of urine, Elizabeth stood by the rusting iron bars clutching her handbag to her chest. Tears rolled down her cheeks as she shook with terror. In the far corner, on the floor that was too dirty and too wet to sit upon, a woman was curled up in the foetal position, her body against the wall and her clothes torn around her. She hadn't moved or made any sound since two police officers led Elizabeth down the corridor past other cells full of men and shoved her into the cell. An hour had passed since then. Elizabeth's voice had become sore from shouting her pleas of innocence through the bars. Only other detainees responded, declaring their own innocence or warning her to stop before they broke into her cell to fuck her until she shut up. The police didn't come. She stood by the bars, clutching her bag to her chest, shaking with fear, afraid of the male detainees in the other cell, and of the officers when they returned for her.

An unopened bottle of schnapps in his hand, Ibrahim stood in front of his officers in a room in the back of Bar Beach police station – officers who had gone with him to the operation at Fiki Marina; desk officers who never left the police station; battle-trained officers of the special task force, Operation Fire-for-Fire; and officers who were off duty but had heard the news and returned to the station. Sergeant Hot-Temper was among them, still in his undercover gear, his eyes red from crying. A few of his Operation Fire-for-Fire colleagues patted his back. Some of them also needed consoling.

'My friends,' Ibrahim said. 'My brothers, my sisters, my family. We have lost one of our own today. Fati is no longer with us. She has fallen in the line of duty. The bagas that took her from us have fled like the cowards they are, and they have gone into hiding. But if they enter water...'

The officers answered, each in their own emotion-laden voice, 'We will swim and fish them out.'

'If they enter rock...'

'We will break inside and bring them out.'

'If they grow wings and hide on trees, nko?'

'We will turn into winch and chase them down.'

'And if they die so that they can hide in hell?'

'We will follow them and tell Satan to hand them over to us.'

Ibrahim twisted off the cap of the bottle in his hands, poured some onto the ground, then took a swig and handed it to the female officer standing next to him. He sang the first line of a requiem in broken English and before he was done, the other officers had joined in. Their voices echoed through the corridors of the police station. The detainees listened in silence in their cells. The officers passed the bottle of schnapps from one to another, each giving Fatima her share before sipping theirs.

Two police officers walked between cells while suspects hurtled to the bars from where they watched the officers passing. The officers stopped at the last cell. Elizabeth's face was streaked with tears. She shook her head, pleaded with them to help her even as she backed away to the cold wall. An officer unlocked the door and pushed it open.

'Are you ready?' he said.

Elizabeth shook her head. Tears rolled down her cheeks and her belly felt weak. She couldn't walk. The woman who was curled up on the ground raised her head and looked at the officers. They entered the cell and lifted her to her feet.

From behind his desk, dressed in the same combat gear as the men from Operation Fire-for-Fire, Ibrahim stood strapping on a bulletproof vest. He holstered his pistol then picked up the first of six Uzi magazines lined up on his desk next to the submachine gun. Combat-ready officers stood in silence around the room, and out along the corridor. The ragged woman the officers had collected from the cell pushed past the men and entered the office. She saluted.

'Anything?' Ibrahim said. He picked up another magazine. Files were piled high on his table. On one end was an empty beer carton containing a framed picture of Ibrahim in ceremonial dress, a miniature Nigerian flag and another of the Nigerian police force.

'She called someone called Felix. I think it was her brother. She asked him to come to the station. She told him a woman and some men in a Lexus stopped to talk to her at Yaba. The woman said her husband had arranged to meet his girlfriend in VI and she wanted to catch him. The woman gave her twenty thousand to take an okada to Fiki Marina. The woman was sending her text messages telling her where to go.'

'So she's innocent.'

'I think so. But we must still check her phone. We will get the woman's number.'

'Good. And when her brother comes, arrest him too. Keep him here till we return.'

'Yes, sir. Sir?'

'Yes?'

'Why are you packing your things, sir?'

Ibrahim had just rolled up the cable of his laptop's charger. He held it in his hands as he stopped to look at the officer dressed in rags, then he placed the cable in a box.

'You understand that this is an illegal operation we are about to carry out?' He turned and addressed the rest of the officers. 'You all understand this is an illegal operation? Including the operation that took Fatima's life. I did not get clearance for it. You are all safe, you were taking orders from me, so you are protected, but when this is over, maybe even before it is over, I will stop being your boss. Fatima's death is my fault. We are going to avenge her now, but that won't bring her back. I asked her to follow me on an illegal mission and she trusted me. Now she is dead. I am asking you also to follow me on another illegal operation. I hope none of us dies, but you must all understand what this is. Please, brothers, sisters, if any one of you doesn't want to come, I will not think less of you.'

'All this talk is too much,' Hot-Temper said from where he stood leaning against the wall, next to the door. 'Let us go and get the bastards.'

The officers followed Ibrahim out of the station and up the dirt road to Ahmadu Bello Way. Two officers stood in the middle of each lane and held out their hands to stop traffic as the others crossed the road. Pedestrians and motorists watched the throng of men in body armour and armed with an assortment of weapons, cross the road and walk along the sandy path where there was meant to be a pavement. The officers passed the entrance to the Navy Senior Staff Quarters to reach the blue and white gates of Wilmot Point where Navy ratings waiting for them held open the gates.

73

Sisi unlocked Malik's office at The Harem and stepped inside. She pulled her hair back, gathered it into a bun, and with a rubber band she'd held between her lips, she tied her Peruvian attachment in place.

She went over to Malik's desk, sat on his chair, and felt underneath the tabletop. Her fingers touched a key taped to the underside. She pushed the chair back and opened the first drawer: inside was a silver Smith and Wesson revolver with a long barrel and black handle. Next to it, a transparent box of cartridges. She gripped the handle of the weapon and lifted it out of the drawer. The pistol was heavier than she had anticipated. It made a loud clank as she half placed, half dropped it on the table.

Twigs snapped and dead leaves crunched beneath boots as armed men crept through the forest towards the building surrounded by a twelve-foot-high concrete fence topped with loops of barbed wire. The men spread out, communicating only with hand signals. They extended long telescopic poles with tiny cameras on the ends up to the barbed wire and transmitted the images they captured to the officers beneath who used laptops in thick, black, shockproof cases.

Ibrahim shifted on the thin cushion of his seat in the back of the armoured vehicle parked in the middle of a narrow road in the forest. Two other officers sat either side of him. Facing them were Amaka, wearing a large grey bulletproof vest, Alex, and Mshelia.

Amaka's phone began to vibrate. 'Eyitayo, not now.'

'Switch that off,' Ibrahim said. He checked his watch. 'They should be in position now.' His radio crackled. 'Tell me.'

It was Hot-Temper. He whispered over the radio: 'No movement detected. Awaiting your signal.'

Ibrahim looked at Mshelia. Mshelia nodded.

'Go,' Ibrahim said.

Mshelia banged on the metal plate separating the rear of the van from the driver's cab. The engine roared, the tyres spun in sand, and the two-tonne vehicle lurched forward, throwing everybody back in their seats.

74

Ibrahim's officers lobbed stun grenades over the fence and tore away sections of barbed wire. Men, eager for vengeance, scaled the fence with practiced efficiency, landing in the compound with their guns drawn and their eyes seeking their targets.

Explosions going off, thick smoke spreading, and the pop pop pop of gunfire everywhere, they surrounded the building. They smashed windows and threw stun grenades through them, and ducked. Two men opened the gate and took up positions outside. Sergeant Hot-Temper led a group to the front door. He pelted the lock with lead, then kicked the door and stood in the open frame. The smoke lifted. In front of him, on the marble floor, in the middle of the large foyer, midway between the door and the staircase, lay a blue trunk, five feet long and three feet high, with shiny aluminium edges and locks.

Hot-Temper stepped into the building and glanced up the staircase. Behind him, officers ran into the house in pairs and four peeled off, past the trunk and up the stairs.

Hot-Temper walked to the box, inspecting it from every angle. Soon, the men returned to the foyer having found that the house was empty. Hot-Temper relaxed his grip on the rifle, removed his helmet and scratched his head. 'Wetin fit dey inside this thing?' he said.

75

Traffic built up at the Lagos end of the Lagos-Ibadan Expressway as vehicles heading into the city were funnelled into the last police checkpoint. Street-food hawkers and beggars darted between cars to beat rivals to anyone who looked at them from the windows of cramped buses. Impatient drivers held down car horns and revved engines, spurting smoke, amid a cacophony of voices.

An Innoson 23-seater bus was in the long queue of cars. The made-in-Nigeria vehicle had been retro-fitted with tinted windows, and inside, the driver, a rotund man in knee-length trousers and a white singlet, had beads of sweat along his hairline despite the air conditioning. He moved his head from side to side like an anxious chicken, and reacted with a jolt, followed by cursing, any time another motorist in the holdup felt the need to use their horn near his bus.

Two police officers in riot-gear had strayed from their checkpoint and were making their way between the immobile vehicles. They kept their eyes on the bus. The driver scanned ahead and looked nervously in his mirrors. The sight of police officers had never worried him before when his bus was filled with girls, all dressed up, all made up, and the cab would be scented with a heady mix of their perfumes. It would be dark and he would be delivering his cargo to a party thrown for a senator, or a governor, or a general, or just some wealthy man somewhere, and an escort would ride in front with him – a police officer, a soldier, an SSS man, even an Army Colonel once.

It would be the job of the escort to turn inquisitive police officers away. But today he had no escort, and when he rushed to the house as his boss had instructed him to, the girls had run into the van, many of them undressed and clutching their clothes, as if pursued by ghosts that had finally descended upon the house in the middle of the forest. The building always made him uneasy; a mansion in the middle of nowhere, surrounded by forest and the spirits that live in forests.

Most of girls that hurried into his bus were white, and they were the ones who had on the least clothes, or no clothes at all. He had watched in the mirror as the girls shared pieces of surplus clothing with those who had nothing to cover their nakedness, but still the clothes were not enough to go around. Now, stuck in traffic in daylight on the express, two police officers were approaching his vehicle.

The girls looked scared. He was scared. It had to be the tinted windows that had attracted the officers. Even if he was not the original focus of the police officers' attention, the windows had given them an excuse to shake him down for a bribe. And when they looked inside, they would see all the girls looking scared like he was going to use them for rituals, white girls among them, and they would ask him who the girls were and where he was taking them, and he would not be able to answer because he was more afraid of his boss than he was of the police.

The two police officers got closer. The driver kept staring at them. The officer in front looked up and locked eyes with him through the windscreen. The driver switched off the engine, left the key in the ignition, unclasped his seatbelt, and opened his door. Then, he jumped onto the road and ran.

For a moment the girls sat still in their seats, then one of them stood, opened the door, and disappeared as fast as she could in the same direction as the driver. The other girls hurried to the door, rushed out onto the road and ran in different directions between idling cars, beggars, and hawkers.

76

The Nigerian Navy armoured personnel carrier rolled through the open gates. The men got out and Ibrahim held his hand out to Amaka, but she got out by herself and the heels of her shoes sank into the gravel. The compound was large, just as the girls had described it. The building stood in the middle, as big and elegant as any mansion in Ikoyi, but this one was in the middle of the forest, closer to Ibadan than to Lagos.

Armed men were everywhere; gravel crunching beneath their heavy boots. There was no threat in the building. The front door of the house, framed by two large columns, was open and more officers stood inside, just beyond the door.

A naval officer who had waited for the vehicle to park walked up to Mshelia and presented him with a silver revolver. He took the weapon and checked it wasn't loaded. Then he wrapped his hand around the handle, held out the gun in front of him and closed one eye to look down the barrel as if aiming into the ground. He handed the gun to Ibrahim.

'The house is empty,' the naval officer said. 'We found the firearm on a desk upstairs. It looks as if everybody left in a hurry. We also found fresh tracks here; a large vehicle. They must have been tipped off.'

'So this is it,' Ibrahim said. He shielded his eyes with his palm to look up at the building.

'Naomi,' Amaka muttered. She walked towards the door.

Mshelia, Ibrahim, and Alex followed, and behind them two officers from the armoured car, the only ones still holding their weapons battle-ready.

Hot-Temper stepped aside. Ibrahim looked at the blue trunk. 'What's inside?' he asked.

'We never open am,' Hot-Temper said. Other men were standing around in the foyer, all facing the trunk from several feet away.

'Good call,' Mshelia said.

Amaka looked up the stairwell. She walked round the trunk and climbed the stairs. On the first floor she looked down the corridor. Doors on either side were open. She walked into the first room. There was a white poster bed in the middle; its rumpled white sheets lay half on the floor. She switched on her phone, and as she did she saw that she had missed several calls. She opened the camera app and held it up to take a picture of the bed.

Amaka walked along the white, deep pile rug to the end of the room where another door was open. It was a bathroom; three toothbrushes and a tube of toothpaste sat in a glass cup on the sink. She looked inside a wicker basket by the toilet bowl: wet condoms and their torn packets lay on top of a pile of crumpled tissues. She pointed her phone's camera lens at the dustbin and clicked, then checked the pictures she had taken. Three of the missed calls were from Eyitayo; one from a withheld number. The phone began to vibrate. Eyitayo again, Amaka assumed, calling at Chioma's behest. But she couldn't deal with the Chioma situation right now. She rejected the call and scrolled through the call log; there was yet another from a withheld number. The entry showed a talk time of five seconds.

'Amaka,' Ibrahim called from the corridor. She stepped out of the bathroom and into the bedroom.

Ibrahim was standing in the doorway. 'You have to see this,' he said.

Amaka followed him and an officer up to the second floor to a large door. Ibrahim pushed it open. 'After you,' he said.

Amaka walked into a dim room. The only light was from shaded lamps surrounded by unlit candles on stools in each of the four corners of the room. The walls and the carpet were red, and there were no windows. The ceiling was covered in mirror tiles that reflected the black massage bed below. Open handcuffs with long chains secured around the legs of the bed lay on the leather top, and next to the bed on a trolley lay an assortment of whips, ropes, and melted candles.

Amaka walked slowly round the bed.

'At least we know it's the right place,' Ibrahim said.

Amaka picked up a black horse whip and inspected it before placing it back next to other similar whips.

'Come, there is more,' Ibrahim said.

77

Sisi stopped on a quiet residential road with tall fences and engaged the handbrake of her red Audi TT. Naomi sat next to her, her hands on the bag in her lap. The AC was on but the sun's rays through the glass were still hot.

'Why did you help me?' Naomi said.

'I didn't help you. I helped myself. You already told your friend how to find The Harem. He would lose his business and he would see me as a loose end. You have no idea how dangerous he is.'

'You do?'

Sisi nodded. 'I do.' She used the mirrors to look around. 'I told him I caught one of the Ukrainian girls with a phone. I said I took it from her and saw that she had sent the location to a number in Nigeria. He told me there was a pistol in his office. He said I should get everyone ready for the bus, then I should get the pistol, take the girl to the back yard, and shoot her.

'Florentine is not the first girl that has vanished. There was this girl, Wumi. She was eighteen. He wouldn't let her out of her room anytime we had guests; said he was keeping her for someone special. One day I noticed I hadn't seen her all day. I mentioned it to him and he told me to mind my business. I went to her room and her things were still there. He found me in the room. He locked the door and told me he had warned me to mind my business. She never returned and I never learnt what happened to her.

'There have been others. They just vanish overnight. I have never had anything to do with it, Naomi, you have to believe me, and you have to tell your friend. I had no part in any of it.'

Naomi stared straight ahead.

'I'm leaving Lagos tonight.' Sisi said. 'I have to see my daughter. Then I'll fly to Dubai.'

'I didn't know you had a daughter.'

Sisi fetched her bag from the back and removed her purse. She showed Naomi the photograph that had been laminated in plastic.

'She looks like you,' Naomi said.

Sisi put it back in her bag and placed it on the back seat. 'What about you? What will you do now?'

Naomi sighed. She leaned her head against the window.

Sisi reached under Naomi's seat, pulled out a large brown envelope, and removed a brick of fifty-dollar notes.

'Take,' she said.

Naomi held the cellophane-wrapped cash and stared at it.

Sisi looked around; there was no one on the road.

'Malik's money,' Naomi said.

'Money,' Sisi said. 'He told me to get it from his safe. If he contacts you, the story is we got stopped at a checkpoint, they searched the car and took the money.' She tucked the envelope back under the seat and retrieved another from under hers. 'Take.'

'What is it?'

'There are hidden cameras in all the rooms. He makes videos of the clients. He uses them for blackmail. If his clients know about the tapes, they won't protect him. Give them to your friend, but make sure you watch them first. You might be on some of them.'

Naomi looked in the envelope and put the dollars in with the CDs.

Both women sat in silence.

'Are you sure this is where you want me to drop you?' Sisi said. She looked at the tall fences.

'Yes. It's my grandparents' house. My daughter is in there.'

78

Chioma sat at the dressing table, staring down, pen in hand, eyes drained of tears. Her face was as blank as the piece of paper beneath the pen; the one she'd stared at for thirty minutes since she asked Eyitayo for a pen and an envelope. It had been an hour and thirty minutes since the phone call; an hour and thirty minutes since she made up her mind, and yet she still couldn't find the right words to explain it. But she had to. She owed Amaka that much.

She heaved a sigh and began to write:

Aunty Amaka. I have gone to Oshodi to see Kingsley. He said he was there at the market because he was trying to save Matthew. He wants to explain everything to me in person. I did not tell Aunty Eyitayo and Uncle Gabriel where I'm going because they will tell you and you will tell me not to go. But I know what I'm doing. I have to see him. Thank you for everything you have done for me.

'She's still not answering,' Eyitayo said, placing her phone on the stool by her chair. 'Let's give her some time.'

Chioma shook her head. She was dressed in a boubou Eyitayo had given her. In her hands she held the white envelope. 'I have to go,' she said.

Gabriel watched from the door to the kitchen, a mug of coffee in his hands.

'Is that the letter for Amaka?' Eyitayo asked.

Chioma nodded.

'Can't you see your pastor another time? And, do you really have to stay there for the night vigil?'

Chioma nodded.

'But you're coming back here first thing in the morning?'

Chioma nodded again.

Someone knocked on the door. 'That must be the taxi,' Gabriel said. 'Are you sure you don't want me to take you there?' he asked.

'No, it's OK.' Chioma said, standing up.

The gateman who had gone to get a taxi opened the door from outside. Eyitayo looked at Gabriel. He placed his mug on the dining table and walked over.

'At least wait to see Amaka before you leave,' Gabriel said.

Chioma shook her head.

Outside in the sun, the taxi idled and the gateman held the gate open. Eyitayo and Gabriel stood in front of Chioma by the back door of the car.

'Are you sure about this?' Eyitayo asked.

Chioma nodded. She was still holding the envelope in her hand.

'OK. Call us as soon as you get there.' Eyitayo embraced her, then Chioma gave her the envelope.

As the taxi drove out of the compound Eyitayo looked at the envelope in her hand. It was sealed.

Chioma turned in the back seat of the taxi and watched the gate close. She turned back, leaned forward, and placed her hand on the driver's shoulder.

'We are not going to Apapa,' she said. 'Take me to Oshodi market.'

She dialled a number. 'Hello, Kingsley, I'm on my way... No, I didn't tell them where I'm going... Yes, I'm coming alone.'

Eyitayo sat opposite Gabriel at the dining table and placed the sealed envelope down on the table between them.

'Should we open it?' she asked.

Gabriel shook his head.

'What do you think she wrote?'

'Thanking her for what she's done, I guess.'

'Do you think we should have let her go?'

'We can't hold her against her will.'

79

'What do you think they do in here?' Ibrahim said.

Amaka walked between the chains hanging from the ceiling. She pressed her hand into the white padded leather wall. Chains rattled behind her as Ibrahim held up a length and looked at the metal hoops in his hand. 'Do you think they tie themselves to these?' he said.

Hot-Temper stepped into the doorway. 'Oga Mshelia say make you come downstairs.'

Amaka took pictures before they left.

Outside, Alex and all the officers were looking in through the doorway; Mshelia was in front of them, one end of a blue nylon rope in his hand, and excess loops of it in the clutch of his other. The rope led across the floor to the banister of the staircase from where it looped back to the lid of the blue trunk.

'You think it's a booby trap?' Ibrahim said as he stepped out of the door.

'Don't know, but not taking chances,' Mshelia said. 'Get back.'

Everyone moved out onto the gravel-covered front yard and watched. Mshelia backed away, letting more of the rope fall to the ground until he backed up to the fence. He looked behind him and grinned. The men put their fingers in their ears.

Amaka did the same. Mshelia began pulling the rope, gathering the loops in his other hand. When it stretched tight across the ground, he paused. 'Ibro,' he said. 'If anything happens to me, I have a case of Petrus under my bed. I will it to you.'

'What is Petrus?' Ibrahim asked.

'Very expensive wine,' Mshelia said. 'Amaka, this one will not appreciate fine wine. I will my custom seizure to you. OK, people: three, two, one…'

He pulled the rope and the lid of the blue trunk lifted. When it was almost vertical, he gave it a tug and it fell backwards. Two Navy officers stepped out and walked along either side of the rope that led into the house. Once they were past the foyer they slowed down and approached the open box as if it was a rigged bomb.

'What's inside?' Mshelia called to the men.

'Oga, you have to come and see,' one of them said.

Everyone crowded round the trunk. In one end was a woman's head – Caucasian, with silky brown hair. The blue eyes were wide open, as was her mouth. Her large lips covered in hot red lipstick formed an 'O'. The rest of the naked body was partly buried under different sizes, colours, textures, and shapes of gelatinous dildos, the largest ones up to twelve inches long, fat as an arm, and ranging in colour from dark brown to jet black; the others were every colour from cream to blue to neon green.

Two navy officers reached inside from either end. One reached through the soft sex toys and clasped his hands under her legs; the other put his arms under her armpits and together they lifted up the life-sized silicone doll as dildos fell away from its belly.

They laid the sex toy on the floor in front of the trunk. It was the size of a real woman; its large breasts had pink areolas and hard nipples; its lifelike vagina had minuscule dots as if it had been shaved.

Some of the men reached into the trunk and held up wobbly prosthetics, teasing one another with them. A few would neither touch the toys, nor laugh at the others. Some were frowning, looking on in disgust.

'It's definitely the right building,' Ibrahim said.

'Yes, 'Mshelia said. 'And someone left this here on purpose so we would know we have the right house. They know we are here.' He turned to Amaka. 'You've found The Harem. What do you want to do now?'

Amaka looked around, and up the stairs.

'Burn it down,' she said.

80

Malik's gate opened. Down the road, Shehu sank low in the seat of his wife's car. A white Range Rover Sport inched out of the gate, held open by the same security guard Shehu had spoken to earlier. The SUV stopped midway through and the darkened window rolled down. Malik was at the wheel. He spoke to the gateman then continued out of his compound and drove away, up the road.

Shehu started the Prius. Without a sound from the engine, the dashboard lit up. Malik turned left at the end of the road leading out of the estate. Shehu waited till the gateman had closed the gate then he pulled out and followed Malik.

81

Officers found a half-full drum of diesel in the generator building. Keeping it upright, two men rolled it along the ground at an angle. Other officers helped get the drum through the front door into the mansion. An officer inserted one end of a rubber hose from the generator building into the mouth of the drum then sucked on the other end till the fuel collected in his mouth. He clamped the hose with his thumb and spat diesel into the trunk of sex toys and onto the sex doll.

The men walked through the house dousing chairs, beds, chests of drawers, and carpets. They tore curtains off the windows, dipped them into diesel and lit them, then they threw the burning fabric onto the beds and retreated only when the fire had taken hold.

By the time the men gathered outside the building, thick smoke seeped out of the windows, curling over the roof.

Standing just outside the door, Hot-Temper lit the wick of a Molotov cocktail he had made and flung the improvised weapon onto the floor inside. Orange flames spread throughout, engulfing the sex toys and the blue trunk.

In minutes, fire was raging behind every window. Through the open front door, flames curled and leapt from every surface, rolled up the staircase, and danced over the walls. The building was soon consumed by fire. The sky darkened behind the inferno; black bits sailed up with spirals of smoke from the burning roof. Everyone watching had to step back and shield their faces from the heat, then the wind changed and the smoke descended upon the party.

'That is one big house on fire,' Mshelia shouted over the noise of the burning building.

'Yep,' Ibrahim said. 'Time to leave.'

'Yes.' Mshelia looked around for Alex. 'We were never here. Remember that when you write your report. OK?'

Alex nodded.

'Do you think we'll ever find him?' Mshelia asked Ibrahim.

'He knew we were coming. He's on the run. Amaka, have you been able to speak to the girl?'

Amaka looked at her phone. She had new missed calls from Eyitayo but nothing from Naomi. She tried her number.

'Her phone is still off.'

'What now?' Mshelia said.

'Whether or not she tipped him off, we find her, we find him,' Ibrahim said. 'Where is her place?'

'1004,' Amaka said.

'Let's go.'

82

Following the white Range Rover was simple, but the notoriously clogged highways of Lagos were free flowing, which meant that Malik could spot a car following him. Twice, when he turned off major roads, Shehu drove on, stopping a few metres ahead then reversing to take the same turning; each time hoping he'd find the Range Rover parked beside a fence and not behind a closed gate. But Malik navigated deserted residential roads and joined the same main road again, much further along. It occurred to Shehu that he was avoiding rioters or the police; either of which could be bad news.

The white Range Rover slowed down on Aromire Avenue, allowing other cars to overtake.

'What are you doing?' Shehu said, looking at the SUV two vehicles ahead. He overtook them and watched the Range Rover in his rear-view mirror. Malik had slowed down so much that a line of cars was beginning to form behind him. Had he seen Shehu following him?

Shehu came up to the Allen roundabout. A column of black smoke rose from Allen Avenue about a hundred metres away. Shehu continued round the roundabout, turning his head to watch the Range Rover. Malik had started moving again. Shehu passed the Obafemi Awolowo Way exit just as Malik took the roundabout and Shehu ended up behind him.

Malik continued onto Allen Avenue and Shehu followed. When a danfo wanted to edge in between the two cars, Shehu dropped back.

The smoke was from smouldering tyres that had been dragged to the side of the road leaving black entrails behind them. Soldiers were waving on the traffic. Malik passed them. Two cars later, Shehu was also waved on. Malik continued up the road, then changed lanes and pulled up in front of a used car dealership. Shehu passed him, continued a while, and pulled up on the side of the road, just after the open gates of another used car lot. He watched through the mirror as Malik got out of his car and walked into the compound. 'What are you doing now?' he said.

The soldiers waving on traffic ahead were looking at him. Two of them spoke among themselves then one began to walk towards the Prius. 'Fuck,' Shehu said. In the mirror he saw Malik return with a man in a sky-blue tracksuit. Together they inspected the Range Rover.

A soldier tapped on the window.

'Is anything wrong?' the officer asked.

Shehu kept his eyes on the mirror. 'My car is overheating,' he said and popped the bonnet.

The soldier inspected the inside of the car then stepped back to let Shehu get out.

Shehu held the bonnet up and watched Malik over the top of it. A black Mercedes-Benz ML drove out of the lot. The driver got out and handed Malik the keys. Malik, in turn, passed him the keys to his Range Rover and climbed into the Mercedes.

Shehu turned his head as Malik drove past.

'Where are you going?' Shehu muttered to himself, before swiftly closing the bonnet and hurrying back to the Prius while the soldiers looked on.

Shehu turned into 1004 Estate moments after Malik. He searched for the Mercedes as he drove up the road then turned into the main car park and looked between parked cars. He stopped when he spotted it, but it was empty – parked between two cars in front of a block of flats. Shehu looked around. Malik had gone.

'Where are you?' Shehu said to himself, looking up at the balconies. 'And what are you doing here?'

83

The driver looked at Naomi in the rear-view mirror of his taxi. Since he picked her up from Ikeja she had not said a word other than to tell him the destination: 1004.

When he told her the hiked fare, three times the standard rate because other taxi drivers were afraid of the riots, she just nodded and got into the back. She was now staring out of the window, as she had been doing all through the journey. She was dressed like an ashewo returning from work, so she should have money, but she looked like a worried prostitute; one who had been robbed of the money she earned during the night. What if they arrived at her destination and she refused to pay him? If he tried to insist on being paid, she could say she already had. She could start shouting and screaming, and when a crowd had formed, she would tell them to check his pocket for the crumpled notes she paid him with – and they would find crumpled notes in his pockets. Taxi drivers always have crumpled notes. Or she could offer him sex in lieu of payment. He arched his neck to see more of her exposed legs in the mirror. He looked at her face. Her eyes were red and moist. He was right. She had been robbed of all her money. He had picked up a prostitute who did not have any money to pay the fare.

He bit his lip and cursed his luck. He would take her number and give her his. He would tell her to call him anytime she needed a driver. If she did, he would make his money back; if she didn't, he might find a passenger in VI. If she offered sex, he would tell her he was a born-again Christian - the same lie he used when his family begged him to get a girlfriend who would one day, God willing, become his wife.

Malik walked along the balcony on the sixth floor and stopped in front of a door. Shehu watched him from inside his Prius. Malik pressed a bell, looked about him, and knocked on the door. He looked through the peephole then turned his back to the door and scanned the car park below. He walked back along the corridor, went down the stairs, and returned to his car. He sat inside and looked up at the flat he'd just visited.

84

A police van, followed by a Nigerian Navy bus and an armoured vehicle, drove into 1004 Estate, drawing attention as they sped over speed bumps and screeched to a stop in front of a block.

'What's going on here?' Shehu said, watching armed officers alighting from the vehicles. He looked at Malik's car. Malik's head slid down in his seat.

The back of the armoured vehicle opened and its occupants alighted, among them, a woman Shehu recognised.

'Wait a second,' Shehu said to himself. It was Amaka Mbadiwe. 'Is that the reason you're here?' he said looking at Malik's car. Malik was also watching her from the window, his hand over the side of his face.

Amaka stood facing two men who appeared to be in charge. A third, younger man, stood between them, listening to what the three were saying.

Amaka squinted at the sun as she looked in Shehu's direction. There were four rows of cars between them.

Accompanied by two police officers brandishing weapons, Amaka, Ibrahim, and Mshelia stopped in front of Naomi's flat. Amaka knocked on the door, pressed the bell, placed her ear to the wood and listened. She shouted through the kitchen window on the side of the building: 'Naomi, it's me, Amaka.' She knocked again, then put her phone to her ear.

Ibrahim looked down from the balcony and saw a group of residents from the estate looking up at them.

Amaka ended the call. 'It's still off,' she said.

Ibrahim nodded at one of the men. The officer moved in front of the door, took a step back and levelled his weapon at the lock. The bang was followed by screams downstairs. It took two more shots to defeat the locks.

Amaka was about to step inside, but Ibrahim held her back and the two officers went in first.

Minutes later, Amaka, Ibrahim, Mshelia and one of the armed men returned. Ibrahim shut the door behind them and together they all began to walk along the balcony.

'Five go in, four come out.' Shehu said.

Ibrahim, Amaka, and Mshelia gathered beside the armoured vehicle.

'He caught her and he killed her too,' Amaka said.

'Or she tipped him off,' Mshelia said. 'Either way, he's in the wind now. We may never find him.'

Amaka's phone vibrated. She looked at the display. It was Eyitayo. She let the phone ring out. 'I need a car,' she said. 'Can I borrow yours?'

'My car?' Ibrahim said.

'The girl from Oshodi. There's something going on with her. She's been trying to get in touch all day.'

'Where is she?' Ibrahim asked. 'My driver can take you.'

'She's with friends. A policeman was responsible for her brother's death. Seeing a policeman will spook her. I need to go alone. Please.'

She looked up at Naomi's block. 'I thought I finally got Malik,' she said. 'I really thought I was going to get to look into his eyes and let him know it was me who took him down.'

A female police officer pulled up in Ibrahim's red Camry. She handed the keys to Ibrahim, who handed them to Amaka.

'Drive safely,' Ibrahim said.

Amaka got into the car. As she adjusted the seat and mirrors, the officers got into their vehicles, revved their engines, and drove out of 1004 one after the other. Amaka pulled out behind them and drove, slowly at first, testing the brakes and readjusting the mirror.

Shehu released the handbrake just as Malik drove past him, following Amaka.

'Hello, Eyitayo?'

Amaka turned the steering wheel with one hand, holding her phone to her ear with the other.

'Amaka, where have you been? I've been calling you all day.'

'I'm on my way back now. How is Chioma doing?'

'That's why I've been calling you. She said she was going to Apapa to see her pastor. She said she's staying there for a night vigil. I tried to stop her.'

'That's all right. Maybe that's exactly what she needs now. I got videos of the lynching from people at the market. When she returns we'll see if she can identify Kingsley in them.'

'You want to show her a video of her brother being killed?'

'You're right. I'm not thinking. It's been one hell of a day. Maybe I'll ask her for a picture. I'll see if I can find him in the videos myself. Did she say when she'll be back?'

'First thing in the morning. Amaka, I tried to stop her.'

'It's ok, Eyitayo.'

'No, you don't understand. She was being very cagey. I have a bad feeling about this. She left you a letter. Should I read it?'

'You haven't?'

'It's sealed. I'll get it.'

Amaka switched hands and moved the phone to her other ear while Eyitayo fetched the letter.

'Oh my God,' Eyitayo said.

'What?'

'She's gone to meet him.'

'Who?'

'Kingsley. Her ex-boyfriend. She's gone to Oshodi to meet him.'

'What?'

Amaka put her foot hard on the brake. The car behind came to a screeching stop. She looked in the mirror. The Mercedes had almost rear-ended her and it would have been her fault. She wound down the window, held out her hand to apologise, and continued driving.

'What do you mean she's gone to meet him?'

Eyitayo read out the letter.

'He wasn't trying to protect her brother,' Amaka said. 'He killed him and he's going to going to kill her too. Fuck.'

She dropped the phone onto the other seat and accelerated. The Mercedes SUV had overtaken her. She looked in the mirror. A Prius was following closely behind. She had to pull out; she had to get Oshodi before it was too late.

The Mercedes was too close. She pressed the heel of her palm onto the horn and braked but it was too late. Her body flung forward, the seatbelt tightened across her chest, and the airbag inflated just in time to stop her face smashing into the steering wheel.

When she raised her head, a sharp pain tore through her neck. The airbag had deflated and flopped over the steering wheel leaving a mist of white powder. She coughed, covered her nose and waved in front of her face. She unclasped the seat belt and opened the door. A car drove by without slowing. She held the back of her neck and groaned. The front bumper had meshed into the rear bumper of the Mercedes. The driver was still in the car. A little further back, the Prius had also stopped on the road. She staggered a little as she approached the Mercedes but couldn't see what had made it stop suddenly. Perhaps there was something wrong with the driver. A medical emergency? A heart attack?

Amaka knocked on the car window. The driver was slumped over the passenger seat. She looked about for help, saw the door of the Prius opening, and pulled the handle of the Mercedes. The door opened. She looked back. The driver of the Prius was now walking towards her. She recognised him; it was retired navy commodore Shehu Yaya – the man with Chief Ojo the night she spiked his drink.

'Hello Amaka,' the man in the Mercedes said.

Her eyes darted to him. He was sitting up, grinning, and aiming a silver pistol at her chest. It was Malik.

85

Shehu stood next to Amaka on the dual carriageway. He looked at Malik. 'I thought we agreed she was mine,' he said.

'Did you follow me?' Malik asked him.

'Yes. From 1004.'

'What were you doing there?'

'Following her.' Shehu said. 'What were *you* doing there?'

'Looking up a friend who lives there.'

'Florentine?'

'No. She's dead. She's buried not very far from The Harem.' Malik looked out the rear window, past Amaka's car at the parked Prius. 'We really don't have time for chit-chat,' he said. 'We've got to get off the road.' He reached back to open the rear door and waved his gun at Amaka. 'Get in.'

Amaka stood still. Shehu grabbed her arm and shoved her towards the open door. He followed her into the car and closed the door.

'What about your car?' Malik asked.

'Move, before we attract attention.'

Malik closed his door and placed the gun in his lap.

'You better give me that,' Shehu said.

Malik looked at him in the mirror. 'You don't need it,' he said. 'We're not going far.'

They were soon on the Lekki-Ajah Expressway, speeding away from Victoria Island.

From the back seat, Amaka watched Malik's side profile. 'What did you do to her?' she asked.

He did not answer.

'Who is she talking about?' Shehu said.

'Oh, just the snitch who told her how to find my club. They burnt it down.'

'The Harem?'

'Yes. Burnt to the ground. I sent a boy to check on a situation there. He sent me pictures of my lovely building on fire. Then my associate lied to me that it had to do with the Ukrainian girls, but I know it's our friend here. She likes to play detective all over Lagos. And now I also know she was working with the girl at 1004. Her name is Naomi. She was there last night while you were there. You would have liked her. Pretty girl. And intelligent. I was going to ask her some questions, but I don't have to anymore. I'll get everything I need out of this one.'

86

'Where are you taking me?' Amaka asked. 'Are we going to Lekki Phase 1? Is that where you live?'

'You should reserve your energy,' Malik said, without taking his eyes off the road. He joined a queue of cars waiting to enter the housing development.

'Is Malik your real name?'

'We'll have enough time to get to know each other later.'

'Or is it a fake name?'

'Make her shut up,' Malik said, looking at Shehu over his shoulder.

Shehu looked at Amaka. 'She's afraid,' he said. 'Talking is her coping mechanism.'

'I don't feel like hearing her voice right now,' Malik said.

'What do you want me to do?' Shehu asked.

Amaka looked out her window. 'You live in Lekki Phase 1?' she asked.

With his left hand crossed over his right shoulder, Malik pointed the gun at her. Both Amaka and Shehu moved apart. He placed the gun back on his lap and looked around. 'Your voice, I find it grating. And I have a migraine. Don't make me shoot you inside this car and dump your body in a gutter.'

'Like you and Ojo dumped Florentine on the express?' Amaka said.

Shehu reached over to touch her arm. She flinched.

'Young lady,' he said. 'Try to do as you're told.'

'Your name is Shehu Yaya. Retired navy commodore Shehu Yaya. You are Ojo's friend. You saw me with him. Is that why you are involved with this? Ojo sent you to get the videos I have of him sleeping with underage girls?'

'I really think you should keep your mouth shut,' Shehu said.

Malik watched them in the mirror. Amaka continued. 'Chief Ojo, a man who is running for governor, almost beat Florentine to death. You, Malik, you helped him dump her body. I found pictures and videos of little girls on Ojo's phone. That's why he wants me dead. That's why Malik wants me dead. But you, what is your part in this? Why are you helping them?'

'You should have left trouble alone when you found it sleeping,' Shehu said.

'One of you lives in Lekki Phase 1. Which is it?'

Security guards stopped the Mercedes. One wrote the registration number down in a worn notebook while another approached the driver's window.

Malik looked at Amaka before he wound down the window. 'Behave yourself,' he said.

Amaka's fingers crept towards the door handle. Shehu gripped her forearm. 'That is a bad idea,' he said.

The guard standing in the sun looked into car then stood away. Shehu wound the window up and continued onto Admiralty Way.

'Bisola Durosinmi Etti Drive,' Amaka said. 'I have friends on this road.'

Neither Malik nor Shehu responded to her.

Amaka turned to look out through Shehu's window. 'Abike

Animashaun,' she said. Malik turned again and slowed down. 'Ayo Jagun Street. Is this where you live?'

Malik turned towards a white gate.

'No 28B,' Amaka said. 'Is this where you killed Florentine?'

'Shut up,' Shehu said. And to Malik: 'Whose house is this?'

The Mercedes was idling. Malik pressed the horn twice.

'It's a guesthouse,' Malik said.

The ten by ten-inch square on the gate slid open and a face peered through the hole. The panel slid back and a moment later a shirtless young man opened the gate.

Malik drove into the compound and waited in the car till the man closed the gates and stood by his door.

'Is anybody inside?' Malik asked, pointing at the building.

The boy shook his head.

'Lock the gates and don't let anyone in.'

The boy nodded.

'Yours?' Shehu asked.

'A joint venture,' Malik said. He got down and opened Amaka's door. The boy looked up from securing the padlock on the door and saw the weapon pointed at Amaka. He suppressed a scream and Malik looked at him and put his finger to his lips. The boy mimicked him and nodded.

'What's wrong with him?' Shehu asked.

'Deaf,' Malik said. Keeping his pistol on Amaka, he stepped back and let her out. He waved the gun at her. 'Inside.'

Amaka did not move. He aimed the weapon at her head. 'Don't try me,' he said.

Amaka stared down the barrel into his eyes. She looked at Shehu, looked at the deaf boy, looked back at Malik, rolled her eyes at him and turned towards the building.

87

Eyitayo, still in her housecoat, held her phone to her ear. In her right hand she held a pen over an open notebook on a stool in front of her.

Gabriel stood, bent over her, his phone also pressed against his ear, reading what Eyitayo had written and relaying it over the phone.

Eyitayo crossed out Abike Animashaun, like she had crossed out Bisola Durosinmi Etti Drive above it. On a new line she wrote: Ayo Jagun Street. Then, after listening, she added 28B in front of the street name and underlined the address.

Ibrahim took the phone away from his ear and covered the mouthpiece with his hand. His body rocked in the front cab of the police van speeding down Ahmadu Bello. He shouted over the noise of the sirens: '28B, Ayo Jagun Street.'

Bakare, his driver, shunted out from behind a white Peugeot 504 and floored the throttle. In the open back of the van, armed police held on to whatever they could grip to stop being thrown onto the road. The driver of the Peugeot beeped his horn in protest at the dangerous manoeuvre. Sergeant Hot-Temper in the back of the van pointed his AK-47 at the motorist's windscreen. The Peugeot screeched to a halt on the road, other cars swerved to avoid running into it, and the police van sped on, siren blaring and lights flashing.

88

'Open the door,' Malik said, his pistol pressed into Amaka's back. Shehu was standing by his side in the corridor on the first floor. Amaka didn't move.

Shehu reached past Amaka and opened the door. It was a bedroom. There were two camera lights on tripods looking down on the bed and between them was a third tripod with a video camera. Black cables ran from each tripod to the ground and along the floor to a black extension box that was plugged into a wall socket. Above the bed's headboard was a metre-wide framed picture of a Great Dane sitting on a golden cowhide rug. The walls of the room were covered in white wallpaper with silver rose petals falling off bunched bouquets. Sunlight shone through the two windows behind thin white curtains.

Malik pressed the weapon into Amaka's back. She walked into the room followed by Shehu, then Malik, who closed the door behind him.

'Take your clothes off.' Malik said.

Amaka had stopped just behind where the video equipment was set up. She turned and stared at him.

Malik raised the gun to her head.

'I said take off your clothes.'

'Why?' Amaka asked. 'What do you want to do?'

'Do you know you talk too much?'

'I hope you're thinking of your mother when you fuck me.'

'I never knew my mother.'

'I'm sure you can't even get it up.'

He lowered his gun to his side, looked at Shehu and laughed, then in a flash he brought his gun hand up and across his chest and smacked the side of Amaka's face with the butt of the weapon. Amaka fell backwards onto the ground, taking the camera down with her.

'See what you made me do?' Malik said. He reached towards her and Amaka recoiled. He grinned. 'I'm not touching you,' he said. He lifted the camera tripod, set it back upright and checked that the camera was working. 'Take off your clothes,' he said as he continued inspecting the camera.

'What do you want to do?' Amaka asked.

'What do I want to do? Do you know why the Romans nailed Jesus to a cross like this?' He spread his hands wide and Shehu moved away from the barrel of the pistol. 'It was not to punish him. They crucified him and planted his cross on top of a hill so that everybody would see 'this is what happens to anyone who tries us'.'

He switched the camera on. A red light blinked.

'By the way,' Malik continued, 'I need to thank you. You did me a big favour today. My house that you burnt – the insurance on that building is worth more than ten times its value. Just like this one. Just like every property I own. You saved me the trouble of burning the place down myself. Now I really need you to take off your clothes and get onto the bed.'

Amaka propped up her body with one hand, touched her mouth, then looked at the blood on her fingers.

'You brought all of this upon yourself,' Shehu said.

'Get up, take off your clothes, and get onto the bed,' Malik said. Amaka got onto her feet. 'No,' she said, spitting blood onto the white rug.

'But why?' Malik said. 'Because I hit you? I already

apologised for that. Or, didn't I? My mistake. I'll just do it again and this time I'll make sure I apologise.'

He stepped away from behind the camera and took a step towards her. She flinched and stepped backwards until her feet hit the edge of the bed.

Shehu held Malik's hand. 'Miss,' he said, 'there is only one way this is going to end, but I can make it fast. A single shot to the back of the head and it would be over. You won't feel anything. You won't even hear it. Or it can be the other way. His way. The choice is yours. Tell me who else has seen the videos and the pictures you took from Ojo and I'll make sure it's quick.'

89

Amaka spat more blood onto the rug and stared into Shehu's eyes.

'Fuck you. I'm not telling you anything.'

Shehu nodded. 'Is that so? Alright.' He turned to Malik. 'Ol' boy, I think you should go first. I'll do the filming. Do you have condoms?'

'I'm not fucking her,' Malik said. 'Maxim is.'

'Who is Maxim?' Shehu asked.

Malik looked at the picture above the bed. Shehu followed his gaze.

'The dog?' Shehu said.

'Yeah. Keep her here while I go get him.'

Malik grinned at Amaka. He turned and walked to the door, placed his hand on the handle, then turned to look back and caught Shehu's fist in his face.

Malik staggered backwards into the door. Shehu swung a kick at his face but missed as Malik slid down. Shehu launched forward and tried to grab the gun dangling from Malik's hand but Malik rolled over on the ground. He raised his weapon and Shehu ducked.

As Malik climbed to his feet, Amaka ran forward, threw her body into his stomach and brought him to the ground again. She wrapped her arms around his body and the gun fell away. He put the heel of his hand under her chin and pushed. Shehu ran to get the gun. Malik headbutted Amaka and she rolled off his body. He scampered to his feet and kicked her in the belly. She curled up on the floor. Shehu was standing with the gun in his hand, but rather than aiming at Malik, he was looking down the barrel. Malik laughed. He dashed out the door, slammed it behind him, and turned the key in the lock.

Shehu threw the gun onto the rug, tried the door handle, then knelt beside Amaka.

'Are you OK?' he asked.

Amaka looked at him.

'It was a lighter,' he said. 'I don't know if he has another weapon, but we can't take any chances. Can you get up?'

Amaka nodded. Shehu stood and offered her his hand. She took it and he helped her to her feet. She kept one hand on the side of her belly where Malik had kicked her.

'Move away from the door,' Shehu said. 'If he has a gun, he won't knock, he'll shoot.'

Shehu started to push the bed; it moved a few inches then stopped as the rug gathered beneath it.

Amaka scanned the distance between the bed and the door. 'We have to turn it over,' she said.

Lifting from either side, they flipped it over against the door. They dragged the two sofas in the room up behind it, and, breathless, they retreated to an adjacent wall and sat with their backs against it.

'Do you hear that?' Shehu said.

Amaka listened. 'Yes.' She got up and dashed to the window.

'No,' Shehu called after her.

She looked out of the window. 'He's leaving,' she said.

'What about the boy?' He turned round and sniffed. 'Do you smell that?'

Amaka turned around. She could smell it too. Behind the bed, smoke had begun seeping into the room from under the door. A fire alarm went off downstairs, and another, and another, all screaming out of sync.

90

Shehu pushed one sofa away from the bed. He covered his nose and coughed. Smoke curled into the room from under the door. 'We have to hurry,' he said, turning to Amaka. She put her hand into the front of her skirt, pushed it down, and pulled out her phone. She looked at the screen before bringing the phone up to her ear. 'Eyitayo?' she said. 'Did you get everything?'

'Amaka.' Eyitayo shouted.

'You got the address?' Amaka said.

'Yes, yes. 28B…' Eyitayo grabbed the notebook from Gabriel.

'Ayo Jagun,' Amaka said.

'What's that sound?' Eyitayo asked. 'Where are you?'

'Fire alarms. He set the house on fire. I'm upstairs in a room. He locked the door.'

'What?'

'He's getting away. He's driving a Red Mercedes ML.'

Gabriel was on the phone to Ibrahim. 'Amaka is trapped in the house,' he said. 'He set fire to it. You have to hurry.'

'No,' Amaka said, hearing the conversation down the phone line. 'Tell Ibrahim to go after Malik. I'll be fine.'

Shehu stood up. 'Who is that?' he said.

Amaka kept her eyes on him as she made another call. 'Ibrahim?' she said into the phone. '…No, I'm fine. Go after him. Don't let him get away. He killed Florentine. He confessed it. I'm in a room upstairs. I'm with Navy Commander Shehu Yaya… No, he wasn't with him. He protected me… You can ask him when you see him...We'll be fine… No, Ibrahim, don't come here. Where are you now?... By the time you get here we'll already be dead if we haven't gotten out.'

She tucked the phone into her waistband.

'Is that the police?' Shehu asked.

Amaka nodded.

'Thank you.'

'Ojo told you about the videos?' she asked.

'Videos of him with little girls. Videos that can cost him the election. Yes.'

'And he told you to get them back from me?'

'Yes. And to take care of you. He will do anything to stop you from releasing those videos. And I will do anything to make sure you release them. That animal cannot become Governor of Lagos State.' He coughed. They both looked at the smoke pouring in from under the door.

'We have to get out now,' Shehu said. He moved the bed enough to open the door.

'Stop,' Amaka said.

Shehu looked at her.

'Is it hot?'

'You're right.' He placed his hand against the door. 'No.' He wrapped his fingers round the handle, stepped back, and rammed his body against the door. It flung open and he fell out onto the corridor. Smoke poured into the room. At the end of the corridor, flames leapt up from the stairwell.

91

Sergeant Bakare was driving as fast as the police van could go. All the while Ibrahim kept his eyes on the other lane of the dual carriageway, looking out for a red Mercedes ML. He saw his Camry that Amaka had borrowed, and a Prius, both parked on the carriageway. He turned to look at the two abandoned cars as Bakare raced on.

'Get to the other side,' Ibrahim said.

They would be driving the wrong way, racing into oncoming traffic, but if they didn't – if Malik drove past them on the opposite lane – it would be near impossible to catch up with him. Bakare moved to the inside lane, ready to cross at the first opportunity. Like the rest of the officers in the vehicle, he was determined to catch the man who killed Fatima, their colleague.

A shot rang out from the back of the van. Ibrahim ducked and looked through the window in the back. The shot had been fired by Hot-Temper and the sergeant was aiming again. Another shot cracked from his weapon. On the other carriageway, a red Mercedes ML sped past. Two more shots rang out. Bakare stopped the van to give Hot-Temper a steady shot.

'Hold your fire,' Ibrahim shouted through the door, but Hot-Temper kept shooting till he had emptied his magazine, then another officer fired off a full volley after the departing ML.

Bakare did a two-point turn, caused oncoming vehicles to swerve to avoid hitting the van, then he levelled the car and screeched off, accelerating into oncoming traffic. Ibrahim braced himself at the sight of cars moving out of their path. 'Bakare, slow down!' he shouted, but the sergeant was hunched over the steering wheel, focused on the road. All the officers in the van were bent on revenge.

92

'We can't go out that way,' Shehu said. He covered his nose and waved smoke away from his face.

Amaka stood behind him in the corridor. She turned, opened the next door and went inside, then tried the next room, and the next. Back in the corridor Shehu had inched towards the flames to look down the stairs. 'Come,' she said.

Shehu followed her into the bedroom she had just come out of. She went to the window, turned and waved him over to join her. The edge of the swimming pool was visible to the left.

'Can you swim?' Amaka asked.

'I was in the Navy,' Shehu said. He slid the window open and gripped the metal burglar bars. They were too close together to squeeze through.

'The roof,' Amaka said.

She walked over to a chest of drawers at the side of the room, swept away a vase on top and the glass shattered on the ground. She shook the chest of drawers. It was solid.

Shehu bent down and interlocked his fingers to give her a boost. She took off her shoes before stepping onto his palms and he helped her onto the cabinet. Hunched down, she knocked on the ceiling. It was hollow. She braced her back against the wall and banged on the ceiling with her fist. A crack appeared. Below, on the ground, smoke seeped into the room from under the door. Shehu ran to the bed, yanked off the sheets, rolled the cloth up and jammed it along the base of the door. He returned to the chest of drawers.

'Let me try,' Shehu said. He extended his hand to Amaka and she helped him up. Hunched down, their bodies pressed against each other, they banged on the ceiling causing debris to fall from the hole. A chunk of the ceiling fell away and thick smoke poured down from the hole they had made. Coughing, they both bent down. Shehu jumped off, causing the chest of drawers to wobble. 'Get down,' he shouted. He held his hand up to her while shielding his own face from the black smoke pouring into the room.

93

Bakare swerved onto the other lane of the intersection. The van zigzagged before he regained control. He downshifted and the engine roared as the van leapt forward. The Mercedes came into view ahead of them, stuck behind two cars at a traffic light. The amber light came on and the Mercedes was still metres away.

'Don't shoot,' Ibrahim yelled. In the mirror he could see Hot-Temper bracing himself in the open back of the van and aiming his rifle at the Mercedes. 'Hot-Temper, do not shoot. It is a command.'

The light turned green and the cars ahead of the Mercedes began to move. Bakare pulled up beside the SUV and rammed the side of the van into it. The SUV swerved away. Bakare accelerated, then stopped across the road. Hot-Temper was first on the ground. He levelled his rifle at the windscreen of the SUV. By the time Ibrahim got out, pistol drawn, all the officers from the back of the van had spread out in front of the SUV and were aiming their weapons at the driver's head through the windshield.

'Put your hands up and get out,' Ibrahim shouted.

Approaching cars stopped metres behind the Mercedes. Some reversed away from the stand-off. In the Mercedes, the driver kept his hands on the steering wheel.

'Put your hands up,' Ibrahim shouted again.

A smirk spread across Malik's face as he raised his hands.

'Get out,' Ibrahim shouted. His pistol remained aimed at Malik.

'Can I put my hand down?' Malik shouted back.

'Keep your hands up and get out.'

'I need to put my hand down to open the door.'

A single shot rang from beside Ibrahim. The bullet pierced the windshield of the SUV on the passenger's side and continued through the leather seat.

Hot-Temper returned his aim to focus on Malik's head.

Keeping one hand up, Malik opened the door with his other hand and got out of the car. A phone fell out of his lap and onto the ground. He raised his hands above his head and stepped out from behind the open door.

'Get on to your knees,' Ibrahim shouted.

Malik knelt, one knee at a time, on the hot tar, and as the officers approached, the smirk on his face widened until he was grinning at the faces lined up behind a row of gun muzzles.

'Malik?' Ibrahim said, standing over their captive.

Malik shielded his face from the sun to look up into Ibrahim's face. 'Yes,' he said. 'And you are Ibrahim,' he read off Ibrahim's uniform. 'Can you be so kind as to explain what this is about?'

Ibrahim turned his pistol in his hand so that he gripped the gun by the barrel, then in a blow faster than Malik could dodge, he smashed the butt of the gun into the side of Malik's face.

94

Shehu ran to the door and grabbed the handle but he did not open it. Instead he looked down to its base, to the cloth he had rolled up and used to stop the smoke entering. Thick smoke now poured into the room from the hole in the ceiling. He let go of the door handle and searched the pockets of his trousers and the sides of his top.

Amaka climbed down from the chest of drawers. She stood and watched Shehu searching in his pockets. He looked scared. His eyes were red from the smoke. It was acrid now and tasted of plastic; of chemicals. Something dangerous was burning. The carpet? Synthetic material in some furniture? Wires? It burnt her nostrils to breathe it in. It gathered in the back of the throat where it festered and built, stealing the oxygen from every breath she took.

Shehu looked at her, continuing to search his pockets. 'Amaka,' he said. But that was all he said: her name, a complete sentence, submitting to what was to come. To the smoke. The fire. The inevitable.

'No,' Amaka said, looking at him. 'This is not how I die.'

Calmness came over her like she had never experienced. With smoke clinging to her hair like mist, alarms screaming from behind the closed door, and Shehu panicking right before her, her senses became sharper than ever. She saw everything as it would happen, and she felt it all: the abrasiveness of the mattress against her fingers as she gripped its edges; its weight as she lifted it; the heat of the flames when they opened the door; the bursting pain in her chest from holding her breath through it all.

'Come,' she said.

She went to the far side of the mattress and began to lift it. Shehu lifted from the other side. He didn't ask why. They heaved the mattress on to its side, and moved it to the door. She knew it had to be heavy but it didn't feel so. There they held it steady while Amaka swiped away the cloth at the base with her leg. Smoke rushed in from under the door and she swallowed a gulp of air and held it in her mouth. She poked her head round the mattress to look at Shehu who was holding his breath as well. Then she gripped the handle, turned and pushed.

The sound of the fire was like hissing snakes slithering over gravel. Together they forced the mattress out onto the burning carpet and let it drop length-wise onto the flames. In a puff, they had gained some ground. They lifted the mattress to its full length. It smouldered from a fresh coat of black soot. They dropped it again, fighting the flames towards the stairs. They lifted again, and dropped it again, and they got closer to the flames leaping up from the staircase. Just then a forceful swoosh of white smoke blew up from the stairwell and engulfed the entire corridor. They couldn't see a thing. They dropped onto the mattress and crouched, coughing, choking, flames behind them, a thick cloud of smoke around them, the edges of the mattress beginning to burn.

95

Two men pulled Malik to his feet. He touched his bloodied mouth and winced. The officers shackled him with rusty handcuffs. Another bent down by the open door of the Mercedes and picked up the phone that had dropped onto the floor. He took it to Ibrahim. Sergeant Hot-Temper continued to aim at Malik's head.

Ibrahim looked at the phone. 'Who did you call?' he asked.

Malik sniggered. He looked around at the officers aiming their weapons at him and smiled at each of them. He winked at Hot-Temper.

'Put him in the front,' Ibrahim said.

Two officers pushed Malik into the police van. Ibrahim got in after him and the rest of the officers climbed into the back. Bakare did not look at Malik as he turned the van to face the queue of vehicles that had formed ahead on the road. He drove the wrong way a while, then, when he could, he turned onto the other carriageway and carried on the Lekki-Epe Expressway.

'Where are you taking me?' Malik said. He brought his hands to his face to catch blood dripping from his mouth.

Ibrahim stared straight ahead.

'You're making a big mistake,' Malik said, gurgling a mix of saliva and blood. 'You haven't told me what you're arresting me for.'

Malik looked from Ibrahim to Bakare and back.

'Look, guys, I really don't want to get you into trouble. Let us talk and settle this thing, whatever it is. I can make it all worth your while. I will give you one hundred K each.'

They rode in silence, passing the Lekki Phase 1 roundabout.

'Look, I can make you people rich. All of you. Two hundred K each.'

'Sharap!' Ibrahim yelled at the top of his voice.

Bakare glanced at his boss and continued driving.

96

Shehu gasped, making a wheezing sound as he struggled to breathe. Next to him, also plastered to the smouldering mattress, Amaka coughed. The smoke was so thick that they couldn't see each other.

Another swoosh and a gust of white smoke blew over their backs and cooled their exposed necks.

'Is anybody there?' a voice shouted.

Swoosh. A fire extinguisher ate up the flames clinging to the ceiling along the corridor. Swoosh. Swoosh.

'Yes!' both Amaka and Shehu shouted back. They stood and spread their hands out into the white cloud.

A tall man in khaki shorts, his lean muscular body glistening with sweat, led Amaka and Shehu down a charred staircase and out of the building past men rushing in with fire extinguishers. The gate was wide open. A dog barked in the background. Everywhere there were people tackling the blaze, breaking windows to pour water onto the flames. A woman kneeling at the edge of the swimming pool was scooping water into pails and passing them to a chain of people that extended into the building. More people with fire extinguishers rushed in through the gates: housemaids, gatemen, gardeners, children, and the homeowners of the neighbourhood. The siren of a fire engine grew louder from down the road.

The tall man led Amaka and Shehu onto the road where people surrounded them. Someone brought plastic chairs but Amaka stood. Shehu sat and took a full blast of water in the face from an old lady with grey cornrows. With water from the plastic bowl in her hand, she wiped sweat and soot from Shehu's face.

All around them people were talking and asking questions.

'Madam, is anybody else in the house?' the man who had led them out asked.

'No. Nobody,' Amaka said.

Shehu coughed. The old lady sprinkled more water on his face, backing away from the road to make way for the fire engine.

'My driver will take you to the hospital,' the woman said. 'You, you look familiar,' she said to Amaka. What is your name?'

'Mrs. Bakare, you don't remember me? I'm Amaka, Emma's friend.'

'I thought I recognised you,' the lady said. 'What happened? What were you doing in that house?'

That house, Amaka thought.

Shehu coughed.

'We need to get him to the hospital,' Amaka said, looking into Shehu's eyes. 'He's asthmatic.'

Shehu continued coughing into his hand while the driver hurried off to fetch his madam's car.

'I know about your asthma,' Amaka said in the back of a speeding 1980 Mercedes S-Class.

'How?' Shehu asked.

Amaka looked at her phone, which had started vibrating, as she answered Shehu. 'After I saw you in Ojo's suite at Eko hotel, I found out everything I could about you.'

'Ojo.' Shehu shook his head. 'You need to release those videos. You need to make sure he doesn't have a chance in hell of becoming governor.'

Amaka held her phone out. 'I will do whatever it takes. Listen, I need to take this call. It's urgent.'

Shehu nodded.

'Ibrahim,' Amaka said. 'Yes, yes, I got out. Did you get him?'

She closed her eyes, took in a deep breath and exhaled 'OK. Listen, I'm on my way to Oshodi. Remember Chioma?... Yes. Her ex-boyfriend asked her to meet him there.... Yes, the person responsible for her brother's death.' She turned to Shehu. 'I need your keys.'

'What?'

'Your car keys. I need to be somewhere and it's urgent.'

'My keys?' Shehu began searching his pockets. 'Why?'

'I bashed my car into the back of his. I need a car the police won't stop.'

'Oh. I get it now. But, shouldn't you get checked out at the hospital at least?'

'No, I'm fine. You go to the hospital; I need to get to Oshodi. A girl's life is at risk.'

Amaka caught the elderly driver's eyes looking at her in the mirror. He'd been listening. 'Madam said I should take you to her hospital,' the man said.

Amaka leaned forward and wrapped her hand around the headrest of the passenger seat in front. 'Sir,' she said to the driver, 'our cars are on Ozumba Mbadiwe. You can drop me and take him to the hospital, but you have to drive faster than this.'

The old man searched for Shehu's face in the mirror.

'You heard her,' Shehu said. He turned to Amaka. 'You'll explain later, abi?' He handed her the keys to his wife's Prius.

The driver floored the throttle and the 1980s V6 engine responded with a growl that thrust the two-tonne limousine forward as if it had been at standstill all along.

97

Ibrahim stepped out and his boots sank into sand. The police van was in the middle of a long, straight, narrow road. Mature vegetation grew wild on either side and there were no houses.

'Get out,' Ibrahim said to Malik.

Bakare reached inside and Malik shimmied over and got out through the other door. Ibrahim led him by the arm to the front of the van where the officers formed a circle around them. A cloud of bats flew overhead. The men looked up till the last of the mammals had disappeared over the trees on the other side of the road.

'I will give each of you five hundred thousand naira if you let me go,' Malik said.

The officers stared at him. Nobody spoke.

'One million each,' Malik said. He turned, looking into each officer's face. 'All of you.' He continued turning in the circle. 'I am very rich. I have very powerful friends. I will give each of you ten million naira. Ten million for you, ten million for you, ten million for you.' He faced Ibrahim and pointed at him. 'Just shoot him. Ten million naira for each of you, if you shoot him now. And ten million extra for the person who shoots him first.' His finger remained pointed at Ibrahim. The men stared into each other's eyes.

98

From the bridge, Amaka saw smoke rising from the road. She turned off to descend into Oshodi. A crowd was ahead on the road, moving between cars, wielding sticks and stopping motorists.

'Oh no,' Amaka whispered leaning over the steering wheel. She had seen this before; the sweating, half-naked young men; the spectators lining the sides of the road, standing on the kerb, hands in the air, taking pictures and recording videos on their phones. The men surrounded her car. She revved the engine. Some turned to look at her; one banged on her bonnet. She tucked her phone into her skirt and opened the door; someone ran into it as it swung open.

Gripping the top of the window that had caught him in the chest, a lanky young man bent down and scowled at Amaka. She stared back at him and he hissed, let go of the door, and walked away into the crowd.

Amaka put one leg out onto the road. She stood behind the open door and watched the gathering mob. In their midst, black smoke rose in a spiral. In the air, a familiar smell. She stepped out, closed the door, and walked into the crowd.

99

Malik turned in a circle in the middle of the officers. They all stared at him.

'Take me to a bank and I will withdraw the money for you,' he said. 'Just shoot him.' Wherever he turned, he continued pointing at Ibrahim.

Silence.

'Are you done?' Ibrahim said. 'Who were the people on the bridge? I need their names and how to find them.'

'Shoot him,' Malik shouted. His smirk vanished.

'Who were the people shooting from the bridge?' Ibrahim asked again.

Malik lowered his hand. He looked at the blank faces of the officers staring back at him. 'I don't know what you're talking about,' he said. 'Will someone shoot this man and become rich or what?'

'Fati. Police superintendent Fatima Alao. That is the person who was in Amaka's car. The person you murdered. Our colleague. Our sister. One of us.'

With his hands behind his back, Hot-Temper stepped into the circle. Malik turned to face him. Turning his back to Malik, Hot-Tempet stepped past him and swung around. Malik yelled out, raised his left leg and grabbed it with both hands. Blood seeped through his fingers. He looked at Hot-Temper, searching for the blade that had cut him, but the sergeant's hands were behind his back.

100

Amaka pushed through the crowd. She squeezed past two men and felt fingers grip her butt. She stopped. Anger surged through her and she formed a fist. This was not the time.

She pushed on, continuing through the throng of people between her and the fire; the body sizzled and popped, and that all-too familiar smell of burning flesh and rubber was thick in the air and impossible not to inhale. At the front, she watched as someone flung another tyre on top of the body that was covered in steel belts from tyres that had already melted away. Another shirtless man sprayed petrol from a water bottle. The flames leapt. The crowd retreated. The fire glowed on the faces of the guilty. Their victim's hand was visible under the burning rubber; black like coal. Flames wrapped around fingers that had charred into a claw.

A young boy was recording the scene with his phone next to Amaka. She grabbed hold of his hand. 'What happened?' she asked.

The boy looked at her and then at his hand in her grip. He tried to pull away, but she held tight. 'What happened?' she asked again and tugged, tightening her grip. He looked her up and down, as if weighing her status or authority.

'Na thief,' he said.

'What happened?'

'He snatch that woman gold chain,' he said and pointed.

Amaka followed his finger. On the other side of the burning body, standing behind the people watching and filming, Amaka saw who he was pointing at: Chioma, staring back at her, face blank, hair dishevelled, eyes cold.

101

Malik bled from the cut and he turned to look at his assailant.

With his hands behind him, Hot-Temper continued to circle.

Malik kept turning, keeping his eyes on the sergeant. Without missing a step, Hot-Temper bent to the ground, almost kneeling before rising to his feet again. Malik cried out and fell to the ground, blood staining his trousers from a straight four-inch tear across his right calf.

Hot-Temper stood with his hands behind his back again; and again Malik didn't see the blade that caught him.

'Names and addresses,' Ibrahim said.

Laying on his side in the sand, curled into a foetal position, his hands over his bleeding wounds, Malik squeezed his eyes at the pain. 'Fuck you,' he shouted, spittle shooting from his mouth.

'Names and addresses.'

'Fuck you. I don't know who they are.'

'Cut him,' Ibrahim said.

Hot-Temper brought his hands forward from behind his back. In his hand he held a dagger. From the ground Malik looked at the blade that had inflicted his wounds. Hot-Temper stepped forward. Malik grabbed the sand and pulled himself away. Then he raised his hand. 'Wait.'

Ibrahim held his hand up and Hot-Temper stopped.

Malik crawled further from the sergeant and closer to Ibrahim. 'Wait,' he repeated.

'Go on,' Ibrahim said.

Malik heaved himself up till he was sitting up, his injured legs stretched out before him. He bent over, wiped sand off his fingers and reached forward to touch the skin around his wounds. He shut his eyes and winced.

'You are wasting my time,' Ibrahim said.

'OK. OK. What happens after I tell you?'

'You have been arrested by the Nigerian police on suspicion of culpability in the murder of a police officer. After you tell us what we want to know, we will take you to the station where you will be formally charged. I will personally call your lawyer or whoever you want to come and bail you for the amount of money you have offered me and my colleagues today.'

'So you will take my money?'

'Yes. For bail.'

Malik sniggered. 'For bail. What if I don't have the names?'

'Then you will not be eligible for bail and your case will go to court.'

'OK. I don't have *names*. I have *a* name.'

'I'm listening.'

'It was meant to be Amaka in the car. Someone wanted to know where she was. I told them. I didn't know they would try to kill her. And I didn't know your colleague would be in her car instead of her.'

'So you made a call.'

'Yes.'

'Who did you call?'

Malik looked Ibrahim in the eye. He looked down and shook his head before he answered. 'Otunba Oluawo. You need to keep me alive if you want me to testify in court.'

'You already did.' Ibrahim said. He nodded at a female police officer. She was holding her phone to Malik. Recording.

She pressed a button on the screen and the video played back. From the tiny speakers came Malik's voice: 'It was meant to be Amaka in the car...'

Ibrahim stepped back. 'Now we send you to hell,' he said.

'You motherfucker,' Malik shouted. He looked around at the officers. 'You fucking motherfuckers. You're all going to die poor. You stupid motherfucking bastards. Take the fucking money and let me go. Otunba Oluawo killed your colleague, not me.' The officers backed away. 'Did you hear me? Oluawo killed your fucking colleague. I didn't even know her. Fuck her. Fuck you. Fuck all of you. You will all die poor, you fucking illiterate fucking fools.'

The officers formed an arc around him and racked their weapons, the sliding and locking of metal the only sound on the deserted road. Ibrahim stood at one end, his sub-machine gun by his side.

Malik looked around at the faces gathered in a line in front of him, their guns ready to take his life, and he began to laugh. 'Fucking illiterates,' he said. He laughed from his belly.

102

Across from the circle of murderers, their victim burning in the middle, Amaka and Chioma stared at each other. The crowd heaved while the body crackled and dripped burning fat.

The boy who pointed Chioma out melted into the crowd and Amaka stood alone in the midst of killers and accomplices, her mind in a swirl that drowned out the noises and blurred everything except Chioma standing unapologetically on the other side.

Amaka wanted to look at the body, at the kill, but she kept her eyes locked on Chioma, as if there was a danger of losing her; as if Chioma would merge with the crowd and become as faceless as the other killers.

Chioma began to move, edging her way through the bodies. Her eyes and Amaka's remained locked. Amaka moved with her on the other side, pushing her way through, then she turned, and with her shoulders and her elbows, she cut a path through the crowd.

Amaka stepped out of the mass and walked to the Prius. She got into the driver's seat and closed the door, shutting out the fumes and muffling the noise.

Chioma broke through the crowd and the two women looked at each other through the windscreen. Chioma climbed in the passenger side, shut the door, folded her hands across her body, and stared out of her window.

Amaka sat in silence, watching, but Chioma kept staring out the window. Amaka texted Ibrahim: 'I was wrong. Chioma didn't come to Oshodi. She's not here. She was never here.' She clicked send and looked at Chioma, then inserted the key in the ignition. 'You realise you're now a murderer,' she said.

Amaka pulled out onto the road, used her horn to clear a path in the crowd, then turned around and drove the wrong way like other motorists were doing to avoid the inconvenience of the lynching.

103

Ibrahim felt a vibration against his leg, reached into his pocket and pulled out his phone. He looked at the screen and then back at the officers standing in silence, their guns pointed at Malik laughing on the ground and bleeding into the sand.

Ibrahim turned round and walked away. He answered the call, listened to the voice on the other end, and nodded. 'Yes, sir,' he said. He placed the device back in his pocket and returned to the line of officers, walked past them, and stood in front of Malik.

Ibrahim looked down at Malik laughing like he had lost his mind. He removed Malik's phone from his pocket and threw it down at the laughing man. It missed Malik's head. Ibrahim spat on the wounded man's face, shutting him up.

'We are leaving,' Ibrahim said through gritted teeth. He turned to his officers. 'We are leaving him here. Let's go.'

They neither budged nor lowered their guns.

'Get into the car. We are leaving. It is an order,' Ibrahim shouted.

Hot-Temper stepped forward, his AK47 still trained on Malik who had gone silent and was watching with as much surprise as the other officers. 'Oga, na who phone you?' the sergeant asked.

'It doesn't matter. We are leaving him here. Let's go.'

Hot-Temper jumped in front of Ibrahim and levelled his gun at his superior's head.

'Hot-Temper!' Ibrahim shouted but the sergeant wasn't looking at him. Ibrahim turned to see one of the officers pointing his weapon at the back of his head. Hot-Temper's weapon was aimed at the man's face. One by one the officers took sides with their weapons, Ibrahim in the middle, Malik behind them all, laughing maniacally.

104

Amaka placed her knife and fork on the empty plate, stained red from the rare steak she'd just finished. She drank the remainder of her Coke, picked the napkin from her lap and dabbed her lips. Her date, the Lagos State gubernatorial candidate, was standing by her side in white agbada and blue hat. He held her purse. She looked up and smiled. He offered his hand and she let him help her up and he waited as she straightened her blouse. Then as she reached for her purse, he slid a hand round her back and pulled her close to his body. Her hands went up around his neck and she closed her eyes as his lips touched hers. She slid one hand down his back and pushed the fingers of her other hand into his hair beneath his hat. Their heads alternated directions as their lips remained locked and their tongues entwined.

They kept kissing, their hands exploring each other's bodies, until someone started clapping and all the other diners in the restaurant joined in, clapping and cheering. Still in Babalola's embrace, Amaka looked about. Children, parents, couples, waiters and waitresses, were beaming at them; some were taking pictures and recording the little tryst on their mobile phones. She sank her face into his neck and he patted the back of her head.

Babalola waved as they left the restaurant, his right hand

over Amaka's shoulder, her left hand on his back, a 24-carat Tiffany diamond sparkling from her ring finger.

———

Ambrose looked at the pictures on a tablet. Amaka sat beside him on the sofa.

'You did your part of the deal,' he said. 'Now I'll do mine. I just don't understand why it is so important for you to still do this. You have already done more than enough to earn my trust.'

'Because I cannot afford for Ojo to become Governor of Lagos State,' Amaka said.

Ambrose nodded. 'And you do not trust us to carry out our own rigging?'

'A wise man once told me that rigging is a leaky business. Every naira spent must count. All I'm asking is that I be a part of it. Call it monitoring. To make sure Ojo doesn't win.'

'And to make sure you know our secrets and you can use them against us. Or if we do win, to play the 'I did my part to win this election' card and demand favours from us.'

'I don't want any favours, and I'm not gathering secrets to use against you or Babalola. I'll be complicit in whatever criminal activities I witness. You said it was important for me to compromise myself to gain your trust. Well, I will be doing just that.'

'I know, and that is what bothers me. You are assured of our protection, you have already done us a great service, you can ask for anything, but you ask for this, why?'

'Oga Ambrose, you just have to trust me.'

'Me myself, I trust you, but it is my mind that does not trust you. Don't take it personally, but I do not trust anyone; even the people I trust.'

Ambrose placed the tablet on the cushion between them and lay back on the sofa.

'There are many ways to rig an election,' he said.

105

'Every registered voter has a voting card. On the day of the election, they go to their polling stations to be accredited. During the accreditation process, an official uses a card reader to check their biometric data. If this is fine, the voter goes to another official who checks for their name on the voters' register sent to the polling station and he ticks it off. The voter's hand is then imprinted with indelible ink and they can return later to cast their vote.

'At each polling station there will be INEC officials, opposition agents, international observers in some cases, ad-hoc staff working for INEC, and supporters of each party, not to mention soldiers and police. The opposition agents will be watching you closely, and they know what to look out for because they are doing it too. The days of snatching ballot boxes are over. We have to be more creative.

'Rigging starts long before the election. It all starts with the polling stations. There are some remote, unknown polling stations. Some of them are in people's bedrooms. You can do whatever you want there. We have some; the opposition also has their own.

'One of the first things to do is to reduce the votes of your opponent. You do this by buying voter cards from the opposition's registered voters.'

'How will you know they are opposition voters?'

'Simple. You go to their strong base.'

Amaka sat in the middle of a shallow, narrow, carved-out

canoe. Behind her, the single oar in the hands of a young boy in tattered brown shorts, dipped into the inky black water of Makoko. Dirty plastic waste bubbled around them in hilly masses that stretched for metres. Sitting inches away from the water, the stench of the lagoon - excrement, decay, and death – was suffocating. Behind, another canoe ferried a party official; a thirty-something-year-old man with both his hands resting upon a twelve-gauge shotgun on his lap. Ahead, standing on the edges of wooden shacks on stilts, dozens of men and women, children and adults, held up their voting cards waiting to exchange them for a portion of the money in the bag in Amaka's lap.

'Next is the ad-hoc staff. INEC recruits them from the ordinary citizenry. Anyone can apply. On Election Day, it is the ad-hoc staff that will cause commotion, do abracadabra, and dabaru everything if need be.

'When illiterate voters ask for help identifying their choice, the ad-hoc staff will show them who to thumbprint. You want to buy as many ad-hoc staff as possible from as many polling stations as possible. The opposition will also be buying them, and they will collect money from both of you; you just have to figure out a way to pay more than them without paying too much.'

'How do we do this?' Amaka asked.

In a hot room with unpainted walls and closed wooden shutters, three men in Ankara sat on a low, narrow bench. They fanned their faces with folded newspapers wet with sweat and disintegrating where they held them.

In the sweltering, dusty room, Moses stood in front of the men. He was fixated on the shotguns on the laps of the ones who flanked the one in the middle. An Ankara curtain over the door behind Moses blocked out the rest of the queue waiting their turn in the sun. Moses presented his papers to the man in the middle of the bench - the one with a beer carton of cash in front of him.

The man took the paper, glanced at it, turned it round, and returned it. Moses folded his document along its existing lines and returned it into the breast pocket of his chequered yellow short-sleeved shirt. The man dipped his hand into the box, counted off some notes from a wad of thousands and held the money out to Moses. Moses in turn looked at what was offered, then gazed at the wall to his left.

The man kept his hand and the money up for a moment, then he put his hand back into the box and counted out more thousand naira notes and held the thicker offering up to Moses.

Moses looked down at the man's hand. The men with the gun looked at him.

'Fifty K,' Moses said.

The man in the middle rested the money on his leg. 'We are paying twenty-five,' he said.

'The other party are paying forty,' Moses shot back.

'Go and join them,' the man said, and threw the cash onto the pile in the box.

'Forty-five,' Moses said.

'Are you still here?'

The ones with guns straightened their backs.

Moses swallowed. A bead of sweat ran down the side of his face by his ear, curved under his chin, trickled down his neck, and straight down the middle of his chest. 'Forty or nothing,' he said.

The man in the middle and his armed guards all stared at Moses. Moses did not move.

'Thirty, or leave,' the man said.

Moses turned.

'Wait.'

Moses stopped. He listened to money being counted.

'Take.'

Moses turned around to even more money being held up to him.

'Forty. But don't tell anyone how much I gave you,' the man said.

Moses took the money and tucked it down the front of his trousers. He turned and left, letting blinding sunshine into the hut as he parted the curtain.

He walked past the row of men mopping their faces and necks with handkerchiefs that had become transparent with sweat. The line was kept straight and orderly by men holding shotguns and pacing about. When he had passed the last of the ad-hoc staff waiting to sell their loyalty, Moses sent a message on his phone.

Amaka pulled back the dusty curtain that had once been white. The mosquito net beneath it was thick with dust. Her nostrils twitched. Outside, under the brilliance of the midday sun, a long silent row of people had formed, stretching from around the corner of a similar bungalow whose yellow walls had chipped and faded, across the narrow once-upon-a-time tarred road, to the door to the house.

She let go of the curtain to read the message that had just made her mobile buzz. '40K.' She tucked the mobile into the edge of her skirt and went to the middle of the room where there was a carved wooden stool, about a foot high, between two men standing with AK-47 assault rifles. A large, black Nike travel bag lay in front of the stool. She sat down, unzipped the bag, and spread it open to reveal the cash.

'Let them in,' she said.

'Now, this is more risky. We will also get the voting forms in advance. We thumbprint thousands overnight and stuff them into ballot boxes. Now, listen carefully; this is very important. Every polling station only has five hundred registered voters. When we are filling our ballot boxes, we cannot fill them with more than five hundred votes. And even then, we cannot give ourselves all the votes. Remember this.

The difficulty is how to switch the boxes with the original ones from the polling booths. There are ways, but at the end of the day it boils down to money. You have to bribe everyone at the ward, from INEC officials to soldiers, to opposition agents.

'Lastly, and we only do this as a last resort, if all else has failed and our permutations indicate that we are losing...'

'Permutations?'

'Yes. We do our own exit poll. We will keep a tally of all the centres where we've been successful at manipulating the vote. If we see that we are losing a ward that we should be winning, maybe the opposition have gained advantage over us, we just dabaru everything. Stabbing, shooting, burning, bombing. We stop voting at that centre and make sure they do not take any voting materials away. We burn everything there.'

106

The night before the election.

Someone had fitted the ceiling fan directly over the only light bulb in the room. With every oscillation of the fan, flickering shadows swept over the people, the boxes, and the surfaces cramped with ballot papers. Outside in the night, generators with various capacities rumbled from different distances, and the wind, on occasion, carried the cymbals and singing of a Pentecostal church's night vigil.

Amaka stood by the closed door, her back against the wall, and fanned her wet face with a campaign flyer. Before her, sitting or kneeling on the floor, sharing the edges of a stool or standing over a table, were women of varying ages, all pressing their thumbs into blue ink pads and onto blank ballot papers. Other women gathered the thumb-printed papers and stuffed them into ballot boxes marked with the INEC insignia.

Amaka's phone buzzed. It had been in her hand all night. She looked at the screen and answered.

'Amaka, where are you?'

Amaka kept her eyes on the old women pressing their thumbs onto ballot papers. 'Where I should be, Ambrose,' she said.

'We have been compromised. DSS has picked up ten of our men.'

'Where?'

'Where they should be. Someone must have tipped them off.'

'And the material?'

'Nothing will happen. They are working for the other party. They will keep our men till elections are over. Someone has given the names and the movements of our people. They are simply neutralising our assets. You might have been compromised too. You have to leave where you are, now.'

'How many people do we have?'

'Doing what you are doing?'

'Yes.'

'Fourteen. Fifteen.'

'And ten have been arrested.'

'Detained. They will be released without charge.'

'Only you know my name and location. If ten of us have been detained, it makes the job of the remaining five even more important.'

'I am not the only one that knows your name and location. Just like you, the others may know where we sent material tonight. Someone within has compromised us.'

'But if I'm detained, I'll be released without charge. It's a risk I'm willing to take.'

'No. Not you. Your father's name will make you a big catch for the government. You can't risk it. Get out, now.'

Amaka tucked the phone in her skirt and looked around. The women, none of whom spoke English, continued thumb printing and stuffing INEC ballot boxes. An old woman with grey cornrows was holding a ballot box steady as another pushed folded ballot papers into it. She looked up at Amaka and gave a toothless smile, her face glistening with sweat.

107

Election day.

The white Toyota bus had stopped at a checkpoint with police officers and soldiers in camouflage gear, nets stretched over their helmets. In the back seat of the vehicle, Amaka took a call from Ambrose.

'Amaka, we are losing badly. We need the material in your car.'

'How will I deliver it?'

'Go to Sule's ward. Park and walk away from the vehicle. He will provide another one for you.'

A soldier knocked on Amaka's window. She held up the observer card on the lanyard around her neck. The soldier's smooth black face cocooned within his helmet was the face of a boy; he must have been twenty or younger. He leaned in to take a closer look at the card then turned to other occupants. The driver kept his hand on the steering wheel; the woman in the seat beside him was also holding up her own observer card, as was the man in the row behind them. In the back row, three men in orange vests sat shoulder to shoulder. The one in the middle had a camera around his neck. They all held up badges that read: PRESS. The young soldier walked round the car looking in through the windows, then banged on the boot of the van. The driver moved his hand to the door handle. Amaka placed her hand on his shoulder to stop him. 'He means we can go,' she said.

The driver looked at her, then in his mirror for the soldier and saw that he had turned his back to them.

As they pulled away, Amaka watched the soldiers in the rear-view mirror. The one who inspected the interior hadn't noticed how the men in the back criss-crossed their legs to hide the fact that the floor was higher than it should be.

The bus stopped next to some other cars that were parked between two bungalows where voters lined up in the middle of a sandy field surrounded by abandoned classroom blocks. Soldiers and police officers stood around. Amaka got out, followed by the others. They gathered by the side of the vehicle. A group of soldiers watched them. In the middle of the field, on both sides of those waiting to cast their ballot, soldiers, INEC officials, observers, and police officers stood in groups, talking and mopping sweat from their foreheads, and watched the voters. Some of the officials and most of the voters held umbrellas over their heads - umbrellas with Chief Ojo's smiling face on them.

'Did you leave the key in the ignition?' Amaka asked.

The driver nodded.

Staring ahead, Amaka said, 'Now, we all walk away.'

She looked down at the card hanging from her lanyard, spun it around so it showed her face and the word OBSERVER in bold, then she pulled her sunglasses from her blouse and put them on. She walked straight ahead. The soldiers parted for her. She kept her head high and continued walking as the military men watched her bum from behind.

108

Election night.

Ambrose's living room heaved with party officials, many on their phones, talking or listening, pacing the room. The few men and women who were talking to each other were doing so in hushed voices, as though they were at a funeral. Babalola was alone on a sofa, his face glistening. He tried to listen to the conversations around him and attempted to read the lips of people chatting to each other across the room. His eyes darted from person to person, often returning to Ambrose who was dwarfed by two men whispering into his ears and showing him things on their mobile phones.

A large man in Ankara entered the parlour and looked about. He made his way over to Ambrose who raised his hand so the man speaking into his ear would pause. 'Oga,' the fat man said, 'Iná ti jó wa. We have been burnt.' He showed his phone to Ambrose.

Ambrose flicked his finger over the screen and looked up. Babalola was looking at him.

'Sule, Sule, Sule,' Ambrose said. 'Didn't you use the ballot papers from Amaka?'

'Oga, I delivered them myself. In fact, only the one meant for Banana Island is remaining in the car.'

'So what happened? The INEC boys betrayed us?'

'Oga, I don't know what happened o.'

'You said there is still one box?'

''Is inside the car.'

'Bring it.'

Sule left. Ambrose and Babalola stared at each other.

Otunba Oluawo was alone in the middle of his sofa. Everyone in the large parlour of Peace Lodge was on their feet, shaking hands, embracing, rubbing their hands in thanks to the Christian and Muslim God and to the several other gods they had prayed to and made sacrifices to. They clapped with each new set of results that came in through text messages and phone calls. Ojo was in the middle of the jubilant crowd. Shehu stood next to him. Declarations of 'His Excellency,' and 'My Governor,' preceded every handshake slapped onto Ojo's palm by people who seemed to think it important to seize his forearm before shaking hands with him.

Alone on his sofa, Otunba scribbled in a little notebook. A man in white buba and sokoto came up to him and told him the results of yet another ward. Otunba wrote the new figure in his notepad and looked up. In the room full of celebrations, he was the only person not celebrating.

Sule returned carrying the INEC ballot box high over his head. Everybody watched. Sule placed the box down at Ambrose's feet.

'Open it,' Ambrose said.

Sule bent down, broke the INEC seal and flipped the lid over. The box was stuffed to the brim with folded ballot papers. Ambrose gestured. Sule grabbed a handful in his large palms and held them up.

The men and women watched as Ambrose went through the papers.

Still holding one in his hand, he looked up. 'Where is she?' he said. 'Where is Amaka?'

'I don't know,' Sule said.

'What is the matter?' Babalola asked. Ambrose handed him the ballot paper in his hand and took another from a new handful Sule had fetched.

Ambrose fell to his knees behind the ballot box and began picking ballot paper after ballot paper, unfolding them and scanning them before flinging them away. Faster and faster he went through the ballot papers, his face contorting more and more. He looked up. Sule retreated.

'Where is she? Who is watching her? Find her. Find her now!'

109

The departure hall of Murtala Muhammad International airport was full and the air-conditioning inadequate. A tall, stocky man with deep-set eyes, in the brown agbada and walking with a limp, moved through the crowd of passengers and their families. He got close to the rope barrier separating the crowd from the Air France passengers. He could have moved even closer but he would risk being spotted. He had seen her once at the house; perhaps she had seen him too and she could recognise him.

Amaka checked the time as she leaned out of the Air France queue. There were at least forty people ahead of her, and there appeared to be two lines side-by-side heading to the same place. The official passport checks seemed to be taking longer with each sweaty, impatient traveller. There was nobody in the priority check-in section. She stepped out of the line and headed that way.

'Ticket and passport, please,' an Air France official asked. Amaka showed the man her phone screen. He squinted then looked up. 'This line is for upper class,' he said.

Amaka nodded and remained where she was.

'Your ticket is economy,' he said.

'Yes,' Amaka said. She began searching in her handbag.

'Madam,' the man said.

Amaka retrieved a white envelope from her bag. She held it long enough for him to see the Nigerian coat of arms on it, then she removed the piece of paper inside.

'It's from the Nigerian Foreign Ministry,' she said. 'It says anyone reading it must treat me the same as they would diplomatic staff.'

The man turned his head, trying to read the letter.

'Can you let me through now?' she said. 'I need to do some shopping for my boss in duty-free.'

The man reached for the letter just as Amaka folded it and returned it to the envelope.

'Can I see your passport?' he asked, holding out his hand.

Amaka looked in her handbag again and produced a letter from yet another envelope. 'Emergency travel documents,' she said.

'Please, wait,' he said and turned to his colleague.

'What's the problem?' Amaka asked.

'Please, madam,' the man said, 'just exercise patience.'

'I will if you tell me how to.'

'What?'

'What am I waiting for?' She checked the time and looked around at the crowd. She couldn't shake the feeling that she was being followed.

Ambrose stood up, clutches of ballot papers in his hands. He opened his fingers and let the pieces of paper fall to the ground. 'They are all for the other party,' he said. 'Every last one of them.'

Sule looked at the remaining ballot papers in his own hand then he also opened one up. Other people were picking up ballot papers from the floor, inspecting them, and passing them around. Everybody looked shocked or confused. Babalola looked constipated.

'What does this mean?' Babalola asked, holding a ballot paper in his hand.

'What does it mean?' Ambrose said. Both men looked at each other and said nothing. 'She was working for them,' someone said.

Ambrose turned to Sule. 'What was the count at Ilupeju again?'

Sule retrieved his phone from his trousers and began clicking away at its screen.

'Show me,' Ambrose said. 'You have the rest?'

Sule nodded. He scrolled down and handed the phone to Ambrose. The lights went out. In the darkness of the power failure, the glow from the phone in Ambrose's hand illuminated his face, and as he scrolled, the deep furrows of his frown smoothed out until his face went blank. His party had lost almost every ward. The corners of his lips began to curl. His frown became a grin and then he broke into uncontrollable laughter.

'He has gone mad,' a young party member in a campaign T-shirt whispered to his mate next to him.

Meanwhile, in the jubilant parlour in Peace Lodge, the man in white returned to Otunba with more results. He smiled as he announced the numbers of yet another ward won, then he stood and read the results to the rest of the room while Otunba wrote in his notebook.

Otunba looked up at the jubilant crowd and shifted in his chair. He looked at his book again, then he looked up. His eyes began to bulge with panic. He struggled to get up. The man in white lent him a hand. As he stood from the sofa, the notebook and the pen fell from his hands. A sharp pain shot up his left hand. He grabbed his chest. The man in white tried to catch the old man. Otunba's head shot upwards and his entire body curved outwards. The man in white thrust his hands around the old man. Otunba fell, still gripping his chest.

The man in the brown agbada moved closer to Amaka. He edged his way to stand next to the rope barrier. He half turned his body away and pretended to search on his phone as he listened. She was causing trouble. It could make things easier or worse for him, depending on what he was asked to do. His phone vibrated. He brought it up to his ear and cupped his hand over his mouth.

'Madam, what seems to be the problem?' a different Air France staff member asked Amaka.

'None, whatsoever,' Amaka said, smiling. 'The gentleman is just making sure my emergency travel documents are genuine. He's just doing his job.'

The man took the papers from his colleague. 'What about your ticket?' he said.

Amaka fetched her phone, opened up the e-ticket and held the phone up for the man to see.

'I tried to check-in online but…'

'You won't be able to do it unless you have a passport.'

He looked at the phone again, scanning through the screen, then he returned to the documents in his hands. 'You lost your passport?' he said.

'Yes. Along with phones, money, everything in my handbag. They broke into my car.'

'Oh, sorry, madam,' he said, gesturing to his colleague to let Amaka through.

The man unhooked the rope barrier. As Amaka stepped through, she felt compelled to look behind her. On the other side of the rope barrier, a square-headed man in a brown agbada was staring at her. His phone was pressed to his ear. She hurried towards the only free counter, but a family beat her to it. She looked back and scanned the hall. The square-headed man was gone.

Sule lowered the phone from his ear.

'She's at the airport,' he said. 'Samson is looking at her now. What do you want him to do?'

Ambrose patted his chest to stop himself laughing, wiping tears from his face with his thumb.

'Where is she going?'

Sule relayed the question into his phone, then took the phone away from his ear again.

'She's checking in at the Air France counter. Should Samson tell customs that he has information she's carrying cocaine in her bag?'

The woman at the check-in counter next to Amaka placed her check-in luggage on the conveyor. Behind her, a man at the economy class queue was already stepping forward. The couple ahead of Amaka had several bags. She stepped out and stood behind the woman whose bag was being weighed.

'Madam, your ticket and passport.'

Amaka handed over her emergency travel document then unlocked her phone and presented it to the woman behind the counter.

'Please place your luggage on the belt,' she said.

'I don't have any. Only my handbag.'

The woman looked confused. She looked at Amaka's documents again, then to her right to catch the attention of a colleague.

'Is there a problem?' Amaka asked.

'No, ma,' the lady said. She printed out a boarding pass and handed it to her. 'Enjoy your flight.'

110

The man next to Amaka in her aisle seat had his head against the window, his face turned upwards, mouth open, and his eyes shut. He could be a snorer, she thought.

She looked over the seat in front of her. A female cabin crew member was shutting the door. The seat between Amaka and the man was still empty. She moved her handbag from her lap onto the spare seat and fastened her belt.

She slipped her hand in through the neck of her shirt and pulled out the election observer card on the lanyard around her neck, pulled it over her head, wound it round the card and tucked it behind the airline magazines in the seat pocket in front. The man beside her let out a solitary snore. She checked the time. The aircraft should have begun moving. Why was it taking so long?

'Ladies and gentlemen, the Captain has turned on the fasten seat belt sign. If you haven't already done so, please stow your carry-on luggage underneath the seat in front of you or in an overhead bin...'

Amaka heard her phone vibrating in her bag. She fetched it but didn't answer. Seventeen missed calls, all from an unknown number. The phone began to ring again. This time it was Ambrose. She held her breath and she answered.

'Hello, Amaka, thank you for taking my call.'

She did not reply.

'Amaka, are you there?'

'Yes.'

'Why didn't you tell me?'

She took her time to respond. 'Would you have allowed me?'

'No, no. You're right, I wouldn't have.'

Silence. In the background she heard other voices. Ambrose continued: 'Tell me, our people that were picked up by the DSS, was that you?'

'Yes. But only enough to make a difference.'

'You are one smart lady. I'm so glad you're on our side. I just got word that Otunba has been rushed to the hospital. It sounds like a heart attack.'

'He knows?'

'I'm not sure he suspects it was us. He'll probably blame his own over-zealous boys, but he knows the consequences anyway. The numbers are still coming in. Already they have won by double the number of registered voters in the entire Lagos state.' Ambrose laughed. 'It is pure genius.'

'And without their votes, we had more than 250 votes in the majority of the wards?' Amaka asked.

'Yes. By the looks of it, without their votes, we have won. It is pure genius. Tell me, when did you get the idea to do this?'

Amaka cupped her hand over her mouth and checked on the man fast asleep next to her. 'When you told me that each ward only has 500 registered voters.'

'You were listening.'

'What happens now?'

'Well, one of three things. Either INEC declares the elections void, or they disqualify them and we win. Unlikely. Or they declare them winners and we go to tribunal and prove they rigged. A rerun is the most likely outcome. You know, from our calculations, we would have lost even if you didn't do what you did. Now we are in a strong position. And it is still possible that they will go to court to challenge us and INEC.'

'Not if you call Ojo and tell him you have seen videos of him having sex with underage girls.'

'So the videos are real.'

'Yes.'

'And he doesn't know you no longer have them. Amaka, I have one word for you. Genius. You are a genius. Who else would have thought of that? Rigging the election for your opponent? I will lean on my contacts close to the INEC chairman to guarantee a favourable outcome for us. INEC will secretly talk to them, but with this information, Ojo will have to agree.

'Amaka, for the first time it is really looking possible that we have won this thing. You could just have got a governor of Lagos elected. I doff my hat to you.'

An air hostess stopped by Amaka. 'Madam, please can I put your bag away?'

'I have to go now,' Amaka said to Ambrose.

'I know. You're running away to London. When will you be back?'

'You had me followed.'

'You also have to switch off your phone now,' the hostess said.

Amaka nodded. 'I'll call you when I land,' she said and powered down her phone. She placed her bag on the floor and pushed it under the seat in front of her with her foot.

When the hostess had moved on, Amaka leaned forward and tried to reach her handbag. She unclasped her seatbelt and fetched the bag from under the seat in front. She pulled out her phone again, switched it on and checked on the position of the cabin crew. She shut her eyes.

'Hello? Guy, it's me, Amaka. I'm on a flight to London. Do you think we can start over again?'

The End

Acknowledgements

Very special thanks to Andy Russell, Naomi Beckett, Ojoma Ochai, Jide Olaniyan, Osaretin Guobadia, Mike Timbers, Bisi Ilaka, Sibilla Woods, Gabriel Gbadamosi, Ben and Adeola, Ali, Lise Belperron, Sofia Alexandrache, Steve Willis, Kọ́lá Túbọsún, Boma Tamuno, Bibi Bakare-Yusuf, Jeremy Weate, Emma Shercliff, David Fauquemberg, Lula Verki, Ayo Onatade, Sophie Goodfellow, the lovely people at Daily Goods, Lumberjack, Mono, and Maloko - all great cafés in Camberwell, and Alex Hannaford.

Transforming a manuscript into the book you are now reading is a team effort. Cassava Republic Press would like to thank everyone who helped in the production of *When Trouble Sleeps*:

Editorial
Alex Hannaford
Bibi Bakare-Yusuf
Layla Mohamed

Design & Production
Michael Salu
AI's Fingers

Sales & Marketing
Emma Shercliff
Kofo Okunola

Publicity
Emeka Nwankwo
Lynette Lisk

CASSAVA CRIME

EASY MOTION TOURIST

Leye Adenle

ISBN: 978-1911115069

Easy Motion Tourist is a compelling crime novel set in contemporary Lagos, featuring Guy Collins, a British hack who stumbles into the murky underworld of the city. A woman's mutilated body is discarded outside a club near one of the main hotels in Victoria Island. Collins, a bystander, is picked up by the police as a potential suspect. After experiencing the unpleasant realities of a Nigerian police cell, he is rescued by Amaka, a guardian angel of Lagos working girls. As Collins discovers more of the darker aspects of what makes Lagos tick—including the clandestine trade in organs—he also slowly falls for Amaka. The novel features a motley cast of supporting characters, including a memorable duo of low-level Lagos gangsters: Knockout and Go-Slow.

Easy Motion Tourist pulsates with the rhythms of Lagos and entertains from beginning to end. A modern thriller featuring a strong female protagonist, prepared to take on the Nigerian criminal world on her own.

CASSAVA CRIME

THE LAZARUS EFFECT

H. J. Golakai

ISBN: 978-1911115083

Voinjama Johnson is an investigative journalist for the Cape Town magazine Urban. Her life is a mess and Vee's been seeing things: a teenage girl in a red hat that goes hand-in-hand with the debilitating episodes she is loath to call 'panic attacks'.

When Vee spots a photo of the girl from her hallucinations at a local hospital, she launches an investigation, under the pretext of writing an article about missing children. With the help of her oddball assistant Chlöe Bishop, she's soon delving into the secrets of the fractured Fourie and Paulsen families. What happened to Jacqui Paulsen, who left home two years ago and hasn't been seen since?

The Lazarus Effect is a gripping new addition to the African crime genre from a talented debut author.

CASSAVA CRIME

THE CARNIVOROUS CITY

Toni Kan

ISBN: 978-1911115243

Rabato Sabato aka Soni Dike is a Lagos big boy; a criminal turned grandee, with a beautiful wife, a sea-side mansion and a questionable fortune. Then one day he disappears and his car is found in a ditch, music blaring from the speakers.

Soni's older brother, Abel Dike, a teacher, arrives in Lagos to look for his missing brother. Abel is rapidly sucked into the unforgiving Lagos maelstrom where he has to navigate encounters with a motley cast of common criminals, deal with policemen intent on getting a piece of the pie, and contend with his growing attraction to his brother's wife.

The Carnivorous City is a story about love, family and just deserts but it is above all a tale about Lagos and the people who make the city by the lagoon what it is.

Support *When Trouble Sleeps*

1. **Recommend it.** Don't keep the enjoyment of this book to yourself; tell everyone you know. Spread the word to your friends and family.
2. **Review, review review.** Your opinion is powerful and a positive review from you can generate new sales. Spare a minute to leave a short review on Amazon, GoodReads, Wordery, our website and other book buying sites.
3. **Join the conversation.** Hearing somebody you trust talk about a book with passion and excitement is one of the most powerful ways to get people to engage with it. If you like this book, talk about it, Facebook it, Tweet it, Blog it, Instagram it. Take pictures of the book and quote or highlight from your favourite passage. You could even add a link so others know where to purchase the book from.
4. **Buy the book as gifts for others.** Buying a gift is a regular activity for most of us – birthdays, anniversaries, holidays, special days or just a nice present for a loved one for no reason… If you enjoyed this book and you think it might resonate with others, then please buy extra copies!
5. **Get your local bookshop or library to stock it.** Sometimes bookshops and libraries only order books that they have heard about. If you loved this book, why not ask your librarian or bookshop to order it in. If enough people request a title, the bookshop or library will take note and will order a few copies for their shelves.
6. **Recommend a book to your book club.** Persuade your book club to read this book and discuss what you enjoy about the book in the company of others. This is a wonderful way to share what you like and help to boost the sales and popularity of this book. You can also join our online book club on Facebook at Afri-Lit Club to discuss books by other African writers.
7. **Attend a book reading.** There are lots of opportunities to hear writers talk about their work. Support them by attending their book events. Get your friends, colleagues and families to a reading and show an author your support.

Thank you!